Driving Jesus to Little Rock

Roland Merullo

Praise For Roland Merullo

Leaving Losapas

"Dazzling . . . thoughtful and elegant . . . lyrical yet tough-minded . . . beautifully written, quietly brilliant." — ***Kirkus* Reviews**

A Russian Requiem

"Smoothly written and multifaceted, solidly depicting the isolation and poverty of a city far removed from Moscow and insightfully exploring the psyches of individuals caught in the conflicts between their ideals and their careers." — ***Publishers Weekly***

Revere Beach Boulevard

"Merullo invents a world that mirrors our world in all of its mystery. in language so happily inventive and precise and musical, and plots it so masterfully, that you are reluctant to emerge from his literary dream." — ***Washington Post Book World***

Passion for Golf: In Pursuit of the Innermost Game

"This accessible guide offers insight into the emotional stumbling blocks that get in the way of improvement and, most importantly, enjoyment of the game." — ***Publishers Weekly***

Revere Beach Elegy: A Memoir of Home and Beyond

"Merullo has a knack for rendering emotional complexities, paradoxes, or impasses in a mere turn of the phrase." — ***Chicago Tribune***

In Revere, In Those Days

"A portrait of a time and a place and a state of mind that has few equals." — ***The Boston Globe***

A Little Love Story

"There is nothing little about this love story. It is big and heroic and beautiful and tragic . . . Writing with serene passion and gentle humor, Merullo powerfully reveals both the resiliency and fragility of life and love . . . It is, quite utterly, grand." — ***Booklist***

Golfing with God

"Merullo writes such a graceful, compassionate and fluid prose that you cannot resist the characters' very real struggles and concerns . . ."

.— ***Providence Journal***

Breakfast with Buddha
"Merullo writes with grace and intelligence and knows that even in a novel of ideas it's not the religion that matters, it's the relationship. . . It's a quiet, meditative, and ultimately joyous trip we're on."

— ***Boston Globe***

Fidel's Last Days
"A fast-paced and highly satisfying spy thriller . . . Merullo takes readers on a fictional thrill ride filled with so much danger and drama that they won't want it to end." — ***Boston Globe***

American Savior
"Merullo gently satirizes the media and politics in this thoughtful commentary on the role religion plays in America. This book showcases Merullo's conviction that Jesus' real message about treating others with kindness is being warped by those who believe they alone understand the Messiah." — ***USA Today***

The Italian Summer: Golf, Food & Family at Lake Como
"This travel memoir delivers unadulterated joy . . . [Merullo's] account of those idyllic weeks recalls Calvin Trillin in its casual tone, good humor, affable interactions with family, and everyman's love of regional food and wine . . . A special travel book for a special audience." — ***Booklist***

The Talk-Funny Girl
"Merullo not only displays an inventive use of language in creating the Richards' strange dialect but also delivers a triumphant story of one lonely girl's resilience in the face of horrific treatment."

— ***Booklist***

Lunch with Buddha
"A beautifully written and compelling story about a man's search for meaning that earnestly and accessibly tackles some well-trodden but universal questions. A quiet meditation on life, death, darkness and spirituality, sprinkled with humor, tenderness and stunning landscapes." — ***Kirkus Reviews***

Vatican Waltz

"Merullo's latest is a page-turning novel of religious ideas written with love and imagination. . . . It also sings with finely observed details of family relationships, ethnic neighborhood life, and the life of prayer. The shoulda-seen-it-coming ending is a miracle . . ."

— ***Publishers Weekly***

10 Commandments of Golf Etiquette: How to Make the Game More Enjoyable for Yourself & for Everyone Else on the Course

"The Rosetta Stone for anyone looking to break through the game's clutter of rules and protocols. It combines Merullo's passion for golf with his gift for clear writing, humor and insight."

—Tim Murphy, retired Senior Editor, *Golf World*

Dinner with Buddha

"Sharp character sketches of people encountered on the way and occasional references to current events keep the narrative from floating away in spiritual self-absorption. . .Clearly there's more to come. With six unconventionally religious novels to date, this brave, meditative author has carved a unique niche in American literature."

— ***Kirkus Reviews***

The Delight of Being Ordinary

"Another genre-defying installment in Merullo's engaging series of seriocomic religious novels . . . Admirers of previous volumes will recognize Merullo's knack for depicting goodness without treacle in his deft portraits of the pope and the Dalai Lama, and a La Dolce Vita-esque party scene spotlights his ability to discern humanity in the most decadent circumstances.... moving and unnerving . . . Lucid, unpretentious fiction spotlighting the drama of trying to make the divine part of our everyday lives." — ***Kirkus Reviews***

From these Broken Streets

"The seamless plot is compelling, making this an altogether deeply satisfying work of historical fiction." —***Booklist***

Also by Roland Merullo

Fiction

Leaving Losapas
A Russian Requiem
Revere Beach Boulevard
In Revere, In Those Days
A Little Love Story
Golfing with God
Breakfast with Buddha
American Savior
Fidel's Last Days
The Talk-Funny Girl
Lunch with Buddha
Vatican Waltz
The Return
Dinner with Buddha
Rinpoche's Remarkable Ten-Week Weight Loss Clinic
The Delight of Being Ordinary
Once Night Falls
From These Broken Streets

Non Fiction

Passion for Golf: In Pursuit of the Innermost Game

Revere Beach Elegy: A Memoir of Home & Beyond

The Italian Summer: Golf, Food, and Family at Lake Como

Demons of the Blank Page: 15 Obstacles That Keep You From Writing & How To Conquer Them

Taking the Kids to Italy

The Ten Commandments of Golf Etiquette: How to Make the Game More Enjoyable for Yourself and for Everyone Else on the Course

Moments of Grace & Beauty: Forty Stories of Kindness, Courage, and Generosity in a Troubled World

Driving Jesus to Little Rock

PFP Publishing
PO Box 829
Byfield, MA 01922
publisher@pfppublishing.com

ISBN: 978-1-7367202-7-1
(also available in eBook & hardcover format)

Cover image:
© Tobias Weber/Getty Images used by permission

Publisher's Cataloging-In-Publication Data
(Prepared by The Donohue Group, Inc.)

Names: Merullo, Roland, author.
Title: Driving Jesus to Little Rock / Roland Merullo.
Description: Byfield, MA : PFP Publishing, [2021]
Identifiers: ISBN 9781736720271 (paperback) | ISBN 9781736720288 (hardcover)
Subjects: LCSH: Jesus Christ--Fiction. | Hitchhiking--United States--Fiction. | Authors--United States--Fiction. | United States--Description and travel--Fiction. | LCGFT: Humorous fiction.
Classification: LCC PS3563.E748 D75 2021 | DDC 813/.54--dc23

For Mary and Michael Miller

Author's Note

I was raised as a devout Roman Catholic and, at Mass, heard stories from the Bible every Sunday for more than twenty years. The stories fascinated me then, and they still fascinate me. Later in life, when I became interested in Eastern spiritual traditions, I noticed a tremendous amount of overlap between Christianity and Buddhism especially, but also between Christianity and some aspects of Hinduism and Sufism—religions I don't know as well. I also noticed that the Bible takes Jesus only as far as his teenage years, and then seems to pick up the story again when he's thirty. What happened in those intervening years, I wondered? Why weren't they described, even briefly?

Steeped in the Biblical stories as I am, I often wonder what a modern-day Jesus would look like. How would he dress, speak, and act? (I explored the idea of a modern-day Mary in a novel called *Vatican Waltz*). Where would he come to earth? From which group of people would he choose his disciples? How would the Christian establishment react? How would he be treated by the population at large?

There's a certain amount of irreverence involved in my exploration of these questions, I admit that. Who am I to suggest what Jesus would say if he appeared in twenty-first century America, for example, or somewhere else in the modern world? On the one hand, I have absolutely no right to speculate. I'm not ordained, not a religious scholar, not a monk. On the other hand, I think all of us—Christians and non-Christians, believers and atheists—have our own idea of who Jesus was, if we believe that he existed—and most historical record suggests that he did. As Eddie Val does in the novel, I think of that as the Jesus of our imagination because we really don't have a great deal of factual information about his life. We have the story of his birth, some parables and miracles, the crucifixion and resurrection, sometimes in conflicting versions. Beyond that, our image of him likely comes from paintings and sculptures made by people who were not even remotely close to his contemporaries.

So I've taken great liberties here. I've had Jesus say and do things that might surprise or upset some readers, but I've tried, in my own way, to be respectful. Attempting to fill out, however fancifully, aspects of Jesus' humanity seems to me the act of a reverent person, which I am. It should go without saying that I don't pretend to know what he'd say or do in the modern world, but the question has always interested me. Thirteen years ago, I explored it in the novel *American Savior*, and I decided to come at it from a different angle here.

Roland Merullo

"So you think the fact that she smiled at you was a sign from God?"

"I think it was God."

—from *Humans of New York*

Introduction

My name is Eddie Valpolicella and I make my living writing books. It's a profession as peculiar as my name, and in general I don't recommend it. I mention my work now only because it led to the events described in this story. Strange events, to be sure. Strange and marvelous and, for most people, probably occupying space on the other side of the border of the believable world.

The long and short of it is this: In the early spring of 2018, in a small town in Western Massachusetts, I picked up a hitchhiking stranger who called himself Jesus and who asked me to drive him to Little Rock, Arkansas. That bizarre moment was followed by a string of others, flashes of life, coincidences, encounters, various species of magic. In retrospect, I understand that those images and voices and scenes and tricks all formed part of what some people call "a teaching." Life, it seems to me, works exactly that way. We feel frustration, fear, hope, amusement, warmth, anger, affection—all as if they are isolated moods, snatches of dream that seem to make no sense. In fact, they are ingredients in the elaborate meal we call a human lifetime. *Live and learn,* my aunts and uncles used to say. I had no idea how wise they were.

~ ~

chapter one

I've published a number of books—novels, a memoir, other pieces of non-fiction having to do with golf and travel and food—so many that I've forgotten what order they came in, what year they were published, how much money they made the publishing house, or me, and (except for some unforgivably awful ones) what kinds of reviews they received. I do remember one book particularly well, however, a novel called *Breakfast with Buddha.* I remember it because it has sold enough copies to enable me to support my family by doing nothing other than writing—a dream I'd held for decades. Fourteen years after it was published, it still sells, and I still get invited to go places and talk about it. Open-minded churches, usually. Schools and colleges, public libraries, book groups, community reads.

A few of these appearances pay very well—six or seven thousand dollars. That's a lot of money for a not-famous writer, a lot of money to pay anyone, it seems to me, for spending an hour or two talking, answering questions, signing books. Those kinds of invitations come along only every few years, however; mostly it's library events in my home state, and usually the honorarium—to use a word I dislike because it sounds overly fancy—is something like $500. Still pretty good money where I came from, and sometimes I feel a twinge of guilt thinking I'll be making, for my hour of gab, what some people earn in a week for taking care of an elderly or handicapped person, or for doing physically hard, dangerous, or painfully boring work. Still, I enjoy it, and it's part of how I make a living for myself, my wife, and our kids, and so when people extend an invitation and offer payment, I show up.

In late 2017 I received, through my now-defunct speakers' bureau, an invitation from a progressive and well-heeled Episcopalian congregation in Little Rock, Arkansas. They were starting up a speaking series, and some members of the committee had read my *Buddha* book and found it interesting and perhaps spiritually provocative, and they wondered if I'd be available to come to Arkansas and talk. My agent said the people seemed sincere, and the payment she negotiated (I'd have to take care of my own expenses) was generous. Months in advance, we agreed on an April date, and I put it on the calendar, planning to fly south from my home in Massachusetts.

But then, as the date approached, an odd idea took root in my thoughts (not the first time such a thing has happened; ask anyone who knows me). I wondered if, instead of flying to Arkansas, I might drive. Although I've flown all over the world and have gradually lost my fear of it, I've never lost my distaste for it. The waiting, the cramped seating and bad food, the turbulence and noise, the potentially crazy fellow passengers. There's one good thing about it: it's fast. But we pay a price for that speed, a hidden price. In the service of convenience, of getting more and more done in less and less time, we lose touch with the earth, with each other, and with ourselves; we soar heedlessly over a landscape that might teach us something important if we took our time going through it.

So, I thought: I love driving, why don't I drive? My wife, Anna Maria, a sensible woman, immediately informed me that the idea represented the height of foolishness. My daughters chimed in with a similar sentiment. You're driving, Dad? Why?

Because.

Because they were away and I missed their presence in our home. Because I love the open road. Because, though I'm very far from rich, I do have the great luxury of making my own schedule and doing eccentric things if I dream of doing them. Because I was getting a nice paycheck for the talk and felt I could safely leave the desk for a few days and spend some extra money on hotels and food and gas. Because my kind wife was busy most of every day taking care of her nonagenarian mother, who lived nearby. Because I like warm weather. Because I thought maybe I could bring my golf clubs along and play an off-season round or two. Etcetera.

So, on an April morning on which I awakened to find a thin skin of snow and ice coating my two-year-old charcoal-colored Camry, I scraped for a while, bare-handed in the great New England tradition, sat down for a waffle, bacon, and coffee with Anna Maria, and then kissed her goodbye and headed off, south, toward St. Mark's of Little Rock.

~ ❦ ~

chapter two

The road we live on is a beautiful road, and though we've been there thirty-two years, I never get tired of driving it. It's a typical country road: Two paved lanes that wind between the hills, with streams cutting beneath it and a small river running beside it, with a few houses spread along it, and one large farm presiding over it like a queen. On that road, in the years we've been here, I've seen black bear and great blue heron, owls and hawks and turkey vultures. Foxes, fisher cats, a black mink holding her two kits by the neck and carrying them one by one across the road. Moles, voles, frogs, toads, and wild turkey in abundance. Plenty of deer. Squirrels, skunks, possum. One rabid raccoon, squeezing herself down backwards beneath the guardrail. Snakes large and small, alive and dead. Songbirds of every description. The occasional lost seagull that must have wandered over from the Connecticut River, ten miles to the east. And one bald eagle. I've seen car wrecks and arguments, loose dogs (I caught one and returned him to his owner), stray cats, walkers and runners and even a competitive cross-country skier who trained with wheeled skis each autumn before the snow came. I've ridden bikes on that road and walked there with my wife and daughters and mother and brother and friends. I've picked up paper litter and empty beer cans. I once found a new wallet with no money in it and no ID. I've stopped to move fallen tree branches, I've avoided cow manure splattered from a farmer's tractor, and I've taken nails and screws from the pavement and sometimes helped orange salamanders cross the tar during their annual migration from one side of the road to the other. I've seen bad drivers and good, yelled at people and been yelled at by people. I have a history of intense and complicated dreams, and one night I dreamt I was about to be hit head-on in a particular stretch of that road, and the next day it happened. Or almost happened: the other driver and I missed each other by a foot, exactly in that place. (He was distracted by a yard sale. I swore at him, using a bad word. But clearly the dream had saved me and my daughter in the back seat.)

So, on that cold April morning, still half asleep despite the coffee, I headed off through piles of memories, tooting a half-guilty goodbye to Anna Maria, who I know wanted to come along but couldn't. As I often do, I said a quiet prayer for the happiness and health of our girls, for the world, for my own safety.

After exactly four-point-two miles of this road I reached a larger two-lane country highway, State Route 9, along which stands the handful of commercial buildings that make up our town. A church, a bank, a gas station, a grammar school, a country store, a couple places to eat—it's a picture-postcard town and looks like it was lifted from a movie set depicting an America of fifty years ago. The people are mostly kind and will help you out if they see you're in trouble; they'll pitch in to build a playground at the grammar school; they'll wave a thank-you if you let them cross the street in front of you; they'll hold the door of the bank open on a busy Saturday morning instead of rushing to get in line ahead of you.

I had one errand there—a stop at the local post office—

and then I was truly on my way, cruising slowly east down Route 9, anxious to get into new territory, to see new things, escape the cold, eat different kinds of food, give my talk, play golf, earn my paycheck. In other words, I was driving through both a pile of memories and a mountain of anticipation.

And then, as it tends to do, the present intruded.

Not far ahead, on a stretch of road without any commercial buildings—a river and trees on one side and a few well-spaced houses set behind sloped lawns on the other—I saw a man holding out his thumb. He was a man of color, a relative rarity in rural New England. Middle Eastern, possibly. He was on the tall side, closer to slim than stocky, and if I were to guess his age, I'd say he was in his mid-thirties. He was wearing work boots and jeans and a green army jacket, and he had a backpack looped over one shoulder. Because I'd done a lot of hitchhiking in my youth, and because it was a cold day, and because the local regional buses run only infrequently, and because I'm not afraid of picking up hitchhikers unless they look like murderers, and because I like to help people when I can, within reason, I pulled over a few yards beyond him and waited.

He jogged up, looked in at me through the window, as most careful hitchhikers do, made his quick assessment—I wasn't a creep, wasn't drunk, wasn't dangerous—and climbed into the passenger seat.

"Hi, thanks," he said.

"No problem. Put on your seatbelt, will you?"

"Sure."

That's almost always the opening conversation that follows my picking up a hitchhiker. Sometimes, after asking where they're headed, we ride in silence. Other times we find a neutral topic of conversation—the weather, the Red Sox, the neighborhood. There have been times when the person I picked up smelled of tobacco, or marijuana, or alcohol. Not long ago I stopped for a man a little younger than I am, a ragged-looking fellow, and when I asked him where he was headed, he said the name of the local hospital and then, "I'm a drunk. I'm going there to get help." "Good," I told him, "a good move," and we went the rest of the way without saying another word. Sometimes women will hitch a ride in these parts, which is a testimony either to their carelessness, their courage, or the general safety of the place. I always pick them up because I know I won't hurt them, or make them uncomfortable, and I'm not sure that's true of some of the other people on the highway. Once, in a nearby town, on my way to play an early morning round of golf, I stopped for a blond woman in her forties, so thin she looked as if the air from a passing truck would blow her over sideways. A few seconds into the ride she asked me if I "dated." I told her I was married. Undeterred, she asked if I would like a particular sexual 'favor' I won't describe here. I said no thanks, and then told her she was crazy for taking a risk like that, given the kinds of diseases she might get. A foolish thing to say, of course, but I tried to say it kindly. Once she realized I had no potential as a paying customer, she asked me to take her back to where I'd picked her up, and I did that, handed her a twenty-dollar bill, and told her to get some food. Another foolish gesture, because food wasn't what she was interested in.

So it's possible that all this—the past, the future, the variety of humanity—was in my mind when I stopped for the guy in the army jacket. "Where you headed?" I asked him, and that perfectly straightforward question marked the end of anything remotely ordinary in that whole trip and marked the beginning of a stretch of time that I will remember to my last day.

"Arkansas," he said.

I laughed. A breeze of uneasiness stirred the air in the car. I wondered if maybe, the day before, I'd been looking at the Rand McNally and had tossed it carelessly into the back seat, open to the Arkansas page, and he'd seen it before climbing in. Or if he'd overheard me saying something about the trip during my visit to the post office and was making a weird joke. He was a mind-reader, maybe. A psychic. I turned to glance at him. Or some kind of stalker. He had a not-very-neatly-trimmed goatee and ears that were a bit larger than normal. He was looking back at me. He might have been smiling; it was hard to know for sure because the smile—if it was a smile—was only a tiny mysterious twist at the corners of his lips.

"Seriously," I said. "You heading into Northampton?"

"Little Rock. I'm going to hear a favorite author speak there."

"Really."

"Yeah."

"What's his name?"

"Edward Valpolicella," the hitchhiker said. "He wrote a book I adore. *Breakfast with Buddha.*" Having pronounced those memorable words, he reached into his backpack and pulled out a well worn hardcover. A book. *My* book. I may have been imagining it, but when he opened the backpack, I thought I saw the flash of a knife blade.

"This is some kind of practical joke, right? One of my golf buddies put you up to it?"

"Not at all."

I stopped at the light in Haydenville, a third of the way to the Interstate, and saw that he was holding out his right hand.

"Jesus," he said. "Jesus the Christ."

I shook the offered hand, said, "Eddie Valpolicella," in an automatic way, and then, when the light went green, I drove through it and pulled over to the curb.

I shifted the Camry into park, put on the hazard lights so a lumber truck trundling down out of the hills wouldn't rear-end me, and then turned to look at my passenger. He had green eyes and a crescent scar along his left cheekbone. "All right, Bud," I said, not in an unfriendly way, but in a way that sent a don't-mess-with-me message. Although I'm a quiet country guy now, a meditator, family man, completely peaceable, I grew up in a city where, no matter who you were, you were bequeathed a certain amount of street smarts. Every once in a while, even in my present rather sedate life, that inheritance proves useful. "All right," I said, "what's the deal here? I'm happy to give you a ride, but don't mess with me."

I didn't actually say 'mess', but I'm a little embarrassed to write what I did say. To a man who was calling himself Jesus, after all.

He smiled more obviously. It wasn't a mean smile, wasn't sarcastic, wasn't the smile of some trickster, and certainly wasn't touched by fear. If anything, I'd say the smile was *sad,* as if I'd disappointed him, or as if the world had disappointed him, but he'd resolved to deal with it anyway, try to be kind in spite of all the violence and anger.

He smiled but didn't say anything, which annoyed me. I found myself wondering if he did, in fact, have a knife.

"Why don't you just get out now," I said, in that same tone of voice. "I have a lot going on today and a long trip ahead of me, so I'm not into playing games, or whatever it is you're doing. It seems like you know me. Fine. And I appreciate you buying the book. And you probably read on Facebook or my website that I have a talk in Arkansas and you somehow knew when I was heading out. That's all cool, but I really want to make the trip alone, so please get out now and I wish you well."

The smile shrank. He was nodding, agreeing. I was glad to

see that things weren't going to get ugly. At the same time, he wasn't making any effort to find the door handle, and I suddenly thought I spied a thin line of aggression in the muscles of his face. The scar worried me, too. After a ten-second standoff he said, "I'm Jesus."

"Right, you said that. I'm happy for you. You have a good name, and you seem like a decent guy, but, really, I need to be on the road."

"*The* Jesus," he said. "Jesus the Christ. The Messiah in some circles. Son of Man. At the very least, a wise rabbi."

"You can call yourself anything you want. Just get out of the car."

He watched me for a couple of seconds. I considered my options. I could turn off the car and get out and walk around to the passenger-side, open the door and pull him out. He was a little younger, but I'm good-sized and not weak and in fairly good shape, and I'd taken a couple years of karate and I thought I could handle him if it came to that. . . . Another option was to drive him to the police station in Northampton—five miles down the road—get out there and ask one of the officers to take care of the situation. Probably the wiser route.

"When you were twelve," my passenger said, "your father's father, who lived next door, died of heart trouble."

"Public record," I told him.

"You and your brothers walked up the street to your grade school, weeping."

"I wrote about that in *Revere Beach Elegy*."

"When you were sixteen, you were hit in the right eye, playing stickball with Michael Capone, and you went to the hospital for three days."

"I wrote about that, too. Same book."

He nodded, squeezed the end of his rather large nose between his thumb and second finger, met my eyes again. "When your father died in his sleep, age 66, you were up on a ladder in Williamstown, Massachusetts, in the days before cell phones. Your wife left her job at the museum and came to bring you the terrible news."

"Wrote about that also."

"Right, but you went back and carefully cleaned the brush and closed the paint can and you were crying. Your tears were dripping down onto the tops of your hands. You were thinking that you and your dad were just starting to establish an adult relationship, growing closer. . . . That part you never wrote about."

There was a bad silence in the front seat. I was looking at him and he was looking at me. A lumber truck rumbled past, throwing up a wave of air that slapped hard against the closed window. "What's going on?" I said.

He shrugged, almost laughed.

"What are you, some kind of a psychic, a stalker? What's the deal?"

"I want you to know," he said, and I had the strange sense then that what might be called the 'power dynamic' had suddenly shifted. A few seconds earlier I'd been the sane one, the normal guy with a car, a speaking invitation, a trip planned. Bigger, probably stronger, better off. And he was somebody who couldn't afford his own set of wheels, a wanderer, depending on the kindness of strangers, a little crazy, a little weird. "I want you to know," he repeated . . . "that I don't do this often."

"Right," I said. "Next you're going to tell me I'm so special, such a wonderful, spiritual human being that Jesus—the actual Jesus—chose me, out of the seven billion people on earth, to come visit. Jesus chose my book, out of the millions of books in print, to carry around in his backpack. Jesus wants to ride with me, come hear my talk. I have news for you, pal, I'm sorry to deliver it, but I'm not that special."

"Exactly," he said.

"Meaning what?"

"Meaning you're just another ordinary Edward."

"Right, so please go bother somebody else."

"Are you sure you want that?"

I had been sure. Until about three seconds before he spoke those words, I'd been a hundred per cent sure. I had the trip planned out in my mind. I love my wife and kids, but I also cherish my solitary time, and, as I might have mentioned, I enjoy driving and seeing the countryside. I imagined a string of good meals—I love to eat across the ethnic spectrum—and quiet hotel rooms where I could write a few pages, trying to find a new project that would garner an advance. Down the road there was going to be a little bit of praise and applause, some book sales, a nice paycheck. Then a solitary ride back home that would allow me to visit an old friend in Hot Springs, Arkansas and a beloved aunt in Indianapolis.

But now I was wavering. Slightly. A touch of ego, maybe. A tiny voice was whispering to me something like: *you know, maybe you* are *special. Isn't this what you wanted, some proof, a visit by a holy man, a sign that you aren't really ordinary?* Or maybe a better part of me was doing the whispering, a part that believes not everything is logical on this earth, that inexplicable things happen, that a mysterious element floats through the mundane world like a sweet fragrance, beyond the sometimes not-so-good smell of ordinary life.

"You're wavering," Jesus said. "You had your trip all planned out."

"I did."

"Why are you wavering? Why not just throw me out? Or

drive to the police station in Northampton and let the officers there handle the situation?"

"I might do that."

"I don't think you will. You're deeply religious in your own somewhat eccentric way. You spend an inordinate amount of time wondering why you were put on this earth, what's the point, what, exactly, you're supposed to be doing. And, despite your persona, which seems to be that of a settled family man—the house, the cars, the kids—you have a taste for a bit of risk now and again, am I right?"

"You're not wrong." I squeezed the wheel in both hands. "Who are you, really? Stop with the bullshit."

"I am who am," he said, and he laughed a weird, fully amused, self deprecating kind of laugh, a short tinkling of notes on the right end of the piano keyboard. It sounded like the laugh of a young girl, and, as I watched him and thought about it for another few seconds, I realized that he did have what my daughters might have called some kind of non-binary vibe going. Or, at least, a mix of tenderness and fierceness. "You've pondered that line from the Bible, too, haven't you, Edward? *I am who am.*"

"I have."

"You've wondered what Jesus had in mind when he said it. And also what it would have been like to walk around with the real historical Jesus, if such a person did, in fact, exist. What it would have been like to see Buddha in the flesh, to hear him give one of his talks. You've wondered if the old stories are all made up, merely wishful thinking set down by people who wanted life to have some meaning. Or, on the other hand, if there might actually be people on earth right now who are, what's the way to say it?"

"Not normal."

Another laugh. "*Holy* was the word I was thinking of. And you've even wondered about that: what does *holy* mean? You've been thinking lately that something about modern life, something about the way you, yourself, live, makes even the idea of holiness seem absurd. Correct?"

"How do you know all this?"

"Listen," he said, with some urgency, "How about we ride together for a while, you and I. For one day. You have to swing through New York City for a meeting, and then your good wife made you a hotel reservation in Harrisburg, Pennsylvania, am I correct?"

I nodded, halfway beyond surprise at that point, but wary as could be. I suspected that the hitchhiker/mind-reader had hacked Anna Maria's computer and read our emails. And she was going to be alone in the house for two weeks.

"How about we go that far together?" he persisted. "As far as Harrisburg. I won't hurt you. You must know that. You're not a particularly fearful type, anyway. In fact, it seems to me you're ready to die."

"I am," I said, a small prickle running along the backs of my shoulders. "Or that's what I tell myself, anyway. Though I'd like to live long enough to see my girls grown and settled."

"You will, you will," he said, and I felt an irrational wave of warmth go through me, something that washed right over the chirping doubts, over the cold prickle, and wrapped around a soft spot inside me. "Let's ride together just for the day," he went on, in the tone of a debt-ridden salesman on the verge of closing a deal. "I know you like your solitude but give it a day. If, when we get to the hotel parking lot, you decide I'm a fake, or I'm playing some game you don't like, I'll disappear. I promise"

I could hear the pulse beating in my ears. At that moment

an ambulance hurried past, siren wailing, in the direction of Cooley Dickenson Hospital, the place where our kids had been born and where all four of us, at one time or another, had gone to the ER with various unexpected troubles. My mother had always told my brother, my younger sister, and me to say a prayer when we heard an ambulance siren, a prayer for the person inside, who was certainly suffering, and probably surprised that something bad had happened, who'd had a life all planned out, a day, a week, a stretch of years, and then she or he had tripped and fallen down a set of stairs, or felt a sharp pain in the chest, or been T-boned by a drunk driver. "Life is like that", my mother used to tell us. "People plan, the Lord laughs."

I said the first few words of the Hail Mary, but silently, and watched the flashing red lights shrink. The siren faded away. Jesus's eyes followed the ambulance, too, and then swung back to me, watching, assessing, waiting. And then—maybe because of remembering my mother's words, or saying the prayer, or maybe I was sensing the fragility of human life, or maybe because I was prone to do foolish things from time to time—I heard myself say, "All right. Good." And then, very foolishly, given the circumstances, "Thank you."

~ ~

chapter three

Just at that point on Route 9, there's a small eating establishment set back from the road, diagonally opposite a nine-hole golf course. Bread Euphoria, it's called, a name I've always liked. It consists of ten tables in a plain, high-ceilinged room with exposed beams and large plate-glass windows. They serve sandwiches and salads, various kinds of coffees and teas, beer, wine, and homemade pizzas, and there's a display case of their own pastries, too. The place is rarely empty. At those tables on any given day you might see a quartet of white-haired female friends out for croissants and conversation, or a pair of mothers with their babies in front packs, a couple of tree surgeons on their coffee break, a Smith student doing research or electric workers out for a pre-work sticky bun. I always stop there as I head off on long drives, and I was determined, despite the unusual circumstances, to hold to my routine.

But, however . . . as I like to say . . . but, however, having foolishly agreed to take this So-Called Jesus with me for the first day of the trip, I was hit almost immediately with a kind of buyer's remorse. I felt bamboozled, manipulated, half-hypnotized, a fool. The guy's mind-reading tricks had played a role in my hypnosis, for sure, but there was more to it than that, and as I turned into Euphoria's gravel lot and found a parking space, I was already raking through my thoughts looking for something I could use to defend myself against the voice that was making a case for my idiocy.

The best I could do was to tell myself it was simply another bit of harmless spontaneity, the same kind of impulse that had led me to drive to Arkansas instead of flying. I did things like that. I was known for it in my family, for a kind of benign illogic that, from time to time, conquered my ordinarily rational mind.

Here's one example out of hundreds: Once, in early 1995, before we had children, I was alone in the Venice, Italy, train station (Anna Maria and I had been on vacation together; she had to leave a week early to return to work) and happened to see ZAGREB on the departures board. The train left at midnight. It sounded tantalizing, adventurous—especially given the fact that, though the former Yugoslavia was in the midst of a horrible war, Jimmy Carter had brokered a Christmas ceasefire that was still in effect. And so, instead of the idea of jumping on a train to a war zone seeming like the notion of a lunatic, it somehow seemed reasonable to me. I care about the world. I'd been reading about the war for months. A nation that had been, for most of my life until then, a reasonably peaceful place, had abruptly devolved into madness. That quick and terrible descent made me wonder: Could something like that ever happen at home, in our peaceful, rational America? It made me curious. So I bought a ticket . . . without being able to speak a word of Croatian, without having a place to stay, without a single *kuna* in my pocket, and without knowing what the conditions in the city would actually be like. I made the overnight trip in an empty passenger car, endured the suspicion and low-level interrogations of customs officials at the Slovenian and Croatian borders, and arrived to a not-very-warm welcome of an hour's wait while the good policemen at the station's passport control office tried to figure out why on earth an American tourist would come to Zagreb in wartime. Was this America a spy, a terrorist, a soldier of fortune, a black-marketeer? I waited on the train platform outside the *policija* office, pacing back and forth, unconcerned for some reason, assuming things would work out well. And they did. After the long wait, the policeman came outside and handed the passport back to me, said something I didn't understand, and let me walk away.

I stayed, at first, in a tourist hotel filled with UN peacekeepers. At breakfast, I asked one of them how long the war would last, and he said, "These people will hate each other for five hundred years."

From there I moved to the apartment of a local woman who was renting out a room to help with wartime expenses (her thirty-year-old daughter offered to share the bed with me; I politely declined), passed three peaceful days walking around the city, and then took a train to the seaside town of Opatia, and stayed for another three days in a hotel filled with refugees from the Bosnian fighting.

Nothing happened to me. Beyond that one hour at the station, I wasn't detained, wasn't shot at or kidnapped or thrown in prison or killed. On the train from Zagreb to Opatia I saw some bombed-out houses, and in the hotel I had a long conversation with a man who'd been held in one of the camps and watched some of the other prisoners beaten to death with crowbars. But the ceasefire held, and I spent the time walking around and eating and working on a novel that eventually became *Revere Beach Boulevard.* After a week, I caught the train back to Venice and flew home.

Reminding myself of that decision, and the way it had all worked out, made the idea of riding with So-Called Jesus seem somewhat less crazy. I told myself it was simply another of my odd moves. It would make for a good story one day, maybe even find its way into a novel. Nothing too bad would happen.

I turned off the car and half-turned in the seat to look at my passenger. Something was different. After a few seconds I realized what it was: his eyes had been green; now they were a very dark brown, almost black. It seemed to me, too, and I hadn't noticed this before, that he might have some Native American blood—the high cheekbones, the slightly hooked nose, a certain wise and world-weary look in the eyes.

"Try to stay with the gluten-free offerings," he said, and then he laughed his strangely beautiful laugh again.

"Want something?"

"Locusts and honey." More of the laugh. It was a pleasant sound. It made you feel happy, like a favorite folk tune.

"John the Baptist's food of choice."

"You know your Bible, brother!" he exclaimed.

"Right. What do you want? Coffee? Tea? They have good cinnamon rolls, and a good local chocolate milk. Want to come in?"

"I'll stay in the car, if you trust me not to steal your precious laptop. Leave the keys, would you? I'm chilled from standing out there so long."

"I'm not leaving the keys. And the car's staying off."

"Fine. Ginger lemon tea with honey. And a cinnamon roll. And then let's get on the road! We might have only one day together, I don't want to waste it sitting around.

Inside Euphoria, still beset by doubts and wondering why I felt the need to buy food for every person I met, I found Molissa behind the counter, a veteran of the place and a woman who did, in fact, have some Native American ancestry. "Hey, hi. What are you up to?" she asked.

"Nothing. Same old. You?"

She shrugged. "Waiting for spring. I loved Easter, it made me happy."

"Right. The ham, the hot cross buns you guys sell."

"The whole meaning of it, too. Resurrection and all that. It always gives me hope, you know? This year, especially, for some reason. What can I get you today?"

"Iced coffee, a little room for cream. Ginger lemon tea and a cinnamon roll."

"Coffee *and* tea?"

"Yeah. I have a traveling companion."

"Lucky you."

Molissa rang me up and poured the coffee and tea and carefully placed the cinnamon roll in a wax paper bag. I stared at the multicolored chalked menu above the counter. Never, not once, not in the four hundred times I'd been inside Euphoria for lunch or takeout coffee, had anyone there ever come close to talking about religion with me. A coincidence, no doubt. I thanked Molissa and wished her a good day and walked across the gravel lot carrying the bag in one hand and balancing two cups in the other. I approached the car from behind. Through the side window I could see So-Called Jesus. He couldn't see me. He was holding his knapsack on his lap and rummaging around in it. As I came around to the driver's side door, he hurriedly dropped the backpack between his feet and pushed his knees together.

"Let me have the coffee, changed my mind," he said, as I was positioning things between us. "Smells good. You take the tea, okay?"

I gave him The Eye. "You're getting a free ride here. A free cup of tea. Free cinnamon roll. Now you want *my* coffee. Anything else? Should I give you the car? My laptop?"

"That would be a beautiful spiritual gesture, yes. Give me your car. It will demonstrate a lack of attachment." He was grinning at me in a way I found maddening. I was this close to telling him to take the damn coffee, *and* the tea *and* the cinnamon roll, and see if he could hitch a ride with somebody else. But he said, "I'm sorry, my Edward. I haven't been back here on earth more than an hour and I'm still trying to get used to your etiquette."

"Right," I said. "Sure. Was that a knife in your bag?"

"Why would I carry a knife?"

"Right. Take the coffee if you want it."

"I'll give you half the cinnamon roll in exchange."

"Sure, fine," I said, and I started the car and drove back onto the highway and east toward the interstate, biting the inside of my cheek.

~ ~

chapter four

Northampton, Massachusetts, a pleasant city of about thirty-five thousand souls, perches on the western bank of the Connecticut River. Not too big or too small, and with an atmosphere of acceptance and open-mindedness, the city offers an enchanting array of eating places and music venues and a minimum of crime and traffic, and so, for the past thirty years, it's been attracting young, educated, sophisticated artistic types. Anna Maria and I live in the countryside twenty minutes west of town. We don't often avail ourselves of the music offerings, and I don't have much to do with the young, educated, artistic types, but we have a meal downtown once a week or so, and I often leave the desk in early afternoon and head over to Northampton for lunch. Moroccan, Asian, Indian, Thai, Greek, Japanese, Vegetarian, Italian, All-American—there are plenty of options. There's a bus station and a new Amtrak station, too, and that morning, when I stopped at a traffic light near Smith College, I had what could politely by termed a change of heart. "Jesus, listen," I said. "How about I buy you a bus or train ticket to New York, if that's where you're heading? We've already been arguing a little and it's only going to get worse."

Silence. No eye contact. No acknowledgment.

Before the light turned green, I glanced over and saw that

he was playing with the tab of the zipper on his bag, tugging it back and forth. I could hear the faint *zzz*. I went forward a block, then pulled over to an open stretch of curb. He was grinning at me. The morning sunlight made the skin of his scar look silvery and illuminated a few stray facial hairs just to the left of his goatee. The smallest crumb of cinnamon bun was stuck there, highlighting a poor shaving job. The top of the backpack was open, but he had both hands on his knees, fingers spread. "I don't like that idea very much," he said.

"Why not?"

"Because the police tend to check people in bus and train stations now."

"And why would that be a problem?"

He shrugged. "I have a fake ID They'll assume I'm here illegally and deport me."

"Just tell them what you told me: you're Jesus Christ, come down from heaven."

A shrug. The sad grin. "All right. I get the message." He reached into the backpack and I felt myself flinch. But when he brought his hand out again, it held only a small laminated card.

"Here," he said, reaching the card across the center console. "Take this in memory of me."

Before I could do or say anything, he'd opened the passenger-side door and climbed out. The door closed, gently. In the side mirror I could see him hoist the pack onto one shoulder and walk away. I watched him for a few seconds, fingering the card and waiting until he'd turned south on Pleasant Street and out of sight.

On one side of the laminated card was a yin-yang symbol, the circle split by a curved line, one half shaded, the other half white, with a little dot in each. I flipped it over and saw this:

"*No one saves us but ourselves. No one can and no one may. We ourselves must walk the path."* Buddha

Nothing, no part of it, made sense.

I pulled back into traffic and took the I-91 entrance ramp. Soon I was cruising along at 72 mph, passing and being passed, looking out at the gray hills and telling myself that abandoning the weird hitchhiker had been the only sensible move. While it's true that I like the occasional adventure, I'm not stupid or naive or careless with my life. I didn't much appreciate the glint of steel in the backpack, or the lack of a real ID. For a while, driving through Holyoke and Springfield—two once robust American cities that had been knocked to the canvas and were trying hard to stand up—I thought of calling the local police and telling them to be on the lookout for a hitchhiker with a backpack and an army jacket. I even reached for my phone. But what was I going to say? Hello, officer, this is Ed Valpolicella. I picked up a hitchhiker in Williamsburg and he said his name was Jesus and it seemed like he was more or less psychic, but I'm worried he might be dangerous.

No.

A thin filament of guilt was unspooling behind me as I drove, as if my thoughts were spilling out in a shiny black line. Either So-Called Jesus was dangerously unhinged, or he wasn't. If he was, I should have notified the police. If he wasn't, I should have kept my word and given him a ride. For one day. On and on it went, this nagging, interior dialogue, the chirping of an overactive conscience. I wanted to be good in the world. I wanted to do the right thing—by my wife, my kids, my readers, my fellow man. I wanted it so badly, in fact, that I sometimes found myself tangled up in hypothetical philosophical predicaments: What if I did this? Should I do that? Why hadn't I done it this way twenty-five years ago, made that decision last month, ended or pursued that friendship? It was a big part of the reason I'd stared meditating, to quiet the jittery mind. And it had mostly worked.

But that morning it wasn't working. So-Called Jesus had reached his fingers into my thoughts and loosed a balled-up fishing line, and now it was playing out behind me.

For a while I turned on the radio, but instead of calming or distracting me, it had the opposite effect. Two female talking heads were trying to figure out who would be the best candidate to put up against Donald Trump in 2020. One of them—so aggressive and talking so fast that I suspected she'd downed three cans of Red Bull in the Green Room—insisted that 'likeability' was a sexist term, more often applied to female candidates than to male. "The word should be retired," she insisted.

I recognized the other commentator—Jennifer Granholm, former governor of Michigan (and the woman who, a year later, would end up being President Biden's Energy Secretary). More quietly—perhaps only decaf for her in the Green Room—she said, "Well, I don't know. Likeability seems pretty important to me, in a candidate for president. Or for any office, actually."

I turned it off again. The political circus was so full of lies and hypocrisy—well off elected officials doing everything in their power to take from the poor and give to the rich, to take from the sick and give to the healthy—that my own moral failings seemed only like lizards in a snake-filled jungle. Small, mostly harmless lizards, to be sure—I hadn't tried to suppress any votes, hadn't cheated on my taxes, wasn't friends with any Russian oligarchs, hadn't lied to the FBI, wasn't interested in giving tax breaks to my friends who didn't need them, hadn't paid anyone to dig up dirt on anyone else—but reptilian all the same. A chastising voice muttered on and on: Couldn't you have given one poor, demented soul a ride as far as Harrisburg?

Or even New York City? Did you really care that much whether you had tea or coffee in the morning? Are you that particular, that full of fear?

Winding around all that was the ridiculous notion that maybe the hitchhiker *was* Jesus Christ. If so, I'd just forfeited a one-in-a-million chance to save my own soul, or at least polish it up a bit.

A few miles north of Hartford, Connecticut, I passed a billboard that I'd noticed on other trips to New York. WHERE ARE YOU GOING? It asked in large letters. On the left side was a dreamy picture of sunlit clouds and blue sky, and on the right a bank of scarlet flames. Along the bottom was written HEAVEN OR HELL? And a phone number you could call, apparently to find out which destination awaited you. I wondered who had paid for it, and why they thought they knew.

Like so many millions of others, I'd grown up with that kind of stuff, suckled on existential fear. A single slip up—you missed Mass on Sunday, once, after attending faithfully for years, then, on your way to confession you had a heart attack and died, and *boom,* an eternity of roasting. It was so easy to play on people's fears; the churches did it, the politicians were constantly doing it. I laughed a small, awkward laugh, sped on, told myself I was a good husband, good father, good citizen. Leaving one nutty hitchhiker on a street corner in a very safe city, breaking one small promise—those sins weren't worth the guilty little scraps of thought they were printed on. I tossed the laminated card onto the empty seat beside me and drove on toward the Big Apple.

~ ~

chapter five

My literary agent, Janet Esther Lee, is a giant in the business. When editors at the major publishing houses see her name on their caller ID, they answer the phone. When she presses them for a larger advance, more often than not, they cough it up. JL, as she's known in the business, grew up in Manhattan's Chinatown neighborhood, daughter of a couple who sold fruit from a sidewalk cart on Canal Street and knew, in total, maybe 200 words of English. Janet won a scholarship to Columbia and rode the train all the way uptown for four years, working the fruit stand evenings and weekends to pay for clothes and subway fare. Shortly after earning her degree—with distinction—she talked herself into a job at *The New Yorker* magazine, stayed there a couple of years, impressed everyone with her work ethic and brilliance, made connections in the publishing industry, then left the magazine to take a position in the offices of the now-defunct Mastodon Associates, America's most powerful literary agency in those years, as an 'agent associate' to the famous R.J. McAdams, another legend.

Four years later, just as her career at Mastodon was blooming and she was about to be offered a share in the business and her name on the stationery, she shocked R.J. McAdams and the rest of the New York literary world by resigning from Mastodon and starting a boutique agency in Chinatown, J.E. Lee Ltd. Thanks to a decade of 85-hour weeks, shrewd business tactics, and an uncanny ability to take on authors that were like 20-1 shots at the horse track but ultimately paid off big, within a decade Janet had assembled a stable of successful writers and had four agents working under her. At that point, on a visit to a writers' conference at Kansas State College, she discovered and decided to represent a little-known author named Alice G. Vunder. Vunder, as everyone on earth knows by now, wrote the Lindsay Z. Cabot series, earned herself three-quarters of a billion dollars writing novels about a goofy, sexually overactive private detective, earned Janet 15% of that sum, and by the time I managed, by a stroke of luck and the recommendation of a good friend, to convince JL to represent me, she owned a five-story building near the corner of Canal and Mulberry and was an icon in the writing world.

Once a year, Janet agreed to have lunch with me, and I considered myself lucky to get that much of her time. Her speaking agent had been the one who landed me the Arkansas gig, and so, when I told her I'd decided to drive instead of fly, JL decided it made sense for us to have our annual lunch on my way south.

With guilt and doubt—those twin demons—still unspooling behind me, leaving a thin string of maybes and what-ifs, I followed I-91 to New Haven, merged onto I-95, followed that road through the precious towns of Southwest Connecticut—Darien, New Canaan, Greenwich—and then through the equally precious towns of Westchester, turned off onto the West Side Highway (because I'm directionally challenged and it's the only way I know how to get into the City), took the exit for Canal Street, pulled into an outrageously expensive garage on the Bowery, and walked to Da Giacomo, an Italian place in what was left of Little Italy. The food there was fairly good, and I liked the people well enough, despite the fact that they tossed the occasional "*Si,*" or "*Va bene,*" at tourists so they'd feel they were getting the authentic Italian American experience. Janet was a regular, and a generous tipper, and so we always got the red-carpet treatment: a quiet table in the back room, a free plate of fruit and cheese after the meal, grappa or limoncello on the house.

I made the three-block walk from the Bowery to Mulberry, enjoying the liveliness of Canal Street, the people selling knockoff purses and baby bok choy, the Chinese barber shops and stores offering herbs, tea, and acupuncture services. I loved the busyness of that neighborhood, the narrow five and six-story brick buildings adorned with gargoyles and stone carvings, the small shops and fruit stands, the whole sense of variety and individual industriousness. Capitalism at its finest.

As I turned right onto Mulberry and headed north to the rendezvous, I noticed, on the back of a parked Porsche SUV, these two words in five-inch decals: LET JESUS with a black-and-white image of someone's imaginary Christ glued onto the window above them. I kept walking. But the decals started up that little run of guilt again, and I arrived for the annual lunch in something less than a perfectly peaceful state of mind. Janet was waiting for me, glass of red wine in front of her. She stood, we shook hands, then sat opposite each other and ordered. Chicken cacciatore for me, and, for her, a ten-inch arugula pizza.

She's an attractive woman, with lively and easy to read facial expressions, a fondness for big dangling earrings and intense eye contact. "So," she said, after the briefest exchange of pleasantries, "anything in the works?"

"Nothing," I answered, because I knew it was futile to fabricate. JL saw through writers' fake optimism as if it were aquarium glass in a fish shop. Behind the glass coasted the bloated carp of failed imaginings, stunted attempts, shitty stories slipped into the trash file on a bad morning. "I've tried a dozen or so things, gotten as far as forty or fifty pages a couple of times, and then tossed them aside. I'm stuck."

Our salads arrived. Janet picked at hers distractedly, and, in a sudden burst of terror it occurred to me that she might lift her eyes and tell me it was time for me to "move on." She'd made a fortune in her years as an agent, owned the building in Chinatown, a ski house in Vermont, represented household-name writers with big TV and film deals. What money I made her was chump change in comparison, and if I had nothing finished, nothing for her to sell, what good was wasting time on me?

But I'd always had the sense that Janet wasn't in it for the money, or not only for the money. A practicing Buddhist herself, she had seemed to genuinely admire *Breakfast with Buddha.*

She swallowed, took a sip of wine, met my eyes and said, "Your niche is what I call 'quirky spiritual'."

"A term I've always liked."

"Yes. We've done fairly well with Buddha, Edward, but maybe it's time to move on."

"Move on where?" I asked, suddenly worried again, thinking of the various things 'move on' might mean. Mostly it could mean me, agentless, with a daughter two years away from college. Trying to get something taken by the big New York houses without an agent would be like wandering across the DMZ between North and South Korea without a flak jacket.

My heart was thumping. I kept a pleasant expression on my face.

Our meals were served, but my appetite had slipped out the

door onto Mulberry Street. Janet separated the three slices of one half of her pizza in a delicate way, as if she were peeling the skin from a clove of garlic, just fingertips. We each took another sip of wine, but by then something else had occurred to me. I was starting to get a queasy feeling that had little to do with college tuition payments. By the time she said the next words, I had the cold line of prickles running up both arms and behind my neck all over again.

She twirled the stem of her wine glass. "You might try writing something about Jesus."

With the trembling tines of my fork, I knocked a gravy-soaked piece of green pepper off the side of the plate and onto the white tablecloth. Trying to rescue it, I made quite a mess. Janet watched me make the mess. "You okay?"

"Too much coffee this morning."

"Any objection to Jesus?"

The busboy refilled our water glasses, eyed the tablecloth as if he'd be assigned to clean it before taking the 7 train back to Queens, and pretended not to hear what Janet had said. I shook my head, speared the pepper, deposited it safely back on the plate, looked up. "The problem with Jesus," I said, thinking fast, "is that everybody believes they already know him. Christians and otherwise, everybody has an idea of who he is, what he's like."

Janet had a nice smile. The waiter swung by and said, "*Tutto a posto?*" sounding as if Spanish were his main tongue, and she replied, "*Si, si, grazie,*" in an accent that had more of Shanghai than Naples in it. "Edward," she said when the waiter had left us in peace, and I thought: *here it comes; you are about to be cut loose.* "Want my advice?"

"Sure."

"Make him likeable."

"A sexist term," I said. It just slipped out.

She ignored my foolishness. "People like likeable."

"Right, okay," I said.

"You're right about how everyone thinks they know him, but find a fresh angle. Make his story pertinent to modern life, if you can. We need a new Jesus these days, as I'm sure you'll agree."

"I do. I'll give it a shot."

"You grew up Catholic, didn't you?"

"I did, but I don't—"

"Be irreverent, but not offensive. Make him real."

"Sure."

"You don't sound convinced. Do you have a better idea?"

"No, no, it's fine," I said, but my skin was crawling beneath my shirt. "It's just . . . I have to say that . . . I wonder sometimes, if Jesus actually showed up at my door one day, well, I'm not sure I'd let him in. Which is strange, because I'm a religious guy, in my own way. I guess I feel like the so-called "Christians" have pushed me away from Jesus. The bumper stickers, the hateful rhetoric, the congressmen on their knees at prayer in front of the Capitol, the support of candidates who take from the poor and give to the rich . . . no offense. I guess, at some level, all that has made me not want to associate myself with Jesus. Not that I don't admire him, I do, but I'm a Buddhist now, mainly, if I had to give a name to what I believe. People don't usually screw the poor in Buddha's name . . ."

"My parents were Catholic, did you know that?"

"I thought you—"

She was shaking her head. "We went to Mass every Sunday. The Church of the Transfiguration. Mott Street, four doors down from our house. There's so much overlap, don't you agree, between Buddha and Jesus?"

"Sure, yes, but most people look to one or the other for their—"

She laughed and leaned down to reach into her purse. "A client of mine published this. I brought it for you."

She passed a book across the table, an elegantly designed hardcover titled *JESUS WENT EAST.* I made a show of paging through it, looking at the author photo, reading the introduction, but I was, for some reason, terribly distracted.

"I'm so happy about the Arkansas talk," Janet was saying. "And this is what I mean: a Protestant church inviting you to speak about a book with "Buddha" in the title! How wonderful is that! There's a lot of open-mindedness around, don't you agree?"

"Sure, yes, absolutely," I said, but I wasn't sure. The closed-minded ones always seemed louder, closer to the levers of power, more numerous. I set the book down on the tablecloth, safely away from the gravy stain. Janet finished her main course, but my appetite had wandered farther down Mulberry Street, dazed, drifting, bumping into people and standing on street corners as if waiting for a sign. I picked at the food, took a few small bites for show, spread things around like a kid pretending to eat his vegetables. We lingered for a while over the fruit and cheese and limoncello. I offered to pay, but Janet had already given the waiter her credit card. "I think you're onto something," she said, as if writing about Jesus had been my idea. "I think this is going to be big."

~ ❦ ~

chapter six

I thanked Janet for the lunch, and while she remained at the table to make a few calls, I stepped out into the April sun. Little Italy had shrunk to a shadow of its former self. In the early and middle part of the 20th Century, it had covered twenty square blocks and was a teeming hive of food markets and eating places, with a mafia den or two thrown in for good measure. What remained of that now was a mini and partially-fake Little Italy, a couple of streets with a dozen or so restaurants, guys standing out front, inviting you in, and souvenir shops selling T-shirts and name tags and baby onesies with things like "Yes, I'm adorable, and I'm Italian, too!" or coffee mugs with various sayings from mob movies. It was more sad than offensive to a person like me, someone whose grandparents had emigrated from the hilltowns outside Naples, and who'd grown up in a tight little world of Italian Americans.

Chinatown seemed to have had better luck retaining both its population and integrity. In addition to a host of other small businesses, sprinkled everywhere from lower Mulberry to Bayard to Grand to Mott, were places offering foot and backrubs for prices that seemed shockingly low. Anticipating the long drive ahead, I ducked into one of them, down a white-painted set of metal stairs, along a short hallway with a sign, in

English and what I guessed was Mandarin, that read NO SEXUAL SERVICE. Fine by me. I turned left through a pane-glass door into a tiny reception area that fronted a warren of narrow rooms with beds in them, curtains instead of walls. The woman at the desk did not speak English well at all. After a couple of fruitless exchanges, I pointed to the price board—fifteen minutes for twelve dollars—and she directed me into one of the back rooms.

There were plastic hooks for clothing and a small sign in both languages: YOU MAY TAKE OFF YOUR SHIRTS AND PANTS BUT *PLEASE LEAVE ON YOUR UNDERWEARS.*

I took off my shirts and shoes. In a few seconds a man entered and gestured for me to lie face-down on the paper covering the table. I pointed to my upper back and settled in. He began to work on me, pressing down hard on the muscles in a fast rhythm, then moving onto the vertebrae, then the sides of my neck and the soft tissue behind my ears. Scalp, shoulders, ribs. He said nothing. It was warm in the room. It seemed to me he was finding the exact places where my muscles were knotted up, and I tried to relax under the energetic kneading and not worry about what Janet had said, about what I should be writing next, about bills and books and kids in college, and if the hitchhiker had been anything other than a scam artist. I tried not to worry at all. At the end, the man gave a series of light karate chops up and down my back, then tapped me once on top of my head to signal that the treatment was finished. He left the room. I sat up and gathered myself. I felt thirty years younger.

I tucked in my shirts, laced up my running shoes, and refilled my pockets with the usual cargo—iPhone, Swiss Army Knife, paper money, coins, a pen, a folded receipt from Bread

Euphoria. I sighed, parted the curtain, and went out into the tiny reception area.

There, sitting on one of the leatherette chairs and smiling up at me, was So-Called Jesus. "I'll have the fifteen-minute treatment, also," he said to the woman. She seemed to understand him without any pointing or gesturing. And then he said to me, "Wait for me, would you, Edward?" Before I could answer, he'd jumped to his feet and disappeared into one of the massage rooms.

I paid and went out the glass-pane door, up the metal steps, and stood on the sidewalk of Grand Street, watching the world. An elderly woman, barely able to put one foot in front of the next and leaning on a cane, shuffled along in a stream of faster walkers. Car horns sounded. Drivers waited impatiently at the light, then surged forward, switched lanes, checking phones and adjusting radio dials as they went. A man set navel oranges in a pyramid on his fruit cart, polishing them one by one with his bare hands. Garbage trucks, police vehicles, two motorcycles, a limousine, a fire engine rolling by in no great hurry. The sights, the sounds, the smells, the blue spring sky flashing behind cottony clouds—what I loved about New York City was that it pushed the world up against the skin of your face. On one block, in ten minutes, you could hear a dozen languages, see people of every race and size and shape, old, young, healthy, crippled, tremendously rich and desperately poor, perfectly sane and awfully troubled, the workers and the cheaters, the satisfied and the miserable. If you weren't too obsessed with getting somewhere in a hurry, if you weren't too concerned about your health or career or money situation, or that of your loved ones, if you weren't hungry or in pain or wrestling with an emotional crisis of one kind or another, then New York—lower Manhattan, especially—encouraged you to ponder the fact that you were alive in a body on a spinning ball of stone in space.

It seemed to me that, from the time I was a little boy, wandering the fine gray sand of Revere Beach with my mother holding my hand, watching seagulls with clams clasped in their beaks flap up into the sky and release their payload, hoping to break the shell and have access to their meal, watching jets from all over creation glide in toward a landing at Logan Airport, part of me had been obsessed with the strangeness of it all, the meaning of it all. What was I supposed to be doing? Why was I here? Later, in Sunday School, I'd batter the nuns with questions like that. Even then, their platitudes—*God wants you to love Him, Edward, and love your neighbor*—didn't settle my mental wanderings. As an adult, stepping away from the rigorous RC rules, I'd become a regular reader of the mystics of every tradition, assembling a small library of books that offered various explanations and answers. I'd more or less come to be at peace with all of it, more or less reached an understanding of the limitations of thought. I'd watched my children be born; I'd watched my brother die; I'd written novels that orbited the hot star of some central mystery.

And yet, still, enough puzzlement remained to keep me curious. It was part of why I'd wanted to drive to Arkansas, not fly. I wanted to watch life being lived. I wanted to lie down beside the mystery and make love to it.

That obsession—and that's the right word—had given me a writing career and a meditation practice. It had also landed me there, on a sidewalk in Chinatown, trying to decide whether I should walk away and retrieve my car, or wait for a shady character who called himself Jesus and was apparently able to read my mind and follow me wherever I went. Beside what I'd said to Janet about the "Christians" having spoiled Jesus for me, the problem was that, while the man who'd been in my car seemed magical, he did not seem particularly *holy,* to use a loaded word. There was no halo, no sense of overflowing kindness, no aura of Biblical miracles. He was a rather shaggy citizen of the modern world, in an Army jacket, with a backpack. Badly shaved, rough-featured, scarred, sometimes almost macho and other times weirdly girlish—to use another loaded word. Despite his remarkable tricks, he didn't fit the Jesus of my imagination, and so, there was, even with his sudden reappearance, a not-so-quiet voice of skepticism muttering between my ears. Part of me wanted to believe in signs and miracles and accept the idea that I was being offered a rare gift, a chance to finally figure things out at the deepest level. And another part of me, the more educated, cynical, logical part, worried I was losing my mind . . . or being had.

Still and all, for some unknown reason, I decided I would wait for him.

~ ~

chapter seven

After a quarter of an hour, Jesus bounded up the stairs and stopped beside me. "Incredible, wasn't it? Does your neck feel as good as mine?"

"Very good."

"Ready for the road?"

I nodded, but, in spite of the relaxed neck, it felt like my skull was filled with ball bearings, clanging metal, excess weight. Any movement caused a certain confused clanging. We walked east, toward the Bowery and the parking garage. "One thing about me," So-Called Jesus said after a few steps, "one thing they get right: I'm endlessly forgiving. I give people a second chance, and a third chance. An infinity of chances."

"That's not the message I grew up with," I said.

"Well, that's part of why I'm here, to help you edit those messages."

I was tempted to ask about the other parts of why he was there, but *guarded* was the word for how I felt then. Guarded, wary, unsure. I found myself processing the lunch with Janet and, at the same time, waiting for the next odd coincidence—a car going past with *Leave it all to Jesus* painted on the back window. Or someone handing us a *Jews for Jesus* pamphlet at the corner of Mott Street. Or Jesus asking if he could use a credit card, just for a second, in one of the souvenir shops we passed. Wariness wasn't a feeling I liked. In fact, I prided myself on being open, mostly fearless, amenable to whatever life set in front of me. Amazing how fast things can change. And amazing what a vast different there can be between who you are and who you think you are.

We retrieved the Camry and headed out (I gave the attendant a two-dollar tip, and, strangely, saw Jesus slip him something, as well), working our way through the maze of Lower Manhattan and into the Holland Tunnel. The tunnel had been opened to the public in 1927 . . . and looks it. The pitted roadbed, the dirty tiles, the lights that seem to be shining through a few yards of Hudson River silt—you half expect the ceiling to crack and water to start spurting through, or an entire nation of rats to appear in front of your car, marching along in formation.

"Guess where it gets its name," Jesus said to me as we went along. The dust, the grit, the noise, the drivers straddling lanes as they wrote an urgent text and steered with their elbows.

"If I have my history right, the Dutch purchased Manhattan from the native peoples. I'm guessing the name comes from that."

"Bad guess," Jesus said, in a tone that irritated me.

"Well, it sounds like you know."

"I do know," he said, and then he fell silent.

We bumped and sped along. I was anxious to get safely out into daylight and I was thinking this: He can't be Jesus, because the real Jesus would never be so obnoxious.

"The other thing I know is that people are sent to earth to perform specific tasks."

"Makes sense."

"Clifford Holland, for instance. Chief engineer for this project."

"Really."

"Really. Died two days before the people digging from the Jersey side were going to meet up with the people digging from the Manhattan side. Age 41. Heart attack. People say it was caused by the stress of overseeing a project like this, but it was simply the case that his work in this dimension was finished. At one point, cutting through stone, they were moving at the pace of one foot per day, imagine?"

"What makes you say that, about people sent to earth to perform specific tasks."

"Because that's the way it's all set up."

Part of me wanted to say, sarcastically, *I guess you know everything about how it's all set up.* And the other part wanted to . . . ask how it was all set up. I don't want to sound too wishy-washy here, I'm not that way usually, but I'm trying to get at the exact truth of how I felt then, and the truth is, the two halves of me were at war. The wary, sensible, educated half was whispering a steady stream of counsel and mockery in my left ear: *He's a human being, a master trickster. You're an idiot for letting him ride with you. Not only are you putting your own life at risk, you're risking the future of your kids, your family's financial stability . . . and making a fool of yourself into the bargain. Maybe he has some special abilities, sure, fine, but Houdini had some special abilities, too. That didn't qualify him to answer questions on the eternal truths.*

In the other ear, a quieter voice was presenting a different case, a stream of thought that started with *what if. What if he isn't an ordinary guy, or a trickster? What if, after decades of wondering, puzzling, questioning, reading, meditating, trying to be good, you're being given an extremely rare opportunity to understand the meaning of life on another level? What if he's going to help you get ready for death?*

Near the end of the tunnel there was a little preparation—a

glimmer—and then an explosion of daylight and what felt, even though we weren't breathing it, like suddenly cleaner air. A sense of freedom, too, and hope, as if we'd survived something difficult and were being given our reward. Maybe—I thought—the way we'd feel after our time on earth was finished.

Just beyond the end of the tunnel, you come to something called St. John's Roundabout, an ordinary traffic circle as far as I was concerned, but it prompted So-Called Jesus to say this: "John was a friend."

"Really."

He nodded. "He was the only one there at the crucifixion, he and mother and Mary and my yoga friend."

"Your yoga friend?"

"John was the only one who focused on the miracles when he wrote up my story. The only one who said so much as a single word about the water and wine at the Cana wedding. The only one who wrote about the Samaritan woman at the well."

"I don't remember that one," I said, playing along, stalling.

"It's an important moment, and it leads to something even more important. . . . I'll tell you about that later. She'd had many lovers. These days you might call her promiscuous, or worse, but she was a woman of real faith and we had an instant connection. After we chatted for a while, she went back into the town and spread the word: "He told me everything I've done, so he must be the Messiah." That's what trust looks like, my friend. That's a line you should ponder."

"Why's that?"

"Because she was mocked and ridiculed, the bottom of the social order, and all she needed in order to believe that I am who I am was one comment—I told her she'd had a lot of husbands, which was a kind of code for the fact that she slept around. No miracle, no long lecture. She looked at me, heard me reveal one surprising truth, and that was it."

We rose up then into the clamorous landscape of northern New Jersey, a scene I've loved since the first time I saw it. Acres of refineries, huge shipping cranes, airliners taking off and landing at Newark, choked roadways, warehouses, here and there polluted canals and estuaries lined with patches of yellow reeds. People make fun of that part of the world, but it seems wonderful to me. *Muscular* is the word that comes to mind. Steel and oil, engines and the rusty old superstructure of bridges—nothing anybody would want to paint or photograph, maybe, but, if you look at it a certain way, it's the stuff that feeds us and keeps us warm. It speaks to me of sweat and ingenuity, of the *real.*

I had the sense Jesus wasn't particularly interested. He seemed focused inward, eyes lowered and half closed, concentrating on something other than the musculature of North Jersey.

"There's so much *not there* in what you people call 'The Bible'," he said quietly.

"Really."

"Sure. You know it pretty well, don't you?"

"Pretty well."

"Much of it is fairly accurate," he said in a sad way.

"These days people would kill you for that *fairly accurate,* you know. Literally kill you. The Bible is said to be divinely inspired. People stake their whole life on that, their whole system of belief. Wars have been fought over that idea. People have been tortured, burned at the stake, sent to prison."

A sad nod. "There's a great deal of wisdom and truth in those pages, but there's a missing section. Some important sections have never been found. Many, in fact. You know what I'm getting at, right?"

"I haven't the faintest idea."

"But you say you know the Bible."

"I was raised Catholic. We went to Mass every Sunday. Heard two readings every week for something like 25 years. Plus Sunday School and two years of Catholic high school. At some point, I was sixteen or eighteen, I read the whole thing start to finish."

"And you never noticed anything peculiar?"

We were leaving the craziness of those roads then and heading west on I-78 into the forested suburban hills. Someone in a white Ford Escalade pulled into the middle lane in front of me, and then slowed down. Exactly the kind of move that turns me from calm meditation practitioner to angry citizen. I said a word I shouldn't have said, pulled into the passing lane and pushed down on the pedal. "Unbelievable!" I muttered under my breath and then I hurried along for a minute or so until I calmed down and remembered that Jesus had asked a question.

"Peculiar? Sure. There are a lot of "thees" and "thous" which, speaking as a writer, can make it sound a little dated. God can seem pretty brutal at times. And then you come along. The sermon on the mount is hard to take. I like the parables, mostly, though the prodigal son has always bothered me because—"

"I'm not asking for a book report. I'm asking if you noticed anything peculiar, anything missing."

I considered that for a few seconds, still off balance. "Well, there's not much sex, and what sex there is is all adultery, kinky stuff, and prostitution."

"That shows where your mind is. It reveals your principal chakra."

"What!"

"Anything else?"

"Nothing I can think of right at the moment, with these idiots on their phones and cutting—-would you look at this ass!"

"About seventeen years."

"Right. That's how long it will take me to get to Harrisburg if we keep having people going 55 in the fast lane, calling their broker to make a trade!"

"Seventeen years are missing. From the life story of a certain central character."

By a supreme exertion of will, I forced myself to calm down. I scraped around in my memory. "There's that scene where you get upset at your mother. You were a kid, a teenager, teaching or talking in the temple, right? They set off in the caravan without you and realized you weren't there and had to turn around. "Woman, don't you know I have to be about my Father's business," you said to your Mom, when she was upset at you. That's the last we see of you until—"

"Until I'm thirty and come back to Jerusalem."

"Right, I remember now. The palms, the donkey. I always loved that—"

"Doesn't it seem at all strange, Edward? You're telling someone's life story, and you take him from birth to age thirteen and then you start up the story again when he's thirty and no editor says, 'Hey, Valpolicella, are there a few missing chapters?' No critic says, 'Valpolicella's novel is captivating, but fatally flawed by an enormous chronological gap?' "

"I never thought of it that way. Was it ever written down, the missing part?"

"By five different people. Some put it on the wrong kind of parchment and it turned to dust after several hundred years. Some left it in caves in odd places—northern Malta, for example. The Bodrum Peninsula in Turkey. India, Tibet, Afghanistan. Those manuscripts will likely never be found, that's the terrible truth. And if they are found, they'll be suppressed. I can promise you."

"So what happened in those years," I said, still basically humoring him, stalling, trying to focus on the road circus. "Tell me."

"I plan to. That's the reason I came to see you, my Edward! This is your whole professional purpose!"

~ ~

chapter eight

Even when three-quarters of you is wondering if the person speaking them is a trickster, a criminal, an escapee from an institution of one sort or another, you can't hear words like "*The reason I came to see you,*" and "*This is your whole purpose*" and just drive along Interstate 78 as if it's an ordinary April morning. I tried to do that, however. I have this unadmirable habit—my wife will tell you—of ignoring difficult situations and hoping they'll disappear. It doesn't go on too long; once I realize the problem isn't going away, I deal with it head-on. But too often my first impulse is to hit the pause button, take no action, pretend I didn't hear or see something that I know, at some level, I heard or saw. In fact, I'd been doing exactly that for the whole day, dealing with a guy who called himself Jesus and knew some psychic tricks and wanted me to take him all the way to Arkansas, and pretending that was all more or less acceptable. I knew I'd have to take action at some point, either decide to let him ride with me the whole way or kick him out onto the street, but for the time being I was hitting the pause button.

So-Called Jesus had fallen quiet. I sneaked a look. He had a strong profile—powerful chin, large nose, prominent cheekbones, his long brown hair hooked behind his ears and hanging down as far as the collar of his army jacket. His hands were wide and thick-fingered, yet somehow graceful, and as we went along he kept them folded in his lap, which adorned him with an aura of peacefulness, as if he were totally relaxed and had nothing on earth to worry about.

As long as I'm confessing here, I should add that, although I think of myself as a decent person—good husband, devoted father, thoughtful citizen of the world—from time to time I notice an ugly thought slithering through the pasture of my ordinary musings. A viper in tall grass. Here's an example: glancing over at my passenger, seeing how relaxed he looked, how carefree, I sensed a poisonous voice whispering something like this: *sure, easy for him to be relaxed; all he does is beg rides from people who work for a living. Anybody can be that calm; all you have to do is let other people take responsibility.*

Etcetera. Etcetera.

In order to silence this unattractive musing, I turned on the radio. Which was, for a person hoping to encourage a more positive line of thought, a mistake. Months earlier there had been another school shooting, this one in Florida. The surviving kids had tried to do something about it. They were appearing on TV, protesting, marching, making appeals to various elected representatives in the hope of changing the horrid situation.

And this tells you more about the moral state of the nation than anything else: because of their well intended activism, they were the targets of death threats and hate tweets! The news report was focusing on that. Jesus didn't seem to be listening, but I couldn't bear it. I actually enjoy target shooting. I admire people who hunt for their meat instead of buying it in a bloodless, plastic-wrapped package in the supermarket. But I cannot tolerate people who make death threats because they absolutely have to have their AK-47s or AR-15s in case the Government comes to their home one day and they need to put up a fight and defend their family and swimming pool. There they are with their ammo and automatic weaponry, firing out of the bedroom window, and the Government is outside with tanks and trained soldiers and bazookas and so on. But they're going to make a stand! No damn government is going to tell them what to do!

It's not only idiocy of the highest order, it leads to the death of children.

I snapped the radio back into silence.

Somewhere near Bedminster, New Jersey—where our president at the time had one of his golf courses—Jesus said, "Take this exit."

I didn't like his tone of voice. A gentle command, as if I were a hired driver and he were on his way to an important business meeting. My bad half was wondering if this might be the moment when he'd direct me down a dead end side street, where his friends would be waiting. I'd be mugged or carjacked, my computer stolen, my beaten body left in a dumpster behind a tattoo parlor.

"Bathroom stop?" I asked, with a little edge.

He turned to look at me. I could feel his eyes. But I had to concentrate on the exit ramp, an overloaded pickup right in front of me, looking as if it were about to drop a rusty pipe or an old toilet seat from the top of a pile of junk in its bed.

"Take this right," Jesus said.

"A detour?" I asked, again with that small edge. "I have a schedule to keep, you know."

"You have five days to go fifteen hundred miles."

"Right. But I was hoping for a little time here and there to relax, see the sights, take America's pulse, that kind of thing."

No response for a minute, then a couple of directions—

"Right at this intersection. Next left." We passed a sign for the USGA museum, went another mile, and then he said, "turn in."

A parking lot. A dumpster. I looked around for the tattoo parlor.

"Stop here. It will take only a minute."

Jesus got out and walked across the newly paved lot. I watched him. He looked around, looked up, and then knelt there, leaned over, and pressed his face against the tar. If I've seen stranger things, I don't remember them. I sat watching him through the passenger window. A minute. Two minutes. Another slithering snake of mental energy said—*just leave him here, he's a nutcase.* But some better stream of thought trumped that one, and I realized it was not in my nature to do such a thing. He was maybe sixty yards away so I couldn't be sure, but it seemed to me that his upper body, bent over that way, was shaking. It was a violent shaking, as if he were laughing crazily, but then I saw him straighten up—still on his knees—and wipe the sleeve of his jacket across first one eye and then the next.

Another minute or so and he stood, let his chin hang down to his chest so that his hair swung forward and blocked his face from view. And then he turned and made his way slowly back to the car and got in. "Hurry back to the highway and get on your schedule," he said in a flat tone.

I made the ten-minute drive back to I-78 not in the finest of moods. I don't mind doing favors for people. And I don't need to hear 'thank you' every time. But . . . "That's not a very nice tone of voice," I said.

"Sorry."

"What was that all about?"

A pause. I could see him blinking and wiping at his eyes, and I was wondering if it was some kind of act.

"The school shootings," he said quietly.

"I'm pretty sure there wasn't a school shooting in that parking lot. Or anywhere in Bedminster, New Jersey. If there was, I never heard about it. And I pay attention to those things. I feel for those kids, for their parents, for the ones who die and the ones who live. I wonder how God can allow it. And I wonder why it happens here so much more than anyplace else on earth."

Silence. The wooded hills, an occasional large, wood-frame home here and there but mainly trees by the millions, not yet in bloom. I was thinking about what it would feel like to watch your friends shot with an automatic weapon, watch them bleed to death . . . and then to get death threats. "You seem to know how it's all set up," I said, "so give me the explanation. God loves us, okay? Why does He or She or It let that happen?"

Nothing. Not a word. Jesus was looking straight ahead, so still he seemed not to be breathing.

I drove on. It occurred to me then, not for the first time, that there exists a gulf between words and reality's deeper layers. I'm a person of the word; I make my living that way. I tell stories, and by telling stories try to make sense of things. To a certain extent it works. You read a book, or a newspaper, or listen to or watch the evening news, or you go online and scan the latest articles, and it's through words that you get a sense of what's happening around you. Words are indispensable. And yet, there's another way in which those sentences, those letters lined up on a screen or page, can't get a grip on the deeper truth. They *approach* it, the way music does, and poetry does, and painting does. They suggest something. But they can't really reach it. It's like speaking with someone on the phone, or via Skype; it's not the same as being in the room with them, or holding them. And even then, even being in the room with someone, even holding that person, even making love with another human being, there is a level of *inaccessibility*, to use a word. A mystery. A hint of something else going on, their presence, your presence. I had my hand on my youngest brother's leg when he took his last breath. Try capturing that in words. You can say "he died" or "I was there when he died" or "I had my hand on my brother's leg when he died" and that indicates some layer of reality, of course it does. But not all of it. Try using words to describe what the kids in Florida went through.

No, there's a layer of reality that remains unreachable, and as Jesus remained silent and I put some miles between us and the Bedminster parking lot, I was considering that. In word-thoughts.

~ ~

chapter nine

Another half hour or so and I started to see signs for Bethlehem, Pennsylvania.

"We were talking about the Gap," Jesus said, breaking his long silence and pronouncing the word as if Gap should be capitalized.

"What gap?"

"The Gap in my so-called story."

"Why 'so-called'?"

"Because it's inaccurate. In certain places."

"The Bible, you mean."

"The so-called New Testament."

"What about it?"

"There's a Gap."

"A big one, from the sound of things."

"Too big," he said.

"You sound angry."

"Frustrated."

"No one likes to be partly remembered."

It was a weird thing to say, a little burst of thought that had come out of my mixed feelings about the guy, and not in my kindest tone. So I tried to soften it. "We want the real story told about us. We want to be remembered correctly. I'd hate it, for example, if someone told my grandkids the story of my life and left out a big chunk. If I had grandkids, which I don't."

"You will."

"Thanks. You predict the future, I guess."

A pause, and then, "Delaware NV 6014."

"Huh?"

Another dose of his silence. *One weird dude,* I was thinking. *One very strange dude.* On we went. Seven or eight miles ahead, a green Honda Civic with a *CHRISTIE 2020!* bumper sticker cut so sharply in front of me that I leaned hard on the horn. The driver swerved back into her own lane.

"On the phone! Naturally!" I said, maybe a little too angrily because I was trying to cover over the fact that the Honda's license plate was NV 6014. Delaware. Another psychic trick. "What about the Gap?" I said, so as not to have to acknowledge anything.

"Painful."

"Please elaborate, sir."

He laughed. It was that tinkling-piano-key sound again, and it brought a breath of good air into the car. "Matthew has me until I'm thirteen, and then *poof.*"

"Right, I remember. It always struck me that you were a little harsh on your mom in that last scene."

"You were rather harsh with your mother, were you not?"

"I was. I was seven. We had a little fight, and I used the *c-word.* But I'd just heard it on the streets, I didn't know what it meant."

"Still wrong."

"Yes, my father came home and, you know, it was the only time he—"

"I know what he did, Edward."

"But Jesus isn't supposed to do things like that to his mother. She came back looking for you, the way any worried mother would, and you gave her some line about being about your father's business. Seemed cold."

"It was wrongly written down. I would never in a million lifetimes speak to her rudely. I still don't."

"She's still around then."

He swiveled his head and looked at me. "What a stupid question that is, Edward. And asked sarcastically on top of it all. Where do you suppose she could go, that beautiful spirit? Beyond creation? Into a dimension unreachable to me?"

"Sorry." When he pronounced my name, a little shot of something went through me, a chill. At the same time, I had almost 100% resolved by then not to stir up the waters, to pay for his room for a night in Harrisburg, leave him with some money, and head out on my own. The thought that I'd have to deal with him and his preposterous imaginings and psychic tricks for five days was more than I could, or wanted to, bear.

"You're cherishing a doubt," he said.

"Listen, okay? You're obviously psychic and I appreciate that, admire it even. An amazing trick, figuring out where I was in New York and getting there. Plus, the car from Delaware. Really incredible. And you have a great name. And you and I feel the same way about what happened in Florida and the other mass murders of kids. But I am an ordinary, sane, normal, late-middle-aged guy. A wife, a house, kids, a two-year-old car, bills. I play golf, for God's sake! I like to eat. And you clearly seem to be pretending to be the historical Jesus who, I might add, in many circles is considered to be God."

"Or his son," he put in.

"Whatever. I'm just not into it, as my kids would say. I'm not down with it. I don't buy it."

"You are within your rights to express that opinion."

"Thank you."

"What would it take to convince you?"

"Nothing."

"Really? Nothing?"

"I'm a doubting Edward. I need more than the Samaritan woman at the well. I need to put my hands into your wounds, and then, you know . . . maybe."

I half-expected him to reach one bloody, pierced palm across the gearshift and let me put my fingers into it, much as the Biblical Thomas is said to have done. Instead, he "hmpfd" and kept his eyes straight ahead. "So you're going to drop me at the hotel, give me a little cash and go on your way?"

"I haven't decided. Not completely. But probably, yes. You'll just have to find another Edward out there someplace, another writer you can tell your story to."

A pause. The latest in a series of irritating silences. The roadway and the hum of the tires. Two or three minutes of a bad air in the Camry's front seat, a sign saying there were three exits for Bethlehem, and then Jesus said, "You didn't eat much during your lunch with Janet. Are you hungry?"

~ ❦ ~

chapter ten

If the mass shootings are America's #1 disgrace, then the fact that some of our countrymen are hungry is, in my humble opinion, #2 on the bad list. Hungry kids, especially. I take such pleasure in eating, that the idea of anyone going hungry—especially in a nation as abundant as ours—fills me with a bad mix of shame, anger, guilt, and frustration. Every year I offer online book sales to raise money for the local food bank, and I try to give street corner beggars something to eat or drink rather than money (I have an addicted sister who used to beg on street corners so I'm wary about handing over cash). I'm never painfully hungry, never really wanting for food, and so what little work I do for the hungry doesn't seem close to enough. As we pulled into the city of Bethlehem, Pennsylvania, I found myself wanting to ask Jesus about hunger—why it happens, who's to blame, how to fix it, how best to respond—and then I remembered I'd mostly made up my mind that he was some kind of scam artist and I was going to get free of him by the following morning. Why would you ask a scam artist for his thoughts on America's troubles?

I *was* hungry though—I'd basically had salad and limoncello for lunch—and I imagined Jesus also might be, if he hadn't eaten since the cinnamon roll from Euphoria. Once or twice in my travels, I'd stopped in Bethlehem. I remembered a decent Thai place, there. It's a great cuisine, and I love Thai iced coffee, and Jesus had taken my coffee that morning, so I felt he owed me. We could have duck with green curry, or pad Thai, a sweet iced coffee there and one for the road. I found a parking spot not far from the restaurant, fed the meter, and at that moment, Jesus, walking an imaginary tightrope on the curbstone like a kid, said, "We have to get a cheese steak, my Edward."

I like cheese steak, though I've found it harder to digest as I get older. But most places that serve cheese steak don't usually serve Thai iced coffee and, as I said, I had my mind wrapped around that drink and didn't feel like peeling my thoughts away from it. I'd sacrificed enough coffee for one day.

"Cheesesteak is a *Philadelphia* specialty," I said. "We're an hour and a half from Philadelphia."

"This is steel country," Jesus answered, as if one could eat metal, and as if I didn't already know what Bethlehem, Pennyslvania, was famous for. "Iron, coal. The I-beam was invented here, did you know that? Without it, a lot of New York's skyscrapers wouldn't ever have been built."

"I was thinking Thai."

"Thai would be good if this were Bangkok," he said, and he put an arm around my shoulder and squeezed me against him in a friendly way. He smelled faintly of cigar smoke, though I hadn't seen him light up. "We're in the Keystone State, so let's have the local delicacy. I'm paying."

"I'm not that hungry," I lied, but he didn't seem to be listening.

A stray dog—part Doberman, part Lab, it looked like—trotted past, then stopped, came back, and nuzzled Jesus' right leg for a few seconds. My companion reached down and scratched it behind its ears, on and on and on, while I stood there watching. I like dogs, love them in fact, and I've been known to pat the occasional stray. But this must have gone on for a full minute . . . and I was hungry. At last we started off again, the dog standing there, watching us.

Two blocks west of where I'd parked we came upon a place

called Jinky's, with a ratty little sign out front that once might have been neon, smudged plate-glass windows, and a hand-lettered square of cardboard taped to the door that read:

> THOSE SERVEY'S ABOUT 'BEST OF BETHLEHEM' ARE RIGGED. COME ON IN!!!!!

"This looks good," Jesus said, and reached for the door handle.

The interior of Jinky's made the exterior look like the front of Google Headquarters. Mismatched chairs stood around three Formica-topped tables, vintage Before-I-was-Born, (or as my kids like to say "BCE" Before the Crazy Eddie). Cracked linoleum floor. Dried out pizza slices in a glass display. A menu on the wall so old it might have been written in Aramaic. And the finishing touch: behind the counter, a fellow who looked like he'd just retired from—or been thrown out of—the local Hell's Angels chapter. Big everything. Big head, big neck, big bare arms ballooning out from the sleeves of a stained white T-shirt and decorated with cheap- looking tattoos of pistols and swords. Big fat hands spread flat on the Formica countertop as if he were trying to keep it from blowing away in gale-force winds. On the speakers—I'll swear to this—Lady Gaga was singing, "I've got a hundred million reasons to walk away!!!"

I was going to suggest to Jesus, quietly, that there must be another Philly cheesesteak place in the neighborhood, but he charged forward and stood at the counter, gazing up at the menu in a minor-league ecstasy.

"What can I do you for?" the guy behind the counter said. "I'm Jinky. Welcome to my place."

"Two cheese steak hoagies."

"I'm not—" I started to say.

"Drink?"

"What do you have?" Jesus said.

"Coke or Pepsi."

"You have both?"

Jinky nodded. "Weird, huh? The distributors give me a hard time, but some people like a different one. You gotta offer variety."

He emitted a noise that was more bellow than laugh, and from the kitchen—visible through a glassless window beneath the menu and directly behind Jinky—came an almost perfect echo of the laugh.

"Pepsi," Jesus said. He turned to me. "What'll you have?"

"Not sure," I said.

Jinky was tapping the end of his pencil on the countertop. Two sets of eyes on me.

"Reminds me of a parable," Jesus said after a bit. "There was a man who came into a place that sold Philly cheesesteaks. He could not make up his mind what he wanted. The Lord looked upon him with disfavor because he was holding up the other customer, who was hungry and thirsty, and also trying the patience of the cook and the establishment's owner. Eventually, the restaurant closed for the day, and, instead of eating a delicious meal, the man was left to wander the city with an empty belly."

I thought this was one of the weakest attempts at a joke I'd ever heard. Jinky, however, seemed to find it hilarious. He sank his soccer-ball-sized head down in front of him, bellowing away and then, when he'd caught his breath, called over his shoulder, "Lester, we got Bible sayins goin' on out here."

"I heard," came a voice from the kitchen. "Looks like God, too, the guy."

Jinky lifted his eyes to Jesus' face, smiling, nodding, and I was so sure he was about to say something incredibly offensive like, "Nah, Jesus is white!" that I practically shouted, "All right, a cheese steak and a Coke for me then!"

"Onions?"

"Sure!"

"Lester, two steaks, twice on the onions!" Jinky busied himself pouring one Pepsi and one Coke into ice-filled paper cups, and Jesus and I carried them over to a table.

"Nice people," he said to me.

I looked out the window. "How'd you know to say "Hoagie?""

"Local lingo. When in Rome."

The subs were served promptly, and they were . . . succulent. Of course they were. The steak fresh and not too chewy, the cheese of high quality, not sprayed from a can, and melted perfectly into the meat. The onions in perfect balance, too, neither overpowering nor flimsy. I watch my weight, my teeth, my stomach, and hadn't had a Coke in over a year, but I discovered—or remembered—that it went perfectly with a cheesesteak sub.

Jesus ate slowly and gratefully, the way he'd consumed the cinnamon bun what seemed like a century ago. "I have a proposition for you," he said, halfway through the meal, "if you're willing. A writing job."

"I'm all set with writing jobs," I lied. "People are always saying they have a great book idea for me, but I—"

"I want you to fill in the Gap."

"I don't think so," I said. "The Gap is going to be there forever, unfilled. You can't just add sections onto the Bible at this point."

"I disagree. Take the long view. How's the sandwich?"

"Better than I expected. Thank you for the lunch."

"It's to pay you back for the gas and tolls and so on."

I nodded, but that part didn't matter to me. I don't care about money. Or I care about it very little. Too little, probably. And I would have had to pay for the gas and tolls even if I made the trip alone.

"The Gap job pays well."

"Good."

"You'll do it then?"

"I'm really booked. No pun intended. I have this speaking gig and then, you know, some ideas I want to pursue."

"You'll sell all over the world."

"I already sell all over the world . . . in small numbers."

"You have a child about to enter college."

"I'm aware of that. Thanks. We've put a little aside."

"Not enough."

I was aware of that, also, but didn't want to admit it, even to myself. On those rare occasions when I forgot that we hadn't put enough away for college, Anna Maria reminded me.

Jesus reached across, took hold of the top of my wrist and squeezed gently. "Edward," he said. "These are not good times."

No kidding, I thought. It seemed to me, and to a lot of compassionate, thinking people in America and elsewhere, they we had entered a kind of modern day Dark Ages. Everywhere you looked, from Poland to the Philippines, the levees of democracy and decency were cracking, water spurting through, flooding the basements of libraries, museums, and universities, a not-so-distant grumbling as if a gigantic dam somewhere just behind us was about to burst. (And this, all this, was *before* the Covid epidemic, BCE). The American conversation was a war zone of epithet and mockery, name-calling at the highest levels, protestors refusing to let campus speakers take the floor. Lies had become the new currency of government, with every pillar of civic life—the vote count, the press, the intelligence services, the judiciary—being called into question. Overseas it was at least as bad, the Putins and Erdogans and Dutertes of this world reigning supreme, with critics being poisoned on the streets of London or shot on a Moscow bridge. In certain circles, the whole idea of truth had become suspect. One didn't even want to listen to the news for fear of another atrocity, more arguing in the style of the eighth-grade playground, kids getting death threats. I had two sisters-in-law who were psychotherapists. Business was booming.

"And what," I couldn't keep myself from saying, "you've come to spread a message of peace?"

"YES!" Jesus practically shouted. Jinky glanced over at us from his post behind the counter.

"Food okay?"

"Great, great," I said. "Excellent."

"Baklava for dessert if you want it."

Jesus held up two fingers and Jinky himself carried over to us triangles of filo on paper plates. "On the house," he said. "Make sure you come back."

"We're passing through."

"Pass through more often."

When the proprietor retreated, Jesus squeezed my wrist again and let go. He leaned toward me across the table, the eyes—green again now—practically sparking. "What," he said, "are you afraid of?"

"Wasting my time," I answered. "Professional ridicule. Bankruptcy. Associating with scam artists. Loss of house, wife, and the respect of my kids."

He laughed, touched a fingertip to a flaky crumb of baklava on his plate and, before suggesting we take the dessert with us and get back on the road, said, "You were a fearful boy. You've almost grown out of it. Make that next step now, Edward. Move into the realm of true spiritual courage."

I *had* been a fearful boy. That part was true. God knows why. Swimming, roller coaster rides, fighting, asking girls on dates—it seemed my imagination was programmed to give me the worst possible outcome, in vivid detail, and my strategy had always been to duck into an alley, slip aside, take refuge in solitude, sports, and studies. But then, little by little, I started to shed those fears. I suppose I grew tired of being afraid. I learned to swim and to feel comfortable in water. I stood up to a couple of bullies—on a Boston subway late at night—rode a roller coaster (all right, only once, but once was enough!), developed an active dating life, eventually married. Every now and again I'd even do something moderately brave, leap off a fifteen-foot wall into water, get a tattoo (two small ones, kids' birthdays), calm a frightened neighbor on a rough plane flight, slip into wartime Croatia on the midnight train. Still, there was a residue of carefulness. I worried too much about my daughters. I sometimes drove like an old man, even though I wasn't quite. Lately I'd been having motorcycle-riding fantasies, not out of some late-life crisis of masculinity, but because it frightened me—I could imagine the accidents in exquisite detail—and I didn't want to be ruled by fear.

So Jesus' comment touched a nerve. I wasn't afraid of him physically, it wasn't that. The idea of writing a book that online critics might eviscerate was mildly worrisome, but you can't make a living as an author and fail to grow a thick skin. Not everybody is going to like what you do, and there were myriad new ways to say so in public. It wasn't that. I wondered, as we sat there eating baklava in Jinky's, if the reason for my reluctance might have something to do with a residue of my Catholic upbringing, the idea that if I dared to address the Gap, the

Biblical seventeen minutes on Nixon's tape, if I started to let myself think that Jesus was Jesus, and not an imposter, I might be falling into the Divine Doghouse, never to emerge. It occurred to me that all the way through the Holland tunnel and across the muscular landscape of North Jersey, I'd been worrying a loose string on an old scarf of papist fearfulness.

And then I had this thought: maybe it's not fear at all, just common sense, logic, rationality. Maybe I'd picked up a psychic con-man, who'd work me and work me and play all the angles until, eventually, at some point in Kentucky or Tennessee or just outside Little Rock, he'd pull the trigger on his weird little game and steal my car or my identity or embarrass me in front of the crowd at St. Mark's by shouting out that I'd sexually molested him, or his sister, or that I said racist things in private. Maybe I'd offended him with some of the millions of words I'd published and he'd been plotting revenge for a decade, combing my books, articles, and online posts from his prison cell in Colorado, searching for scraps of information that would make it seem like he knew my secrets and my past. Maybe he was a kind of hacker, intent only on invading my life and finding out something he could use to blackmail me. Or just messing up my files for the perverse fun of it.

Fear, it seems, can wear a hundred disguises, speak in a hundred convincing voices, sound so rational.

I stubbornly shook my head, and Jesus let the subject drop. We finished Jinky's excellent baklava. I dropped the paper plates into a wastebasket, our cans into a recycling bin. Jesus paid from a thick wad of cash and left a tip equal to the bill. As we were turning toward the door, Jinky called out, "Bethlehem, Baby! Birthplace of God and American steel. You guys have to come back for the Christmas lights!"

~ ~

chapter eleven

I travel a fair amount for various presentations and talks, and for research, too. Sometimes Anna Maria comes with me, and sometimes she does not. We've been married a long time and have developed a fair system of sharing work around the house, and we've also learned to allow the other to do what he or she does best. For instance, Anna Maria is good with details, with planning, with finances, with giving directions. I am not. So when I travel, she makes the hotel arrangements online and sends the address to me in a text. I plug it into my GPS and follow the directions, and about 80% of the time I avoid getting lost.

For that first night she'd found a Holiday Inn outside Harrisburg, which is an hour and a half southwest of Bethlehem. During those ninety minutes, Jesus slept. I pondered things like this: fear, meaning, God, trickery, death, violence, money, my next writing project, Janet Lee's words, and why I had eaten a second lunch.

In the end, the Camry's GPS led me to the Harrisburg Holiday Inn without trouble. I pulled into the parking lot, still on the fence as far as the So-Called Jesus situation was concerned, and shook him gently awake. He didn't respond. I thought for a minute that he was dead. How would I explain it to the police? A long-haired stranger with fake ID, dead in my car. "Jesus," I said quietly, rocking him by the shoulder. "Hey."

This was the trick then. He knew I'd eventually run out of patience and go inside and register, and he could hotwire the car and drive off into the Pennsylvania wilderness, where his associate was waiting with fake license plates, a fake title, fake ID. Good way to make a quick twenty grand.

I shook him again, harder. He opened his eyes. "Meditating, not sleeping," he said calmly.

"We're here. I'll get you a room and we'll meet for breakfast and then, honestly, I'm probably going to head out alone."

"Fine," he said. "Done trying to convince you, my friend. Thanks for the room. I appreciate that. Try to get 306 if you can."

"Sure," I said, but I had zero intention of asking the hotel clerk for a particular room. I'd take what I got, as I always did. Non-smoking, yes; but floor, bed size—none of that mattered to me when I traveled without my wife.

Jesus got out. I rolled my small suitcase and he carried his backpack and . . . when I checked in, the clerk told me we'd been assigned rooms 304 and 306. Non smoking. One king bed in each room. Free internet.

"The cheesesteak is going down kind of slow, so I'll just grab a bag of chips out of the vending machine and see you at breakfast."

"Fine, good," he said. We were standing near each other in the hallway. A father came out of the elevator, a strong-looking man carrying a pretty little girl with her hair done up in corn-rows. As they passed, the girl swiveled her head, and kept staring at Jesus as if he had a puppy crawling out of his shirt collar. "Daddy, look!" I heard her say, but her father's response was lost to me and they disappeared into a room at the far end of the corridor.

"Sweet dreams," Jesus said. I opened the door and was, at last, alone. I fell backwards onto the bed and stared up at the dark ceiling for a while, and then assumed my favorite position, back on the floor, lower legs hooked up over the mattress. I find it relaxing.

It had been too weird a day. Much too weird. I was used to giving talks, sometimes in front of hundreds of people; I wasn't nervous about that. At the same time, those kinds of presentations do take a certain amount of energy and focus, and I did like to cultivate a stretch of peace of mind beforehand, and peace of mind was not the atmosphere of the moment at the Holiday Inn. I must have drifted, eventually, into a shallow sleep because I was awakened by the phone buzzing in my pants pocket.

"Hey hon. *Cosa dici?*"

"Hey. Weird day. I was about to call. You?"

I sometimes think that, instead of measuring married life, as we most often do, in terms of years, we should measure it in number of conversations. Anna Maria and I had been married 38.4 years at that point and, since we both work at home, it's probably true that we'd had more conversations than most couples. Twenty a day? Forty a day? It depends on what you consider a conversation. But even twenty a day would add up to something like 7,000 a year. Multiply that by 38.4 and it's possible we'd had 268,800 conversations. Roughly. Which means we finish each other's sentences and can pretty much guess the response to something we say. I knew, for example, that once I said 'weird day' she wouldn't tell me about her day but would want to know what had been weird about mine.

"Why weird, Eddie Val?"

I took a breath, because, again, I had a pretty good idea where things were going. "I ended up traveling with somebody."

"What! Who! I can't believe this! Are you bored with me? What's going on, Eddie! What the Christ?!"

"Hon, I—"

The connection was broken. On her end.

I tried to relax into the carpeted floor and let my legs lie heavy on the mattress. It's a semi-yoga position, restful and spiritually healing after a day behind the wheel. I looked at my cell phone to make sure that she had, in fact, hung up, and then I placed it face-down over the middle of my chest, looked at the ceiling and subconsciously began to count. Subconsciously, because I was thinking: it's not a good idea to have two people with Italian blood marry each other. We're too emotional, too explosive. There had been times, in the eighteen years together before our kids were born, when Anna Maria and I would have epic arguments. There was never any physical violence involved, and we almost always steered clear of the harshest comments we could have made (*almost* being the key word here), but there would be two or five or fifteen minutes of yelling, back and forth, back and forth, me slamming a palm down on the table, she stamping a foot, swinging her long black hair this way and that in a fury of frustration. In those early years we didn't know the meaning of mild disagreement. The fumes, the eruption, the hot lava flowing over the kitchen floor, or the seat of the car, or the bedroom.

These enchanting interludes would be followed by the silence of the dead. Fifteen minutes, an hour. Once or twice an entire night and next day. Then we'd make up, and shortly after making up there would be epic lovemaking, nothing sedate there either.

Lying on the carpet of the Harrisburg Holiday Inn Express, I was thinking I should have married a good WASP woman from a quiet Connecticut family. Sane, low-key, stable. We could have had the lovemaking, still, but there would have been long stretches of harmony, the occasional tiff, all quiet words and facial expressions.

But would I have published any books?

Subconsciously I was counting, 28, 29 . . . The phone vibrated against my heart and I answered immediately, the way Italians answer the phone, by saying, "Ready!"

"*Pronto.*"

"I'm sorry," she said. "What's going on?"

"It's a man, not a woman," I said.

"Oh my God almighty! Eddie! Now you're gay! I never would have guessed in a million years. Are you bisexual? What—"

"Hon, stop. I'm not gay. I'm not cheating on you. I picked up a hitchhiker in Williamsburg."

A few quiet seconds. Then: "You do that. I told you it's crazy. He could be some nut. Are you being held hostage? Should I call my brother? He'll kill the freaking guy! He'll drive down there and tear his freaking arms off!"

"I know he will. I know your brother very well. Listen to me, would you please!"

"All right, don't yell."

"Sorry. Listen. I picked up a guy in Williamsburg, thinking he was just heading into Northampton on a cold morning and didn't want to wait for the bus. I was going that way and he looked like he needed a ride and maybe a couple of bucks for coffee or something."

"Your heart is too big, I'm telling you. I've always said it's going to get you in—"

"Hon, please. He says he's Jesus."

"Oh for Christ's sake, Eddie! This is worse than being gay, and worse than if you were with some babe. You're crazy. You're cracking. You're really losing it now, you—"

I hung up. I didn't intend to, I just did it. To even things out, maybe. To preserve a balance in the relationship. It's so easy to do: you just tap the little red circle at the bottom of the screen. I lay there, phone over my heart, watching a tiny spider creep across the ceiling. It had been a long, tiring day and I didn't want to be yelled at, but I shouldn't have hung up and after drawing and expelling two breaths I called her back and apologized. "It's been a long day," I said. "I'm tired. Please don't yell at me and please let me explain."

"Just tell me you're not losing it. You have books to write. We have a college tuition to pay."

"I'm not losing it."

"Good, alright. What then?"

"I know it sounds bad, but this guy . . . something's going on. He calls himself Jesus, and he kind of looks like Jesus, if Jesus looks like the pictures we grew up with."

"He's not white," Anna Maria hastened to say. "He couldn't have been."

"Right. He isn't. He's wearing an army jacket."

"That's weird."

"What's really weird is that he seems to know things about me."

"He's read your books, that's all. I told you you write too much about yourself. He's been stalking you on the internet. He's not in the room with you, is he?"

"No. Next door."

"You paid for the extra room, I bet."

"I did. But I'm thinking of cutting him loose tomorrow. He wants to go all the way to Arkansas with me. What's completely strange is that he told me that the minute he got into the car, and he had a hardcover copy of *Breakfast with Buddha* in his backpack. Not only that, but he knows things that he couldn't know from the books or the Internet." I thought of telling her about Jesus meeting me in New York at the massage place, but

I decided not to because I knew what would happen: Anna Maria would suspect I'd gone into the massage place looking for a Happy Ending, for sex. I'd plead innocent, we'd argue. She'd remember it always. Years into the future we'd be having a tiff, and she'd say, "Sure, here's Mr. Holy, the guy who goes to New York to get a handjob!"

"Knows things? Like what?"

"Like what I'm thinking sometimes. Like something I said to my mother when I was a little kid that I've never written about or even told you about."

There was a long silence. "You still there, hon?" I said.

"Yeah." More silence. "Maybe he's, you know, God."

My turn to be silent. "Hon, be sensible."

"Well, maybe he is."

"Right, and God came down to earth wearing an army jacket and hitching to Little Rock."

"Don't be sarcastic. God can take many shapes. You've said that yourself a hundred times."

"Yes, but I didn't mean it this way. I meant you can see the divinity in people if you look close enough. In dogs, animals, trees, clouds."

"Maybe he's the actual Jesus," she went on, as if, not for the first time, she hadn't been listening to me.

"Now who's the crazy one?"

A long pause. I could see Anna Maria in my mind's eye, sitting on the couch in our house in the hills, glass of red wine on the table beside her, Sudoku puzzle on a folded section of newspaper on her lap. I could see the small gold cross and a silver yin-yang symbol around her neck, the two thin rings—one gold, one with a bit of sapphire—on her long, slim finger, the first from our marriage, the second to mark our 25th anniversary. In that moment it was as if all the many talks we'd had about religion and faith and spirituality and our upbringing were being replayed in her mind and in my own. I was sure I knew what she was going to say then, something like, "Yeah, you're right. It's too weird. Why don't you just slip away early tomorrow morning and leave him twenty bucks at the desk or something?"

But after half a minute or so she said, "You've spent so much of your life writing about spiritual things, and thinking about them, and meditating and everything. I think this is some kind of *visitation*. It's kind of cool in a way, but a little scary."

"I think he's a flake."

"Well I think *you're* the flake, Edward Valpolicella! My God, what would you like, an engraved invitation? You're the one who's always saying mysterious things happen, that we shouldn't be so limited by science and logic and all that. So now something finally happens that's outside the boundary of rational thinking and you're Mister Doubt all of a sudden."

"I am."

"It's because you don't think you're a good enough person for something like this to happen to you."

"Maybe I'm a bad enough person."

"There, see! I'm going to hang up and call the girls. Allie and Juliet, will—"

"Please don't."

"Why not?"

"Because, you know, the tattoos, the motorcycle fantasy, the yelling at the soccer ref that one time."

"You went out on the field!"

"It was halftime, kids were getting hurt."

"They wanted to kick you out of the stadium."

"I know. And the tattoos are discreet . . . as tattoos go."

"Still."

"Okay, but the point is they don't need any more evidence that Dad's a kook."

"Maybe Dad's getting a special blessing."

"It would be spiritual egotism to think that."

"Maybe it would be the opposite."

"Meaning what?"

"Meaning maybe it *isn't* happening because you're such a good, special soul. I mean, you are good. I love you, you know that. But maybe it's just . . . something you're supposed to learn or do or figure out, and you're being chosen, not because you're so special or good or anything but because it's your job, your *thing*. Maybe you're supposed to write something about meeting him."

"He hinted as much."

"See."

"It makes me extremely uncomfortable."

"It shouldn't. God asks different people to do different things. Be a nurse, a teacher, a mother, take care of an old person, invent something."

"Build a tunnel and die two days before it's finished."

"Huh?"

"Nothing. Okay, I hear you. But God doesn't literally come down to earth and sit in their car and call himself Jesus and ask them to do something that way."

"How do you know?"

"Did that ever happen to you?"

"Actually, it did. When I was having Allie. I never told you. Twenty-two hours of labor and in the middle of the night, I felt someone, a spirit or a ghost or something, come down and lie in the bed next to me. I thought it was my grandmother. But it felt like God."

"You never told me."

"I didn't want you to think I was weird or something. Special. She—it was a she—told me not to give up, that I was supposed to have the baby, that was my job right then."

"You did it well."

"Twice."

"But that was a fleeting visit, the sense of someone or some spirit. This is a guy in an army jacket who likes Philly cheesesteaks!"

"Even so," she said. "I think if you ran away from it, you'd be sorry later. It's not childbirth. It's not painful. Just go with the flow and see what happens. And call me every night and let me know, because otherwise I'll worry."

"Okay, but don't tell the girls yet."

"Promise. Love you."

"Love you, bye."

That night, before going to sleep, I opened the Bible to the Book of John and read about the miracle at Cana and the woman at the well. I knew the first story, and remembered once having known the second, and neither of them were particularly surprising or enlightening to me. I returned the Bible to its drawer, opened the book Janet had given me and read the first two short chapters and then a page here and there toward the middle and end. The writing was only passable, and the thesis seemed absurd, the author claiming that the young Jesus had spent many years in the East, studying Buddhism, Taoism, and Hinduism. There was even something about the crucifixion being an elaborate trick he and his friends had played on the authorities, that he hadn't died, but had lived for many years, teaching and performing miracles.

I closed the book, buried it in my suitcase, said a Hail Mary and an Om Mani Padme Hum, and fell asleep.

~ ~

chapter twelve

In the morning, I showered, shaved, and went downstairs for the hotel breakfast. Jesus wasn't there. Ordinarily, I do my best to avoid these breakfasts. Too much Styrofoam and plastic, too much waste. Lately, hotels have tried to improve the offerings, at least, even make them a little more on the healthy side with some flavored yoghurt and fruit. Usually, though, the pieces of melon taste like they were grown in Laos two years earlier and shipped across the Pacific in the hold of an oil tanker. The coffee is bland, made from beans soaked in dishwater to wash off the poisonous insecticide. The eggs were cooked on the night shift and have been sitting under a hot lamp ever since. I'm not a food snob, but I am a little bit of a food snob . . . and most of the time I'll skip the free breakfast and go out to a local diner and have eggs poached hard and potatoes and a decent glass of iced coffee and spend ten or twelve bucks when I probably shouldn't. In the early years, before we learned to laugh at each other's quirks, Anna Maria and I used to argue about it.

But the Holiday Inn breakfast actually looked okay. I made myself a cup of tea, put two slices of bacon and a Granny Smith apple on a Styrofoam plate and carried it over to the dining area. Sun streamed through the windows, and there was a pleasant bustle of moms and dads and kids at the other tables, a morning business meeting, three men and two women, all in blue suits; two elderly women sitting across from each other, sipping coffee, CNN on the big screen. The day before, two black men had been asked to leave a Starbucks because they hadn't bought anything. The police had been called. It had turned into a national story, and the Two Americas were arguing over it.

I chewed the bacon, sipped the tea, watched the door. No Jesus. This would be my punishment then: after studying that passage in The Good Book and glancing at the tall tale of Jesus in the East, then spending a night and morning thinking about it, I'd decided Jesus was right—the Biblical gap *was* disturbing—and Anna Maria was right—I should just go with the flow and quiet my cynical side. I still wasn't sure he was anything other than a mind-reading con-man, but I was starting to lean away from that idea, and it seemed to me there was little to lose by letting him ride along for a few more days. What was the worst that could happen?

I finished the breakfast, dumped my trash in the waste container, guiltily, rolled my suitcase out into the lobby and sat on one of the couches there, facing the desk clerk. There was a TV screen on one wall there, too. Fox News this time. Same story, different angle. I was thinking about the two guys in Starbucks, thinking that, if I had been there, I would have bought them each a cup of coffee. Five or six bucks, end of incident. I was thinking we were all too eager to fight these days, too cheap to spend a few dollars, too quick to call the police on someone with a different color skin, too ready to make a big news story out of every less-than-great interaction so readers on both sides of every issue would get upset . . . and keep watching. It was money-driven, so much of it, the pitting of one group against another for the benefit of a handful of rich dividers and Russian hackers. And then, too, we had such a sordid racial history that it wasn't a surprise we'd never been able to stop looking at each other as black or white instead of as sacred human beings, even as the lines blurred, situations changed. I had no idea how to solve it, except in my own tiny sphere, in the depths of my own hidden, less-than-fair mental tendencies. That was hard enough, but thinking about solving the problems that beset America and the world. . . . I'd leave that up to the Great Spirit.

It was a few minutes past nine o'clock. Despite Anna Maria's advice, I was getting tired of waiting. I figured I'd give Jesus until 9:30, do him the courtesy of calling his room, and then, if he didn't answer or hadn't shown up, I'd head out south, and put the whole episode behind me. It would make a good story at a gathering of friends—the day I picked up a hitchhiker who called himself Jesus.

As I was thinking that, who should step out of the elevator but So-Called himself. He saw me right away, big smile on his face. I wanted to smile back, wanted, as Anna Maria had suggested, to be more positive about the guy, but the second thing I noticed, after the smile, was that he was dressed in an expensive-looking gray suit, pale blue shirt and diagonally striped blue and silver tie. In place of the backpack, he was pulling behind him a bright red suitcase large enough to hold a small ping-pong table and the collected works of Fyodor Dostoevsky.

He strode across the lobby. I stood up. He said, "What a good wife you have!"

I wondered if Anna Maria had bought him the suit and luggage online and had it delivered.

But then he said, "I see she convinced you not to run away!"

I flinched. We walked out to the car, side by side, not

speaking. The route I'd planned would take us on I-81 from Harrisburg south through the Maryland panhandle, across a piece of West Virginia, and halfway down the west side of Virginia. I was hoping for the weather to warm up—we were heading south, after all, and an early onset of spring was part of the appeal of the Arkansas drive—but we were in the high hills and warmth did not seem to be in the forecast.

Jesus sat quietly in his seat, fancy suitcoat folded in his lap, hands folded calmly on top of it. He'd put both his red suitcase and his knapsack in the back seat next to my suitcase, because my golf clubs took up most of the trunk. I was partly at peace with the decision to take him along, but not fully, not quite, not yet. Anna Maria had made a good case for it. I trusted her judgment, trusted her to straighten me out on those many occasions when I started to think crooked. Still . . . but . . . even so . . . I'd be lying if I said I was truly at ease. It seemed to me that Jesus was waiting for me to ask where the suit and nice luggage had come from, but I was stubbornly refusing to do that. Another trick. More weirdness. Possibly even another indication of some kind of criminal connections—he had mobster pals in Harrisburg who'd filched a suit from the Brooks Brothers warehouse, and the red suitcase from the local mall. They'd sneaked them up to room 304 at two a.m. "Sorry, Boss, red was all we could get on short notice."

Sometimes an active imagination can be a bad thing.

In order to make the silence between us less uncomfortable, I switched on XM radio and dialed in to one of the cable news channels. There were endless discussions about the Starbuck's incident, the Mueller investigation, the president's juvenile tweets, the Florida kids. It was, in April 2018, difficult to argue against the idea that the fabric of American society was unraveling, that we were becoming less tolerant, more divided, cruder. Journalism had veered toward the *National Inquirer* model. Boxing had turned the corner to Ultimate Fighting, where the gloves had less padding and you could hit your opponent while he—or she—was on the ground. Politics, always a nasty business, had gone the way of divorce court, with each side angling for advantage, demonizing the other, resisting compromise, fomenting hatred, digging deep trenches and filling them with grudges that would be there for decades.

My own political persuasions were off-beat and resisted labels, left-leaning, I suppose, but with speckles of resistance to the leftwardmost rants and nuttiness. It seemed to me that so many of our problems came from one item: the vast and widening gulf between rich and poor. It seemed to me that the places in this world where I'd least like to live were places where a thin layer of the very wealthy sat atop a mound of the working masses. Stable, safe, abundant nations had a large middle class; ours was shrinking by the hour. You had golfers making 50 million a year, and schoolteachers making $50,000. You had a handful of billionaires whose empires expanded exponentially, who made more from a day's worth of interest on their investments than a working person earned in five years. Unlike most Americans, I'd actually spent time in a communist society, had even supervised laborers there (long story; I'd written about it in *A Russian Requiem*). I knew what happened when you paid truck drivers the same as surgeons, when the government tried to force everyone onto the same level. It led to murder, basically. But, driving through Hagerstown, Maryland—a picturesque river city where, if I hadn't been so determined to let Jesus make the first move, I would have stopped for what my father used to call "coffee, and"—I tired of the cable networks and fished around on AM radio for a local channel. I ended up listening to an interview with a mayor of someplace in West

Virginia. He sounded like a sane and reasonable man, an anti-politician. But it was yet another disturbing report. The topic was drug overdoses and there were horrible statistics cited, locally and nationally, hundreds of thousands of lives destroyed. The discussion was an enlightened one, but no one raised an issue that seemed obvious to me: what was it about the way we lived that caused huge numbers of our citizens to take refuge in getting high?

It's a dangerous question, too dangerous. We'd rather keep assuming we have the greatest system ever devised, and simply treat each new overdose, each new school shooting, every new step downward in political discourse as an unfortunate blemish on an otherwise healthy body politic. Great country, yes, I agree; but something seemed badly off-balance.

Jesus talked about his Gap, but I was thinking of another gap just then, a ruinous one. Conservative golf buddies called me inaccurately, "The Socialist." It wasn't a term of endearment. But hadn't Jesus—the real Jesus—been something like that, someone who called for the people with two coats to give one away? And didn't some of those conservative friends call themselves Christians? And wasn't there some kind of reasonable middle ground between the obvious evils of Soviet communism or Venezuela-style socialism, and the evils of feudal states where the rich were idolized and everybody else scrambled for food? Couldn't the pro golfers be happy with, say, *five* million a year instead of fifty? Couldn't we pay teachers more?

As I was thinking this, worrying the thread of a longstanding, working-class-kid's disdain for the super rich, devising economic programs that had their basis in a well meaning ignorance, Jesus finally broke the silence. "I'm taking you to lunch again today."

"Okay, where?"

"West Virginia."

"Fine. I'm sure they have lots of good eating places. Barbecue and so on."

"I don't think the restaurant I have in mind offers barbecue."

"Fine, anything but another cheesesteak. That's still with me."

He laughed and I liked him again, briefly. "Do you have any better clothes?"

"Fancy place, huh?"

"The fanciest, actually."

"I have a shirt and sportcoat for my talk. In the suit bag hanging behind me."

"Let's find a place where you can stop and change. Do you have actual shoes?"

"I do."

"Excellent."

I was thinking, may God forgive me: *Go to hell! I'm giving you a ride, I paid for your hotel room, and all of a sudden you're telling me I'm not dressed up enough for your fanciest of all restaurants!* But one thing decades of meditation—and marriage—have taught me is that thoughts are just thoughts. Flickers of mental energy. Sin, if that's the right word, comes from acting on the bad flickers, following them down a long road of lawyerly evidence that leads to the conclusion: You're messed up! I'm right! I know! It's all about me! And then causing real harm.

Sometimes, in life, in marriage, at work, and when you are driving So-Called Jesus to Little Rock, restraint and a small measure of humility are called for. You can't give in to everything you think. I swallowed the little burst of pride and anger, pulled over into a Burger King, and changed into my good clothes in the bathroom.

Just shy of Lexington, Virginia, Jesus asked me to turn onto I-64 West, and I did so without complaint. By then we'd been riding for close to four hours. I was hungry. Plus, as would be the case with most men my age, especially after having enjoyed two cups of coffee for breakfast, I had to pee. Inspired by my bladder's gentle encouragement, and despite a longstanding nightmare-vision of being stopped for speeding in some small, mean town, I pushed the speed a bit as we crossed the Appalachians. Cliffton Forge and Covington sailed past, and just as I was about to start seeking a place to fill one part of me and empty another, Jesus directed me to turn off. The exit read *White Sulphur Springs, WVA*. It sounded like a place where one might eat.

Left here, Jesus directed me, *straight now, next right,* and so on. I hoped he had a restaurant in mind, not another parking lot. A few minutes, one last *turn here, Edward,* and we were driving up a long, tree-lined access road and onto an oval circle with flower gardens in its center. Directly ahead of us stood, not some local BBQ spot as I'd hoped, but an enormous seven-story building, white as cotton, long as two football fields, with a columned facade. An American castle. The Greenbrier Hotel.

I'd heard of it. The PGA played a tournament on one of The Greenbrier's three golf courses and I sometimes watched a few hours of it on TV. Maybe more importantly, I'd heard of it because The Greenbrier was reported to house secret bunkers, where the United States Congress and President would flee in case of a nuclear war, letting the rest of the population go up in radioactive smoke. These two items—golf and nuclear war—did not mesh well in my mind, but at that point my focus had narrowed, let me put it that way.

Even before the valet approached, I was uncomfortable,

and not just physically. This was the playground of the ultra rich, the 1% of the 1%. Not my place in the world. Not my people. I rolled down the window, and Jesus leaned over in front of me. "Just coming for lunch, Sam," he said. The valet took my keys, practically bowing, and Jesus and I stepped out of the Camry and walked up the massive front steps.

I was thinking: *Sam?*

"You've been here," I noted.

He didn't answer. After a quick bathroom stop, Jesus led me along a carpeted hallway and through a set of beautifully trimmed white doors. He had a word with the maître d', who handed us over to the hostess, who escorted us into a room with thirty-foot-tall ceilings held up by green marble columns and decorated with chandeliers. We sat at a table with a white cloth and gleaming silverware and took up the menus. After a few minutes' perusal, I ordered the Herb Crusted Bay of Fundy Salmon Steak ($28), and Jesus ("I'm into the local specialties.") went with the Maryland Style Pan Seared Crab Cake ($26). I had lemonade, he ordered a chocolate milkshake. The waitress introduced herself as Melanie, said, to Jesus, "Nice to see you again," and carried off our menus. We sat there, not looking at each other.

"Okay," I said. "I surrender."

He turned his eyes. "Meaning?"

"You know what my wife tells me in a private phone call. You carry magnificent suits—"

"A Brioni," he said, fingering the lapel. "James Bond wore Brioni."

"You conjure red luggage out of the air. You know the valet and the waitress at the Greenbrier and they seem to know you. I hereby surrender my logic and sense of normalcy. *I give*, as we used to say where I grew up."

He was looking down at the woven tablecloth, a tiny smile touching the corners of his mouth.

"I'm not saying you're God," I said quietly, though there was no one sitting within thirty feet of us. "I'm just saying I'm surrendering my rational thinking."

"That's an important first step, spiritually. . . . And I never said I was God."

"Talking about "My Father in Heaven" is pretty close."

"Not the same. You could say "my father in Heaven" as easily as I could."

"But I don't. I don't raise people from the dead. I haven't been crucified . . . yet. Who or what are you?"

"The Son of Man."

"Stop that, please! You know what I mean."

"An embodied spirit," he said, just as the waitress brought our drinks. He held her hand for a moment in thanks, met her eyes. "There is nothing," he said to her, "nothing on this earth, as fine as a chocolate milkshake at lunch."

She laughed and told us she'd bring the food shortly.

"An embodied spirit?" I repeated.

"Exactly. Just as you are. Just as Melanie is."

"And we're all the same?"

"Essentially."

"What then? What's the point?"

"A very easy question to answer. In each time and place on the continuum of eternity and in the limitless span of universes, each embodied spirit has a purpose. I mentioned this to you earlier, in regard to the spirit who supervised the construction of the Holland Tunnel. The cruder spirits, those new to this level of creation and still finding their way, cannot see their own magnificence, nor their own purpose. Such souls are temporarily blind to everything but their needs and desires. They rape, they steal, they torture and murder; everywhere they go, they cause pain. Moderately advanced spirits, and there are billions of them on this planet alone, recognize that others in the world also have needs and desires. They retain some selfishness, but they also contribute. They give. Their giving takes an endless variety of shapes, depending on their circumstances, interests, and God-given skills. You write. Others heal, or teach, or give birth and raise children, or tend to the sick, or make music, or build tunnels, or simply wait on customers with dignity and friendliness then go home and lovingly raise their three sons and a daughter, as in Melanie's case. The very highest spirits have transcended their own needs and they lead lives of continuous giving, and they are hiding everywhere in disguise. See?"

"Makes sense," I told him. And it did. I felt the ground beneath my wariness being slowly eroded.

"You are each called upon to do something—many, many things, in fact, some large and some small—and you then have the free will to decide whether or not you will do those things and how diligently."

"What about the child who dies after two days? What about the kids at Sandy Hook, and in Florida, and the rest of—?"

"For a later discussion," he said.

"What about atheists?" I said. "Asking for a friend. What happens to them?"

"Many of them do good. In some ways they deserve more credit for the good they do, because there's no thought of eternal reward. It's not what you *believe* that determines your spiritual progress, Edward; it's what you actually *do*."

"The two are often connected."

"Often, yes. Not always."

"And you know all this how?" I asked, "if you're not God."

"Just doing my job," he said. "Teaching, more or less. And I'm glad you've come to your senses, my Edward. You're a stubborn fellow, anyone ever say that to you?"

"My wife. Four hundred thousand, two hundred eighty-six times."

"More evidence of her wisdom."

Melanie arrived and set our plates down in front of us with a gracious twist. "Anything else?"

"Not one thing," Jesus told her. "And how are your sons and beautiful daughter?"

"Lights of my life," she said. "And Anton wanted me to tell you he'll be here shortly."

My salmon steak was delectable, garnished with new potatoes and small, perfectly steamed heads of broccoli. Jesus seemed to be enjoying his milkshake and crab cakes, and he ate and drank with an attentive gratitude that sparked a small fire of discomfort—almost guilt—in me.

We were halfway through the meal when a man built like a barrel, carrying an oversized alligator-skin purse, and wearing a white silk sport coat and a red shirt open at the collar came striding across the room. Even before he stopped at Jesus' side of the table and slapped a hand down on my traveling companion's shoulder, this man made me extremely uncomfortable. Gut reaction. He smelled of cigar, not necessarily a bad thing in my opinion, but he carried himself with a certain I'm-the-best swagger. He wore cufflinks. His dark chest hair puffed up at the open collar. Atop the barrel-like torso sat a relatively small head. High forehead, graying hair trimmed neatly at the sides. Small eyes, small mouth, big cheeks. Everything—the way he walked, dressed, stood, grinned, even the odd purse—expressed the kind of supreme confidence that leaks out of the edges of the Superior Man. I didn't like him.

Jesus seemed to. He stood up and gave the man a warm embrace, and his face was painted with a smile I hadn't seen at any moment before that. "Anton," he said, "I'd like you to meet my good friend, the famous author, Edward Valpolicella." I stood, we shook hands.

Anton said, "Of course. Valpolicella. Love your work," in a way that made me wonder if he'd flown in from Hollywood. The remark did nothing to improve my opinion of him. He borrowed an empty chair from a nearby table and sat in it, leaning back, hands shoved down in the pockets of his expensive suit jacket and holding it out away from his wide hips, smiling all the while.

"You're looking good," he said to Jesus, and I detected a Russian accent. I may have mentioned that I spent some years working in the former USSR, and I speak Russian well, and that, in a more recent visit and in some European trips, I'd come across a certain New Russian Man, a combination former KGB agent and modern day oligarch. Not an attractive species. Anton fit the bill.

"You also," Jesus said. "Business going well?"

Anton laughed. "Business," he said, as if it were a nasty hobby. *Beeznis.* "You know khow eet ees. What was it Schopenhauer said, "The commercial instinct is morally fatal!" More laughter.

Jesus was smiling. "Not in your case, obviously, Anton. Will you join us for lunch?"

Anton flung one arm out of his pocket and, using two fingers of his other hand, brought his shirt cuff back just far enough to reveal one of those watches that cost as much as three moderately priced automobiles. He shook his head sadly. "No can do. Tee time, khalf an hour."

"A drink?"

Another shake of the head. From the purse he removed a package, roughly the size of a shoe box. It was wrapped carefully in gold, blue, and red-striped paper. "As agreed," he said, handing it to Jesus.

Jesus seemed slightly uncomfortable with the package. He set it down at his feet, out of my view, and did not make eye contact with me. "You're an angel," he said to Anton.

Anton humphed, pulled the sides of his jacket together over his copious belly, turned his eyes to me without turning his head and said, "Vatch out for thees guy," in a joking way. He hoisted himself to his feet, shook my hand, leaned down and kissed Jesus too close to the corner of his lips, patted him one last time on the shoulder, and sauntered off.

Still not looking at me, Jesus immediately started to eat. "Don't let your food get cold," he said.

~ ~

chapter thirteen

We finished the meal in a silence broken only by Melanie's offer—declined by both of us—of dessert. And by Jesus' response, "My friend here has a schedule to keep!"

Jesus insisted on paying. I suppose by then I shouldn't have been surprised to see him remove a thin leather wallet from the inside pocket of his suit jacket and pinch two 100-dollar bills between his thumb and second finger, shifting them back and forth against each other, making sure he wasn't taking more than two of the several crisp bills I could see. I watched him hand them over to Melanie and bring a smile to her face by telling her not to worry about the change. He leaned over sideways and lifted the wrapped package onto his lap, keeping it below the edge of the table and out of my view. "It's important to be generous," he said. "Should be the eleventh commandment." And then, "Are you ready, my Edward?"

I wasn't ready. All the morning's good will had disappeared like ice in a glass on an outdoor table in South Carolina in July. I didn't at all like the idea of driving through West Virginia with a stranger holding a wrapped package that had been given to him by a golf-playing Russian oligarch. But, and this was odd, I felt temporarily incapable of speaking up. Something about the decor, the food, the sense of elegant propriety, something about The Greenbrier made starting an argument seem the act of a petulant juvenile, someone who knew nothing about margins and shorts, a frightened little boy in the world of movers, shakers, and Masters of the Universe.

I have a clear memory of feeling young and small there, leaving the table and walking beside Jesus along the carpeted hallway, stepping out the front doors—held for us by a uniformed doorman. Jesus descending the wide front stairway with the box held against his left hip, and his eyes up, taking in the gardens before us as if he were part owner of the place and was well pleased with how it was being maintained. Another memory of the two of us—yours truly feeling made of metal, a robot, an alien—taking off our sportcoats and hanging them neatly in back. Jesus removing his tie, folding it very carefully and putting it, of all places, into the glove compartment.

Sam the valet was summoned with a casual wave, tipped with a twenty.

"Back to the Interstate" Jesus said, not as a command but in a funny, ironic tone, as if he were an actor in a British drama. I rolled my car slowly around the oval and down the entrance road and then pulled over to the shoulder and hit the button for the hazard lights.

I put the car in park and looked over at him, no longer held in the thrall of the place, no longer small or weak or ignorant of the Market. "Tell me," I said, "that you're not carrying drugs in that box."

The disappointed smile appeared again, beaked nose and dark eyes above it. I noticed that there were no wrinkles on his face. Not one. "That request is a reflection of your thought process," he said.

"Exactly. But tell me there's nothing in the box for which I could be arrested and thrown in prison."

"That's absurd," he said.

"Please answer."

"If you knew what was in there, you'd be embarrassed by your own question. You'd be ashamed."

"I'm sure. But either tell me there's nothing illegal in the box or get out here, walk back to your friends at the hotel, spend the night, and then call in a private helicopter to take you wherever it is that you're really going."

"I'm exactly where I'm supposed to be," he said.

"Please answer."

"Nothing," he said.

"Nothing what?"

"There is nothing in the box or in my luggage for which you will be sent to prison."

"You're sure."

"Utterly."

I put the car in gear and started off. On the highway again, after a suitable period of sulking, I asked Jesus how he knew Anton.

"Old friend," he said, cryptically.

"Pretty well off, it looked like."

"Everybody there is pretty well off."

"So how'd he make his fortune?"

"Family money, at first. Then, as he said, business."

"Russian, wasn't he?"

"You know he was Russian. You speak the language. I was surprised you didn't say a few *zdrastvuite* or something. Or have him searched for contraband. You're a very suspicious man."

I let the subject drop. I concentrated on the driving. I thought of Jesus telling me I'd be embarrassed at asking what was in the package. I wondered if he'd been lying. I turned on the radio and switched it off again. So-called Jesus seemed to be sleeping, or meditating, or calculating the profits from his drug sale. I took a deep breath and made myself focus on the road.

West Virginia isn't made for interstates. Too many hills too close together, too many big trucks, too many sharp turns at 75 mph. We climbed and swooped, gray forests to either side, touches of snow in the shadowed spots and on the tops of the mountains. As we were approaching Beckley, Jesus awoke from his dream and said, "You looked at the Bible last night."

"I did."

"And?"

"You're right, John is the miracle man. It gets you to about age thirteen and then . . . nothing."

He pondered for a moment, during which, after all this prelude, I wondered if he was going to change his mind and keep the Gap secret for another two thousand years, or find someone else, more friendly, more pliable, more skilled, less suspicious, to listen to the story. He looked out the window at the gray hills and said, "Know anything about Selenium?"

"The supplement. I have friends who take it for heart issues. Some of them think it keeps them mentally sharp, too. Anna Maria went through a phase of taking it. Not cheap."

"There's not much selenium in the soil in China."

"Really? Who knew?"

We raced along.

"Among its other properties," he said after a bit, "selenium in grass makes horses bigger and stronger. That one fact—not much selenium in the soil in China—led to the Silk Road."

"I don't follow."

"The Chinese wanted stronger horses, beasts that could carry their merchants for longer distances, and would fare better in war. In the soil of the steppes of Asia Minor there's more selenium, therefore the people there had stronger and bigger horses. So the Chinese were drawn in that direction. And they knew how to manufacture silk, which was another key element. The trade routes kept pushing westward, and then you had Alexander the Great pushing eastward, and then you had the Romans, who got as far east as present day Uzbekistan. It was all about money and power, really."

"Isn't it always?"

"Then the wealthy women of Europe—"

"The kind who would have stayed at the Greenbrier."

"Went mad for silk. And the men went mad for women in silk, so much so that certain heads of state tried to outlaw it. You had streams of gold and gems flowing from west to east, and rivers of silk going in the other direction. Other things were traded, too, of course—jade and spices, and, just as it is today, it started to be in the interest of the large powers to protect those trade routes and keep them open. If you look at human history from a certain distance, it's the same dynamic occurring again and again and again in slightly different forms, with different prominent figures. Look at all the fuss we just heard on the radio about trade—Mexico, Canada, China. A basic repeat."

"Everyone needs bigger horses and sexy clothes."

"Precisely."

"I don't see how that connects to your Gap."

"It's obvious."

"Not to me."

"In those days, you had not only goods traveling along those routes, but ideas. It's not as true now, but if you think about the computer, and silicon, or if you think about petroleum, you can see something like the same thing. You have goods traveling across the world, but you also have ideas and inventions—the Internet, for example. Communism. Democracy. The internal combustion engine. Ideas went from China, across Tibet, as far as Egypt and what is now Israel. Some of those ideas were connected to religion. What isn't talked about, but is actual fact, is that, at the time I was born in Bethlehem, you had Jews in India and Buddhists in Egypt."

"Not talked about at all, in my experience."

"Dig into it a bit and you'll see that it's true. Obviously, the centers of Buddhism and Judaism were thousands of miles apart, but there was a certain amount of cross-pollination."

Exactly at that moment—I remember it because I remember Jesus said "craws-pollination" with almost a southern accent and that seemed extremely odd—a six-point deer leapt over the guardrail into the road. We were in the right-hand of two lanes, going only about three miles an hour over the speed limit. There was an eighteen wheeler in front of me. I was keeping a safe following distance. I might have been very slightly distracted by the tale Jesus was starting to tell, and by the odd tinge of accent that had suddenly appeared in his voice, but I stand by the fact that I was focusing on the road. I saw the deer maybe a second after it came out of the trees and two seconds before it leapt over the guardrail, but there was a car immediately to my left and no place to go. I slammed my foot down hard on the brake and, as I was skidding toward the breakdown lane, hit the deer dead-on. The poor beast flew up into the air and landed on the hood of the Camry—which was still moving forward—and it lay there, gasping pitifully and breathing blood. I brought the car to a full stop, turned off the engine, and we got out.

We were high up on a windswept hill at that point, the Camry safely in the breakdown lane, a steady stream of cars and trucks rushing past a few yards away. We had, as I said, taken off our sportcoats after the Greenbrier meal, and our dress shirts—Jesus's pale blue, mine a striped cream—were little protection against the sharp West Virginia wind whipping over the guardrail. The deer was pressed against the front of the Camry's grill as if glued there. Its eyes were open, chest fluttering, thin sprays of blood coming from its mouth with every stuttering breath. A horrible sight.

It was hard to know what to do. We were standing there, chilled and windblown, staring at the gasping animal in a kind of hypnotic death-watch, when a rusted, peach-colored pickup, vintage 1990, swerved to a stop just in front of us. A man climbed out of the driver's side and hurried over. For one second I thought it was Jinky from the Scranton cheesesteak place because, while shorter, he had the same roundish build, hips wider than shoulders, and the same aura of physical strength. This man, though, early forties I guessed, was dressed in paint-splattered jeans and workboots, flannel shirt and denim jacket on top, and he had dark eyebrows and dark hair that stood up from the top of his forehead as if he'd been wearing a cap or a helmet all day. His legs were widely bowed.

"Lot of this," he yelled into the wind as he strode toward us.

There was about him an almost official air; it wouldn't have seemed odd if a sheriff's badge had flashed under the lapel of the denim jacket. He was confident, all-business, in perfect contrast to my own state of hesitant uncertainty.

He stepped past us and rested a pair of thick workman's hands on the deer's neck, as if to keep the animal from snapping its rack of horns toward his face, and then he leaned a few inches closer and made an examination in much the way a physician might. "Not gonna make it," he declared. In the next second, Jesus had ducked into the car, rummaged around in his knapsack and produced—why should I have been surprised?—

a hunting knife. The blade gleamed in the cold afternoon sun. The stranger stepped aside, Jesus put his hand on the deer's neck just as the man had done a moment earlier, then seemed to whisper a prayer beneath his breath. He took hold of an antler with one hand and slid the knife into a spot high up and just behind the deer's jawbone. The blade slipped in without resistance and the deer was instantly dead. Eyes glazed, one final sputtering breath, a stillness.

"Ya put him out his misry," said the stranger, giving Jesus a look that rested somewhere between astonishment and admiration, as if a longhair in nice clothes shouldn't have been able to do what he'd just done. "You're a hunter," the man said. "We sure kin see that!" He reached out a hand to me, and then to Jesus, saying his name twice to each of us, "Mason. I'm Mason."

"Eddie," I said, squeezing as hard as I could to avoid damage. I noticed that Jesus didn't say his name.

"If you guys don't have no objection, I'd like to take him home. Feed the famly for a good long while with the meat. Allright by yez both?"

We nodded.

"Mind helpin' me then? I see yer dressed up, but if you'd only just hold the legs, that'd work fine. Hang on, let me pop the gate."

He lowered the tailgate of his truck; the hinges made a squealing noise in the wind. Jesus set the bloody knife on a guardrail post and took the front legs in his hands. I took the rear legs. Mason cupped his arms under the deer's torso, left elbow just inside the antlers, and we settled the departed creature onto scraps of old carpet in the pickup's rusty bed. From somewhere in the back, Mason produced a rag. He wiped his hands, cleaned the knife and handed it back to Jesus, raised his eyes to the highway behind us as if searching the traffic for a game warden. The sun was just passing behind one of the higher peaks to our southwest, casting all of us in an odd pinkish glow and touching the air with cold breath. Mason's hair fluttered like a headdress. Jesus, I noticed, had blood on the front of his shirt. I had blood on my shoes. Mason seemed unbloodied.

"Would yez join me and my famly for dinner then?" he said in an odd combination of lilting and gruff speech, not quite a sing-song, but different than anything I'd ever heard. I couldn't identify the accent and am no doubt portraying it poorly here. It verged on southern, but there was something else going on, music of the mountains maybe, even a bit of Scotland.

"We'd truly enjoy that," Jesus said, without asking how I felt about the invitation. And then he added something I knew to be untrue. "We're starving."

"Well, gonna take a bit to git there and then butcher him and grill it up, but you won't be sorry, I kin tell ya that. Won't be sorry!"

"We'll follow you," Jesus said.

Mason nodded, slammed the squealing tailgate, and climbed back into the cab.

I found myself sitting beside a bloodstained Jesus, following a rusty Chevy pickup half a mile along the Interstate and then down an exit ramp, and merging onto State Route 19 in the direction of a place called Oak Hill. I was wondering what, if anything, I wanted to say about the hunting knife. I decided to say nothing.

Once we left the highway, there was a sense, almost immediately, of moving away from the rush and hustle of the modern world. It was as if the Interstate were a Potemkin Village, and the true America lay just beyond its neatly mown edges.

We dipped into a valley, with gray hillsides shouldering up to either side, and clapboard homes—white-painted, mostly—presiding over ragged, dormant lawns. Behind the homes, on both sides of the road, stretched fallow fields, some dotted with the stubble of harvested corn, some planted over with winter grass, one or two showing corrals in which horses nibbled and neighed.

Mason went along at a steady pace and Jesus fell silent again, hands in his lap.

"Your shirt's ruined," I told him.

He nodded, lost in thought.

"You told me you didn't have a knife."

Another nod.

"Why do you carry a hunting knife?"

"Old habit."

"And why did you kill the deer instead of letting Mason do it?"

"I wanted to release this good man from the karma of taking the animal's life."

"Karma's a Buddhist word."

"Hindu also."

"Strange, coming from you."

"Why's that, Edward?"

"Well, if you are who you say you are, then it's Christianity that's named after you, not Buddhism, or Hinduism. Judaic references I could see. That would make sense, but *karma?*"

He glanced over at me and smirked. Mason had stopped at an intersection and, in the gray dusk, the red traffic light glowed with a particular sharpness, mimicked by the truck's one working taillight. We were on the outskirts of a small town. The mood of the place was toward the poorer end of rural-domestic, with not-new pickups in the driveways, and antennas on the roofs. The sides of some of the houses could have used a coat of paint.

Jesus wasn't answering the karma question.

"How did you know where to insert the knife?"

"YouTube," he said without hesitation.

I was starting to sense a pattern of deflection and evasion and I didn't like it much.

"Something's bothering you."

"Just the opposite," he said. "I feel I'm among my people."

"Mason?"

Silence.

The light went green. Mason led us down Route 19 for another mile or so and then, at a sign for Cunard—a small wooden sign at an intersection, with the numeral 6 painted too close beside the 'd'—he turned right, onto a smaller road. I could feel darkness settling down at the houses' ankles and the bases of the tree trunks, and I could see a first star in the sky. Simple people, I supposed Jesus meant. "The salt of the earth," my mother would have called them. Diametrically opposed, it seemed to me, to the people who'd been sitting in the Greenbrier's dining room with us, a claque of well-heeled Masters of the Universe whose kindergarten-age children already knew to ask for their grass-fed hamburgers medium well, with sweet potato fries on the side if possible and, oh, a fresh squeezed lemonade? Mired in my less than holy preconceptions, it wasn't lost on me that Cunard was the name of the ship line that operated the Queen Mary. And that Anna Maria and the girls and I had traveled on it once, Southampton to New York, thanks to a magazine assignment.

This Cunard, however, proved to be a two-block commercial strip with a feed store, a hardware, a cafe, two churches, and a gas station that looked like something out of an Edward

Hopper painting. Beyond the pumps, Mason made a sharp left, then turned toward a range of foothills where the road went to gravel. I fell back a bit to avoid the dust his wheels threw skyward.

Two miles of this and we angled onto a smaller road, gravel again but with a strip of grass down its middle. Stones ticked up against the Camry's underbelly. I worried how much it would cost to repair the damage to the hood and grill, and wondered if I should have called my insurance company and taken a photo of the deer, and then wondered why it was that Jesus had said we were hungry when we weren't, and then wondered how deep into the woods Mason was taking us. We climbed at first, and then the road swerved right and dipped into a shadowed hollow. We passed a small house, a shack really, unpainted wood with a chimney puffing smoke and a woman with bare arms peeling white undershirts off a line strung between two trees and flipping them one by one onto her shoulder.

One last turn, an even narrower road, slanting down now almost in darkness, and I saw a light ahead, then a house, very small, with an outbuilding of some sort off to one side, a junk tractor rusting in the weeds, and a stocky woman standing on the stone step, hands on hips.

We pulled up behind Mason. He jumped out happily, slammed the tailgate down, called to the woman to come see. She glanced at us, suspiciously it seemed. Out from behind her skipped a happy young boy or girl—in the poor light I couldn't tell—and then we were all standing around the tailgate and I could see that it was a girl, with gold-blond curly hair and wide-set eyes. The little girl reached out and touched Jesus's leg, as if assessing the quality of the cloth of his trousers, or as if wanting to make certain that he was real. He reached down and touched her on the head with a similarly tentative gesture, and she giggled and buried her face in the woman's skirts.

Using the same technique we'd used on the highway, the three of us—Mason, Jesus, and I—lifted the dead animal and carried it, at his direction, over to the edge of the yard. There was a light on a pole, a wire running toward the house. The woman fetched a shovel. As the child watched, the woman handed Mason a small knife, the blade half serrated, half not, and, lying the deer flat on its back, Mason began to slice a straight line down its belly. He worked with a surgical sureness, the knife pressed only half an inch or so into the furred skin, cutting and ripping and pulling away as if slicing upholstery from an old sofa cushion. I'll spare you some of the details, but in another minute he was lifting out a greenish sac, tossing it aside, scraping out the cavity with both hands. While Mason worked, the woman, his wife I guessed, dug a shallow hole and buried the mess nearby. "Entrals," he said over his shoulder. "Cain't let them touch the meat."

When the cavity was clean, he and his wife—both of them very strong—lifted the creature by its legs and carried it to a frame made from saplings lashed together with rope. As they held it there, Mason asked Jesus to tie the hind legs to the crossbar with more rope, and Jesus did so, as surely as he'd inserted the knife. A few drops of blood dripped on the leaves and dirt, the antlers just touched the ground, and Mason set to work in earnest in light from the house, first washing out the cavity with a garden hose, then peeling off the hide with delicate, right-handed cuts of sinew, his left hand pulling away and down.

On and on he went as Jesus and I and the girl watched, captivated, and his wife carried away first the hide, then the antlers, then the head. At his direction, we untied the carcass and lay it on a flat soapstone raised up on a wooden platform and

Mason performed more of his artistry, slicing off the legs and setting them aside, running the blade up inside the vertebrae just so and pulling out fillets of steak—"Loin meat," he said. "Best part. Our supper." And then, holding the knife horizontal to the stone, he sliced off a silvery skin of gristle and, one by one, set the fillets aside. He worked at a steady speed, almost but not quite hurrying, the cool air around him touched with a sense of celebration. His wife came outside with butcher paper and string. The legs and rib meat were wrapped and tied. "For freezin," and Mason was washing his hands carefully in the hose water and telling us to do the same and then leading us inside.

It was a simple house, a box with a metal roof, the walls covered with peeling wallpaper, the floors with ancient linoleum. There was a ten-foot-square kitchen that opened onto a room with a table and four chairs, handmade it seemed, from their beautiful irregularity. The girl—she had a peculiar, adult-like way about her—brought forks and knives and cloth napkins to the table and set them there clumsily but attentively. The woman had lit two burners on a gas stove in the kitchen and was putting oil in a pan and salt and pepper on the steaks. Some kind of greens were soon boiling on the second burner, filling the rooms with a smell I'd never encountered before and can't say I liked. Mason pulled a loaf of white bread from a drawer, sliced it and put it into a basket and handed the basket to the girl.

While all this was going on, Jesus and I stood there awkwardly, or I did, at least. In his stained shirt and dress pants, Jesus seemed more at ease, touching the little girl's head each time she walked past, asking if we could help.

"No, no, yer our guests," Mason answered. "And now yer good shirt's all spoilt, lookit." From the moment he'd seen Jesus slip the knife in behind the buck's antlers, there had been an eagerness about him, as if the windfall of the deer meat had lit in him a fire of hospitality, as if he'd been waiting all his adult life to be able to host a pair of well dressed strangers for dinner and had finally gotten his chance. Sturdily built and with freckled skin, his wife, on the other hand, while not unfriendly, gave the sense that she was ashamed or embarrassed, by her clothing, her home, her dishware and cutlery and mismatched chairs, and had been pummeled into silence by the guests in nice shoes and the almost new car with Massachusetts license plates.

I am ashamed to say that my elite, educated-person's preconceptions were firing on all cylinders. This was West Virginia. A hollow, no less. The child, who laughed every time Jesus tapped her head, was probably cognitively impaired, the wallpaper peeling, the pickup rusting. All I needed to complete my foolish and cliché'-ridden assessment was for an uncle to bang through the door with his skin blackened by coal dust and a Make America Great Again hat perched on his head.

But something else was going on and, as the dinner preparations moved closer to climax and Jesus studied an old framed topographical map on one of the walls, I was able to let go of my foolish ideas and sense it more clearly. I watched Mason's wife sear the meat in a hot frying pan and then slip it into the oven. I watched him slicing the bread, placing it in the basket, handing the basket to his daughter. I watched the daughter carrying it into the dining room and pushing it toward the center of the table as if it had to be positioned exactly there in order for the meal to go on. From a wide-mouthed metal pitcher, Mason poured water into five plastic glasses. His wife snapped off the stove and drained the greens over the sink. The girl hugged her mother's leg. I watched Jesus turn away from the map and face the center of the room, then take one rickety extra chair from its place beside the sofa and settle it at the table. He didn't ask to do it, he did it as if he were a relative and entitled or expected to do it, and that small gesture caused me to realize that the family was as unguarded as the skinned deer. What was missing was pretension, the wordy armor of personality. From somewhere in the depths of my memory came a fact from a magazine article I'd once read about the Amish of Lancaster County, Pennsylvania. "The Plain People" they called themselves. It was *plainness* I was feeling, what the third-century monks of the Egyptian desert used to call *spiritual simplicity,* the polar opposite of the elaborate catering to every taste and the complex etiquette of the Greenbrier dining room . . . and so much of my own life. I don't mean to glorify poverty, or even to cast a judgment either way. But as the woman carried in a platter of venison steaks and then a ceramic bowl of greens with an enormous pat of butter melting on top—apologizing all the while for the mismatched dishes—and as we took our seats around the table without a word of direction, and the platter of sliced venison and bowl of greens was passed from hand to hand (Mason served his daughter with so much love it cast me back to the days when our girls were very small and I'd spoon-feed them in their high chairs and carefully wipe their lips with a napkin.) I had a sense of 'space' in the air of the room. It reminded me, so strangely, of the interior space I felt in certain quiet moments of meditation. The run of thoughts had slowed to a trickle. The list of concerns and planned enjoyments had been temporarily set aside. The moment loomed large, simple, magnificent. "Emptiness" is a word the Buddhists sometimes use, a confusing word, it had always seemed to me, but there was a sense of it around the table. Not a lack, but a freedom, and in the heart of that freedom I experienced a sense of surprise at the bare fact of being alive on this earth.

I was sitting across from Jesus. He nodded, as if reading my thoughts. Bowed heads and a spoken grace would have fit my clichéd image, but there was none of that. The woman said, "I'm Emma, and this here is little Ellory."

"I'm Eddie, thank you for having us. Everything smells so good."

All of us turned to look at Jesus.

"I din't never git your name," Mason said. He was watching Jesus expectantly, happily, a morsel of meat already on his fork and in his eyes that same pride of hospitality.

Now, I thought, now he'll make up something, say he's a Mario or a Caesar or a Bill. Joe, Mike, Thaddeus.

"Jesus," he said.

The little girl laughed, and neither Mason nor Emma shushed her. They were, however, eyeing Jesus with a new attention and then Emma said, "That's a fine name. Please eat." And we did.

The food was succulent, the meat with a tinge of wildness to it and the greens bitter as the dandelions I'd eaten at my grandmother's table fifty years earlier, but salty, too, a perfect complement to the venison. With the soft buttered bread and cold well water, the meal fit perfectly into the evening's sense of elegant plainness. Mason told the story of seeing my car at the side of the road and stopping, first, because he thought we needed help, and then seeing the deer. "My mouth watered fairly," he said.

I said how bad I'd felt, hitting the deer.

"Why do you talk funny?" Ellory asked me when her father and I had finished talking.

"Because I live pretty far away."

"Where?"

"Massachusetts."

"We've never been that far," Emma admitted, her forehead pinched into parallel lines.

When Mason asked me what had brought me to West Virginia, I told him I was headed to Arkansas, and when he asked why, I told him it was for a talk about something I'd written.

"Books, you write?"

I nodded, swallowed, took a drink of water.

"We're not much for books."

"We have the Bible, Papa," Ellory reminded him.

"Do you go to church?" I asked her.

"Sometimes we do."

"It's why she laughed at your name," her mother said to Jesus. "We've never met someone with that name. We heard of it only from the Good Book."

"You look like him," Mason said pleasantly. "Do you write books, too?"

"I'm a pretty fair carpenter," Jesus said. "But not much of a writer."

"I hang Sheetrock," Mason said, "In Beckley. When there's work."

"And I sew," Emma said.

It was all pleasant and nice and free, it seemed to me, of the ordinary judgments. Somehow, their simplicity and straightforwardness made what could have been an extremely awkward encounter seem absolutely natural. Emma brought out brownies at the end of the meal and looked at me as if I were truly an alien when I offered to bring the dirty dishes into the kitchen. "I'm making coffee," she said.

"Excuse me for one second," Jesus stood up and went outside.

I asked to use the bathroom and Ellory led me down a narrow hallway, boards squeaking underfoot, to a tiny bath with an old porcelain sink and a bare lightbulb. "Shut the door so we don't see," she said, and when I did that I stood in the room for a moment, leaned on the sink, and felt an urge to pray. Why, I don't know. Sometimes in the course of a day I'll say an old Catholic prayer I like, the Hail Mary. Not for any particular reason, just when there is a certain kind of . . . *emptiness* in the day. A quiet moment, a gap in the rush to accomplish or enjoy. Or I'll try to remind myself of a memory from my daily meditation session, a quietness, a perspective on things. In their bathroom, I got as far as *Hail Mary, full of grace,* and stopped, then did what I'd come there to do and washed my hands and for some strange reason couldn't look at myself in the mirror.

When I came out again, Jesus was back. He took his seat and Ellory jumped onto his lap, ignoring the stain on his shirt, which had dried by then. She leaned her blond head against the middle of his chest and I saw that he was holding something down at the side of the chair. Emma carried in a tray with four coffee cups and one glass of milk. "My friend Edward and I would like to give you this small gift," Jesus said to the girl, "as thanks for the delicious meal, and your family's gracious hospitality." He looked at Emma, and then Mason. "If your parents don't mind."

"No mindin' here," Mason said.

Jesus then lifted into view the wrapped package Anton had delivered to him in the Greenbrier dining room, and, at the sight of the gift, I had a premonition that, as he'd predicted, I was about to feel deeply ashamed of myself for my suspicions. The girl squealed with excitement. Jesus helped Ellory peel away the wrapping, revealing an old, scratched-up wooden box with a small brass clasp. He placed her hand at the clasp. "Open it," he said kindly.

She struggled with the clasp for a moment and then lifted

the lid. She was sitting across from me. I could see her face light up, but I couldn't see the contents until she reached in and pulled out first one string of beads, and then another. Rosary beads, I assumed, and my feeling was it would be another of Jesus's small rudenesses. The man who didn't understand earthly etiquette because he hadn't 'been here long' had given a little girl—who was probably not even Catholic—a set of rosary beads and had made too big a fuss about it. But, when I didn't see any kind of crucifix, I realized it was just a string of beads, not a rosary. With that same look of adult-like concentration—truly it was an eerie expression, and, strangely, I had goose bumps on the skin of my arms—Ellory set the two loops of beads on the table in front of her. They were quite different from each other, one reddish-brown in color and made of wood, the other shiny fake pearls strung together with small loops of metal. She reached back into the box and pulled out three long, thin pieces of cloth—maroon, satiny yellow, and lavender—and set them on the table, too, straightening and smoothing them.

"You can have them all, but choose your favorite first," Jesus told her.

For half a minute she sat there, tilting her head sideways, moving the beads apart with a small index finger, touching the pieces of cloth one by one. I was sure she'd take the glittery beads and the satin yellow cloth, but I was wrong again: she picked up one set of beads—the plainer set—and one piece of cloth—maroon—and Jesus wrapped the cloth around her golden locks in the form of a headband, a gesture that brought out a huge girlish grin. She stretched the beads apart in two hands, kissed them, then turned to look at her mother.

"Pretty," her mother said.

The whole thing was a scene in a bizarre play. I couldn't

imagine one of my daughters—comfortable as they were around people—jumping onto an unknown visitor's lap. Couldn't imagine going into a strange home bearing strange gifts, giving used beads, asking the child to choose. But Mason and Emma sat there, watching with a kind of innocence and acceptance and humility that seemed to be infiltrating the atoms in the air around us.

"Real nice," Mason said. "Say thank you, El."

The girl thanked Jesus, then jumped off his lap and disappeared into one of the back rooms with her gifts.

"Just a small something," Jesus said to her parents. And then, "We'll be in touch again."

They nodded, as if actually believing this Jesus in the Camry would swing by on another evening, accompanied by his weird-talking friend and bringing used beads and strips of cloth for their little girl.

With that, we all stood up. There was Mason's hard handshake and Emma's hesitant one, thank-yous all around. As we were heading toward the door, Ellory emerged from the back room, ran toward us and then stopped and made an odd gesture, perfectly in keeping with the oddity of the day. Two fingers held up against the middle of her forehead, hand between her eyes. A salute. She made a small, perfect bow in Jesus' direction. He bowed back. I had the goose bumps going again.

Her parents stood in the rectangle of light in the doorway and waved to us as we drove off, and I felt as though I were wandering the alleyways of a queer dream, things being done and words being said that made no sense, but carried the essence of some deep truism, some eerie gorgeousness, a miniature, elegant, floating throne, festooned with rubies and red and gold paint, drifting down a river of the subconscious world.

~ ✣ ~

chapter fourteen

We pulled away from Mason and Emma's house in the darkest of darknesses, the sky so full of stars that when we reached the end of their road I stopped, rolled down the window, and stuck my head out to gaze. Somehow, despite the darkness, despite my matchless talent for getting lost, and despite the fact that the GPS had no signal in that hollow, I was able to find my way back through Cunard and onto the Interstate. A miracle.

It required all my concentration, however. While I went slowly along, looking for landmarks in the night, Jesus sat quietly in the passenger seat, still as a statue. It was only when we were back on the highway, being guided toward the hotel in Charleston by the voice of my now-operative GPS, that the goings-on at Mason and Emma's came back into focus for me. I tried to sort it out—the package Anton had delivered during our Greenbrier lunch, the obvious fact that the delivery had been arranged beforehand, the bizarre transfer to a little blond girl in a West Virginia hollow . . . who seemed pleased but strangely unsurprised by it. The salute and bow, the goose bumps. As I drove, I went over this sequence several times, trying to pierce the perplexing crust and reach the center of it. Had Jesus suddenly decided to make a gift to a cute little girl, in thanks for her family's hospitality, as he'd claimed? If so, why give her the wrapped box? And how did he know what was inside? What if it had been a box of Cuban cigars, or Marx Brothers playing cards, or contraband? Had he and Maxim discussed the contents beforehand? Had Jesus known we'd hit the deer, meet Mason, and be invited back to the house where Ellory lived? If so, then why not have Anton wrap up a doll or a toy, something she'd appreciate more?

In the end, hard as I tried, I could not keep my curiosity in its cage.

"Could you explain something to me?"

"Depends," he said, in a suddenly grumpy tone.

"On what?"

"On your willingness to set aside your doubts and consider what I have to say with an open mind."

The GPS voice piped up, "*One mile ahead on the route . . . slow traffic.*"

There was another in a series of difficult silences between us. Even at that hour—just before eight p.m.—the winding, roller-coaster highway was busy with tractor trailers. It was also crossed by strong winds. Not the best time for a driver to have a difficult conversation. A few seconds passed, and then, as the GPS had predicted, the traffic thickened and slowed. We crept along, the grumble and groan of downshifting engines, the sense of something wrong ahead, something unexpected and not good. Soon I could see blue and red lights flashing on the trucks' silvery sides. Another few minutes of slow forward progress and we reached two mangled cars sitting crookedly in a sea of sparkling bits of glass and pieces of plastic fender. An ambulance with its back door open. Two state police cruisers. Someone belted securely onto a wheeled stretcher and wearing a neck brace. And then we were past the scene, cars and trucks picking up speed again, the world back in balance . . . for us, at least.

"I was just curious," I said, hedging.

Jesus paused. I could feel him looking over at me. "A little more than that, I think, Edward."

I hedged again. "It's just . . . I don't know . . . there was something weird about the whole day. Anton. The girl. The strange gift."

Jesus didn't speak.

I kept trying. "Nice people though, weren't they?"

"Very fine people. Exceptional people."

"*Your people,* was the way you put it earlier."

Not a word.

I knew exactly what I was doing, yet I couldn't stop myself. It felt sinful, dishonest, cowardly, the opposite of straightforward, but all that was overshadowed by a kind of devilish pride, an unwillingness to give in to him, to admit—fully and publicly, as it were—that he might be something other than a major-league scam artist, a potentially violent psychic, a stalker. I'm not proud of that. I'm just reporting the truth.

I decided to play the best card in my hand: "You told me more than once that you didn't have a knife, and then it turned out that you do have one. Care to explain that before we go any further?"

"If I told you I had a knife you would have thrown me out on the street."

"Probably."

"I knew I would never harm you with the knife."

"So you lied."

"Yes."

"Are you lying about anything else?"

No answer.

"Do you have a gun?"

Nothing, for a time. I saw the blinking red lights in the mirror, and then the ambulance raced past on our left, a kaleidoscopic reminder of mortality. It was the second one we'd seen so far in our time together. I said another silent prayer.

Jesus took out an elastic band and tied his long hair back in a ponytail. "I'm still waiting to hear you say you're ready to set aside your doubts."

At that moment, watching the lights of the ambulance slip down an exit and toward a small cluster of streetlights to the right of the highway and below; at that moment, with some poor soul breathing his or her last, or in great pain, or traumatized by the crash, or all of the above, may God forgive me, but at that moment I still wasn't ready to set aside my doubts. It occurred to me, as the silence between us deepened and swelled into a prickly discomfort, that the position Jesus had put me in was perhaps a metaphor for our existential predicament: we're continually being asked to believe there is some sense to be made of the very odd situation in which we find ourselves. To believe in the idea that, behind the incredible suffering, the manifest unfairness, the inequity that's visible in every news report on any given day, the apparent randomness of human misery and joy, the repetitive nature of almost everything we do—there is a point, a meaning, a lesson. In the face of all that suffering and monotony, all that pleasure and busyness, the inevitability of our death, we're asked to go on. To try to be decent to one another. We are given every reason not to believe that human life has meaning, and yet so many of us do.

So, instead of answering his question, I asked my own: "Why are people good?"

He laughed and seemed to relax a bit. "Mostly the puzzle is approached from the opposite direction: why are people bad?"

"Okay, but why?"

"I'm not answering," he said, "until you tell me you have set aside your doubts, you are willing to trust me, to believe I am who I say I am."

"I'm not."

Another small laugh. "An honest moment, at least. Fine, then let's just ride along as friends. Or acquaintances. Or fellow travelers, whatever you wish. But it seems to me you're smart enough to realize the contradiction here. You ask me to explain the mysteries of life, everything from Ellory's examination to the existence of goodness, and yet, at the same time, you insist on clinging to your doubts. You worry that I'm a charlatan, a fake, even a murderer."

"I didn't see any *examination!*"

"There is much you don't see, Edward. . . . And, you're trying to change the subject. Do you recognize the contradiction, or don't you? You're so highly educated, so well read and well traveled, so thoughtful, and yet, a great spirit you've been hearing about and praying to for decades comes down to you in the flesh, and you cling to your doubts the way a child clings to a dangerous object his mother wants to take away. You're worried about my having a hunting knife, a useful tool that, by the way, I used a few hours ago to alleviate suffering, and yet here you are wearing your doubts like a turtle's shell, a shield, like armor."

"Why don't you give up on me, then? Why don't you just leave at the next rest area and come down to somebody else in the flesh?"

"Because I don't give up on people. Not easily, at least. If they insist on pushing me away, and keep insisting, and keep insisting, then I might deprive them of my presence for a time. You're not quite there yet."

"Thanks."

"Spare me the sarcasm. And don't ask any more of the great questions until or unless you get to the point where you're willing to actually embrace the answers, without slicing them to pieces with what you think of as your highly developed intellect. Either trust me or don't look to me for answers, I don't think that's too much to ask."

It wasn't, of course, but I couldn't quite admit that. Jesus was correct: I wanted to hear, if not answers, then at least his thoughts on things like evil and the afterlife . . . just in case he was something other than a whacky magician.

That wasn't so unusual, however. The truth is, I've spent so much of my life wondering about these 'great questions' that I'm open to listening to any reasonable person who wants to offer an opinion. I love to read across the spiritual, philosophical, and psychological spectrums, to entertain the various explanations for what we're supposed to be doing here and what awaits us beyond the blink of death. Several of my closest friends are atheists, professing a belief only in the Religion of Randomness. It's all an accident, they contend, all without meaning. That's their credo. Death as dark curtain, the end of consciousness.

I confess to having a problem with that. Even Einstein pointed to the meticulous design of everything from subatomic particles to the arrangement of planets in the various universes, as evidence of some kind of Divine Intelligence. Everything from the arrangement of blood vessels in the body to the spinning of the earth seems to me anything *but* random. Yes, violence and misery appear to be pointless: what sense does the Holocaust make? What kind of God would allow a child to be tortured by cancer or evil parents? Or allow war to exist? Or starvation? But to have all of it—the stars, the creatures of the sea, the link between me and my wife and daughters—stem simply from a spiritless roll of the dice? That requires a different kind of faith, a faith in meaninglessness. I can't go there.

I don't pretend to have answers to the big questions. On the one hand, I can't take refuge in the explanation that it's all random. On the other, I can't quite take refuge in the explanation that God is love and does these things for our ultimate benefit. Which leaves me caught in a no-person's-land between cynicism and simple faith. I respect churchgoers, but don't attend. I admire science, but can't make a god of it.

Still, I'm curious and always have been. I'm perfectly willing to admit that my human intelligence isn't broad or deep enough to understand it all. But it seems to me that some people in the history of our species, a select few, have reached a state of peace and wisdom, a kind of perfection . . . to use a word Theresa of Avila favored. Not merely an intellectual understanding, but a profound sense of . . . what's the way to say it? *A belief in anti-randomness.* An absolute, intelligent, time-tested certainty that the world as we know it makes sense and has purpose. And that they, themselves, have a sacred place in it.

So, of course, I wanted to hear what So-Called Jesus had to say about it, in the same way I'd pick up a copy of the Upanishads, or the Sutras, or read a chapter of the Bible, or an essay by Einstein or Kierkegaard, or something from Theresa of Avila or Thomas Merton. Or have a conversation with a thoughtful friend, or listen to a podcast that dealt with spiritual and philosophical issues.

But, despite everything that had happened in our short time together, all the things he'd done that transcended science and logic, I couldn't open myself far enough to quiet the cynical voice and listen to him.

And the knife incident didn't much help.

"What you want," Jesus said after a while, and the voice that had gone harsh a few minutes earlier was now merely sad, "is for your preconceptions to be supported. If I were a gentle, quiet man in robes, with maybe a halo around my head, someone who didn't carry a knife and didn't like Philly cheesesteak, if I came to you floating in air and saying things like, "Believeth in me and thou shalt have life everlasting," you'd be on your knees in a second. But I come looking like an ordinary guy, just as I did two thousand years ago, and so you indulge your cynical, doubting side, as so many people did then. Your pride. Your ego. Your need to be The One Who Knows."

I felt a crack form in the protective wall I'd built around myself. I might even have admitted that, but just then Jesus said. "Pay attention. This is our exit."

Two seconds later, the GPS agreed with him. I left the highway and saw, a hundred feet up in the air, a neon sign announcing the hotel Anna Maria had found for that night.

~ ~

chapter fifteen

Jesus and I checked in and went to our separate rooms with a sour distance between us. It seemed to me, again, that I'd started out with some kind of advantage, feeling superior without meaning to, the guy with money in his pocket, a nice car, the giver of a favor. And now all that had flipped on its head.

I closed the door behind me, dropped my bag on the floor, and assumed the usual position, legs over the mattress, back on the carpet, phone on my chest. I lay there for a while, twisting in a delicate misery, and then dialed home.

"Hey, Beautiful," I said, when Anna Maria answered.

"You made it to the hotel?"

"It's nice, thanks. Another big room, firm mattress, easy check-in. Give them five stars on Yelp or whatever."

"Hotels.com. Is he still with you?"

"Who?"

"Don't play games, Eddie. Jesus."

"Yes. Still with me."

"Separate rooms?"

"He paid for his own this time."

"And?"

"And what, Hon?" I asked her.

"What is wrong with you, Eddie Val! I spent the whole day

thinking about my husband traveling with Jesus Christ! I've been dying to tell the girls, or my mother, or Cindy, or one of my other friends. I've written three pages about it in my journal. I've checked my phone two hundred freaking times, hoping you'd send a picture of him, or a story, or that there was a miracle or something."

"It's not like that, Hon."

"What do you mean?"

"I mean, it's not like he's some gentle guy in a robe, floating around with a halo who says things like, 'Believeth in me and thou shalt have life everlasting.'"

There was silence on the line. After a few seconds I said, "Hon?"

"Eddie!"

"What."

"That's insulting as shit. Do you take me for an absolute idiot? Do you really think I picture the guy walking around in a robe and a halo and talking like that? Have you been drinking?"

"No, but—"

"I can't believe you said that to me. It makes me want to hang up. It—"

"Please don't hang up. I've had a hard day."

"How can you be with Jesus and have a hard day, would you please tell me?"

So I told her. Sort of. I described the Greenbrier lunch, Anton, the wrapped package, my fear that it contained something illegal. When I mentioned the deer, she interrupted.

"I can't believe you slaughtered an innocent deer!"

"It jumped in front of the car, Hon."

"You murdered it and didn't even get out and try to bury it. I really can't believe this."

"We did get out. And it was Jesus who killed it, actually." I hadn't been intending to tell her about the knife (I worried, she'd worry), but realized I was holding things back, and we'd promised never to do that, so I described Mason, and Jesus's knife, and the trip to Mason's house, and his wife and daughter, and the meal, and then the strange gift. At that point I stopped and waited, exhausted. Wrung out. Alone in the spinning world.

Another few seconds of worrisome silence and Anna Maria said, "It sounds like how they find the Dalai Lama."

"Meaning what?"

"You know, when they're looking for a special incarnation, the old monks have a dream and go out into the Tibetan countryside and find the little boy they dreamt about and they show him objects from the previous Dalai Lama, or the previous Rinpoche or whatever, and the little boy always picks the glasses the Dalai Lama wore, or the beads the famous teacher used, instead of the other ones."

"Right. But this was a little blond American girl in West Virginia, not a little Tibetan boy in the Himalayas someplace."

"Hah! I get it now," she said angrily. "It was *you* who expected Jesus to wear a robe and have a halo and talk funny, not me! And *you* who expects the next holy one to be a boy in Tibet. It couldn't possibly be a girl, could it, Eddie! And not in West Virginia, God forbid! You surprise me, you know that? I thought you were a deeper thinker than that."

"I thought I was, too," I said, and something in my voice must have reached her because all of a sudden she changed lanes and wasn't angry at all.

"Are you all right?"

"Yes," I said. And then, "No."

"What's going on?"

I shrugged, even though I knew she couldn't see me. "Not sure."

"Spit it out, Eddie. Come on. What's wrong?"

"I think," I said, and then I stopped and stared across the perfectly clean, perfectly unsurprising, perfectly like-every-other hotel room, and took a breath. "I think I'm not the man I thought I was."

"Of course you are!"

"I don't think so. I mean, I wrote the Buddha books, and some people like them. And I've meditated almost every day for forty years, and I was a devout Catholic until college, really devout—"

"So was I. We discovered sex, remember, then we stopped going to confession."

"And then I started reading every kind of religious book I could get my hands on, *What the Buddha Taught, The Inner Life, The Upanishads, The Bhagavad Gita,* Merton, Whitman, Buber, the Dalai Lama. And I've tried so hard to be a good husband and good father."

"Check off both those boxes, Babe."

"And we give to charity, and do volunteer work, and try not to use plastic bags or waste food."

I paused. She said, "Are you about to confess some terrible sin or something, Eddie? Do you have a mistress? Other kids someplace? Are you a secret online gambling addict or something? Do you write porno on the side? Is that how we paid for—"

I was shaking my head. "Nothing like that. But down deep inside, I think I've always been trying to go to the next level. Not have some glorious spiritual experience or anything like that, but maybe just feel, I don't know the word . . ."

"Saved," she suggested.

"Bad connotations."

"Holy."

"Not saved, not holy, but . . ."

"Spit it out, Eddie."

"I'm trying to. It's right there in my mind, but vague."

"Un-vague it."

"I think . . . I think sometimes that less educated people, *simpler* people, maybe, but I don't mean that in a bad way—"

"You're thinking of my brother."

"People like him, yeah, but not him exactly. Not educated, not sophisticated, not so aware as we are of the larger world. They seem to have this absolute, simple, straightforward faith. Their minds are like a clean white canvas, and mine is crossed with a million lines and has a billion words written on it, and for everything I believe, or want to believe, there's a smart counter-argument."

"You don't want to be like Reggie, don't say you do. Please don't."

"I don't. I can't. We can't. But it's like he's Adam before he ate the apple, and I'm Adam after I ate it."

"Reggie is a horrible example . . . but I know what you mean."

"You do?"

"Sure. I think of it like the way the girls were when they were two or four, and the way they are now. I love them both ways, but there was a kind of purity then, in their minds, in who they were. Zero self-consciousness. Pure spirits."

"Right, exactly, but I think some adults can be that way, too. And I feel like all the meditating, all the living and reading and thinking I've done, is because I've been trying to get back to that, to a kind of complete peace with who I am."

"Me, too."

"But then, let's say this guy actually *is* Jesus. *The* Jesus, I mean. If he really is, and he's really come into my life, our lives, for some weird reason, if I were the person I've been trying to become, I feel like I'd react differently. I wouldn't be afraid of being hurt or cheated or tricked. I wouldn't have this defensive wall built up around me. But I don't want to be stupid about it, some gullible, sentimental person who . . . I'm . . . I feel, I don't know, caught in the middle someplace. Does that make any sense?"

People were yelling at each other in the hallway. I heard *Shithead!* And *Prick!* And worse things. A woman and a man. I was relieved to realize that neither of them sounded like Jesus. I thought maybe I should tell Anna Maria to give the hotel four stars, not five.

She said, "So if you put down the defenses and just believed he was the real Jesus, what's the worst that could happen? He wouldn't kill you or hurt you, would he?"

"No. At first, I worried he might, but now I don't think so. No. I'm sure he wouldn't."

"So what's the worst thing?"

"That he'd turn out to be something else, and I'd feel stupid, scammed, taken advantage of."

"Money-wise?"

"Not really. He seems to have plenty of money now. Just. . . I'd feel like a fool."

A pause. I could hear music in the background. Often, before she went to bed, Anna Maria liked to play old rock-and-roll tunes on YouTube. She'd play the same ones over and over again, usually songs with great guitar work, because she played that instrument herself. The song I'd been hearing was Pink Floyd's "Wish You Were Here." After a few seconds, she said, "As fears go, that's pretty flimsy."

"It is. Telling you about it made me realize how flimsy it is."

"I'll give you a guarantee," she said. It was one of her expressions. When we were first together, she'd say it sometimes in the middle of the day, and the guarantee she was speaking of was sex, and it always sent a thrill through me, and maybe through her, too. As the years passed, the words had come to mean other things—besides, but not necessarily excluding sex: that we'd have a nice meal at a nearby restaurant, that she'd give me a backrub, that something I was worried about was going to work out fine as in, "I'll give you a guarantee they make you a nice offer for this book, Eddie Val!" Sometimes after we'd had an argument and made up, she'd say, "I'll give you a guarantee that I love you."

I was smiling, relieved, listening to the music in the background and thinking maybe she'd chosen that particular song because she missed me as much as I missed her.

"I'll give you a guarantee," she said again, "Here it is: If you let down the walls and trust him, and if that turns out to be a mistake, and he turns out to have just played you so he could get a ride, or even if he tricks you somehow and takes a little money, or a credit card or something, I won't tell anybody and I won't think you're a fool, okay? I'll never mention it, no matter how bad we fight. I'm not even going to tell the girls what's going on and you don't tell them either, okay?"

"I haven't."

"Good. Just go for it, Eddie. Jump off the high rock into the water and if you look stupid and make a bad splash and sprain your ankle or something, I'll never bring it up and I won't think less of you. In fact, I'll think *more* of you because you tried. Okay?"

I held the phone against my ear. I was thinking: *this is what love sounds like.*

"Okay, Hon?" she said again.

"Sure, yeah, thanks," I said, and then a great spiritual weariness came over me, as if just the idea of setting my resistance aside required my organs to spin and leap across some interior stage in a complex ballet I'd never practiced and had no talent for. "You're the best."

"Eddie."

"What?"

"Did she seem that special?"

"Who?"

"The little girl."

"Yeah. A lot of kids do, but yes."

"In what way?"

"More poised and open than most kids that age. When he gave her the gift, there was an expression of . . . *familiarity* on her face. I had goose bumps going."

"I wish I was there."

"Any chance you could fly down for the talk? You could meet him."

"I'd love to, but Mom needs me here right now."

"You have, as the say, a guaranteed spot in heaven."

"Right. In a gated community of sinners."

"As long as they have golf," I said, and I heard her laugh. "Sleep good. Love you."

"Love you back, Eddie Val. Love you big."

We signed off then, forty years of history playing as background to the words. Great times, bad times, ER visits with the kids, and games of golf on sunny afternoons, places where we matched up perfectly and places where we never would (she doesn't like anchovies, for one example). Two spirits had been brought into the world through us, nourished by us, then set free to find their own way. What a system it is, family life! I have a writer friend who says that, if there were no families, there would be no novels, and probably she's correct.

For a little while after we closed the connection, I went back and forth with the girls via the miracle of the Internet. Little love notes, really, disguised as questions about what they were doing. Studying hard for one of them, visiting temples in the Cambodian jungle for the other. I didn't mention my traveling companion. I'd promised Anna Maria, for one thing, and, for another, I wanted to come to terms with the strangeness of it myself before reinforcing in their minds the idea that their father walked a line somewhere between eccentricity and lunacy. There would be time.

Still, we prided ourselves on being open and honest with the girls, and I felt a twinge.

Maybe because of that twinge, I wasn't ready for sleep, and decided to head downstairs to the bar and see what the Yelp-four-star hotel might have on the drink menu.

~ ~

chapter sixteen

The semi-circular bar, just off the main lobby, had a TV showing a college hockey championship game, and a menu offering hummus and pita bread, among other delicacies. But I was there, I realized, to fortify myself for the challenges of the next day. And not with hummus.

Though I enjoy a glass of wine with dinner most nights, and partake of the occasional pint of Guinness with friends, I limit myself, strictly, to six vodka martinis per year. I save them for important moments—a friend's good health report, Anna Maria's birthday, particularly good or particularly bad news from the New York publishing world, and so on.

At the bar in the Charleston, West Virginia, hotel, after a day that could be described as uprooting, I decided that this was an important enough moment, ordered my martini (Grey Goose, dry, rocks, olive, stirred), watched the man-bunned bartender perform his magic, and then sat twirling the tapered glass in front of me for a few minutes before indulging. All the while I was turning over in my mind everything Anna Maria had said. I knew I'd been behaving in a way that was beneath me, courage-wise. And, after the first sip of what I often thought of as the Nectar of the Gods, I could feel the edifice of my pride dissolving like a kid's sandcastle at Revere Beach at high tide. A pleasant warmth enveloped me. I was going to shed my armor of doubt, and trust that Jesus was who he claimed to be. I was going to humble myself and hope that the rest of the trip south would bring me some new spiritual wisdom.

What was the worst that could happen?

As I sat there, one eye on the game (having played a bit of hockey in my youth, I enjoyed watching the sport, especially at the college level, where it wasn't periodically interrupted by a bare-knuckle brawl with the fans cheering as if they were in the Roman Coliseum and the refs letting it go on for a while, so the ratings would be high) a middle-aged couple came into the bar and sat next to me. We struck up a conversation. They were, they told me, making the long drive to Naples, Florida, where their kids and grandkids were going to meet them for a two-week vacation. "Golf and sun," the man said as his wife looked at him and smiled, "exactly the medicine we need after another Vermont winter."

I was happy for them.

We shared our dislike of the cold months—"house arrest" the talkative male half of the pair called it—and then the conversation turned to what we all did for work. Mostly it turned to what he did for work.

I'm not one of these guys who's ashamed of being a man. I like it, in fact. I've met plenty of good men, and more than enough bad men, and I've met enough good and bad women to have formed the opinion that evil and saintliness remain unconnected to gender. A radical view in some circles these days.

But, however, as I like to say, but however, it does seem to me that more males than females claim citizenship in the Nation of Narcissism, at least when it comes to talking about themselves. Their theme song should be "I am the World." I don't have much tolerance for it. In the case of the Charleston Charmer, though, the story offered a window into a slice of life I knew little about—the world of business—so I listened politely and made the appropriate noises.

The man—I'll call him Albert, although that was not his name—owned and operated a business that had been in his family for several generations: they made ping-pong balls. One product. Apparently, over the decades, they'd developed a formula for the plastic and a way of shaping it into a sphere that combined durability with low price, and they'd run a large factory somewhere in Vermont that employed a hundred or so people who demonstrated, in Albert's words, "A reasonably high work ethic." It sounded to me like Albert and his associates had pretty much chased every other ping-pong ball producer out of the market. Then something happened. What happened was that a very large department store chain that shall go by the initials W-M, became by far the largest purchaser of Albert's balls. Once they'd established that position, they informed Albert that, either his company could, as he described it, "put a can of six balls on the shelf for the cost of one dollar to them," or they were going to find an overseas company that could do so. "Now there's no way on earth we could keep our plant in Vermont and sell them half a dozen balls for a dollar, so we were forced to close. We opened a place in Laos and now we produce the same quality product at a tenth the price. We have people who work for $50 a week and they're really grateful to have the job. We give them lunch."

"You give them rice," Albert's wife, whose name was Masha, corrected.

"Right. They like to bring their own stuff to put on the rice."

"And W-M buys only from you," I said.

"Exactly."

"So what happened to the people in Vermont with the reasonably high work ethic?"

Albert pinched his lips and narrowed his eyes at me. Perhaps, sensing something in my tone of voice, he suspected me of Socialism. "I'm sure they found other work," he said.

"Though probably not for what we paid them," Masha admitted.

I nodded. Sipped the martini. Accidentally let my eyes turn to Masha, who seemed embarrassed. My impertinent question had had the effect of dampening the conversation, not a bad thing, and for a while the three of us pretended to be watching the hockey game with great interest. My thoughts went back to Jesus, to what I was going to tell him the next day, but then, as he gazed at the screen, Albert said, "This guy makes some great saves, doesn't he?" and I had the sense he wanted to keep talking, so I turned to look at him.

"Are you religious?" I heard myself say. It might have been the word 'save' that did it. Out of the corner of my eye I saw the bartender jerk his head in my direction and I realized what I had done, what I sounded like. Now both Masha and Albert were squinting at me. "I'm not some kind of freak," I hastened to say. "Sorry for asking. But I was just having a long phone conversation with my wife—she's home in Massachusetts—and we were talking about that stuff, and it's on my mind, that's all."

The bartender went back to work. Masha and Albert relaxed their eyes. She said, "I am, a little bit. Al isn't much for that."

"*Isn't much for that* is putting it mildly," Albert said. He was already on his third beer.

I nodded in a way I hoped conveyed that I wasn't trying to proselytize and was at peace with whatever their attitude on religion might be . . . which was, in fact, the case.

"My parents were nuts," he said.

"Sorry. I shouldn't have—"

"No, no, they were nuts. I mean crazy."

"Really really bad," Masha put in.

"In what way?"

"Everything was a sin, you know? Drinking, fucking—"

"Al!"

"Sorry, Hon. Drinking, sex, birthday parties."

"Jehovah's Witnesses?"

He shook his head. "Nah. For a while they were members of some upstate Maine cult. They did everything the weird pastor told them to do. Even after the guy was arrested, they still half believed that shit."

"Hard on a kid, I bet," I said.

"Huh! You have no idea. Killed my sister, literally, for one thing."

"I'm sorry."

He nodded, gulped his beer. "Jesus this, Jesus that. By the time I finally got out of the house and went to college, I wanted to punch out the next guy who said the word *Jesus* in my presence."

"He did punch some of them," Masha said proudly. She curled an arm inside her husband's elbow and rested her head against his shoulder for just a second, proud to be with a puncher-outer.

"It's all bullshit," Albert went on. "They weren't having any fun, so they didn't want anyone else to have fun."

"Exactly," Masha said.

"So you think there's nothing?" were the next words that slipped out of my mouth. It might be obvious by this point why I limit myself on the martini consumption. I wasn't drunk, not at all, but the guardrail that keeps me from saying potentially incendiary things had temporarily rusted away. Four or five sips of vodka do that to me. I lifted my chin toward the ceiling, "Nothing at all? Up there, out there?"

"Pure bullshit," Albert repeated. "That's all it is. You have your fun and then you die. End of story."

"You sound like you know," I couldn't keep myself from saying.

"It's obvious, that's all."

"What makes good people be good, then?"

He laughed, two loud "*hahs.*" "Simple: Fear of going to jail."

"And alimony payments," Masha said. She squinted at me again. "Are you a priest or something?"

"He said he was married," Albert told her before I could answer.

"An ex-priest, then?"

"Just an ordinary guy," I said. "I think about it a lot, that's all. I wonder about stuff."

"Let me give you a tip," Albert said. "Don't waste your mental energy."

"You're probably right."

"I'm certainly right," he took another gulp of beer.

I wish I could say here that I'm making him into a cliché for the sake of narrative convenience, but I'm not. He'd suffered, I could sense that: lost a sister, endured a bad upbringing. But I found him hard to be around. I sat there for another minute, looking down at the last few silvery drops in my glass, wondering if it made sense to suggest, however mildly, that he might be wrong. "The unexamined life is not worth living," Thoreau had written. It was entirely possible that I examined too much, but I work, I love, I function. It's not like I wander down the fairway puzzling over the meaning of blades of grass instead of thinking about my shanked six-iron. But on that night the embers of my natural curiosity had been blown into full flame by the presence of a guy who called himself Jesus. The weird happenings, the psychic stuff. The absence of my wife, my home, my usual routine. Her wisdom and love. The martini. I stake my claim to normalcy, to ordinariness, even. But I try not to take being alive for granted. And I try to keep one hand on the idea that I could be wrong about things.

I swallowed the last of the nectar, found a twenty in my pocket and slid it under the glass, as compensation for making everybody uncomfortable. "Good talking with you guys," I lied. "Enjoy the vacation."

"You, too," Masha said. Albert nodded without looking at me. I left them and took the stairs. In my comfortable room, lying in my comfortable bed, staring at the dark ceiling, I thought of the look on Mason's face when he was loading the dead deer into the back of his pickup. The immediacy of his invitation. The pleasure he so obviously took in being able to offer us hospitality in his home. Emma apologizing for the dishes. Ellory setting the table with such care. The simple meal. The bizarre *examination* which, apparently, the little girl had passed. Jesus's remark that he would *see them again.*

I thought about humility. About rich and poor. I mused and pondered, which is what I do, not in a frantic way, just letting my mind roam the mountains and plains of human existence, a traveler on horseback, amazed at all of it.

I was about to be paid six thousand dollars for talking to a few hundred people in a church, for an hour or two. Albert made enough money to take his wife, their three children and eight grandchildren to a golf resort in Naples, Florida for two weeks. Members of the family that owned W-M, already billionaires, put ninety-eight men and women out of work so they could get ping-pong balls onto their shelves for a buck a sixpack. And, in Laos, people were happy to work for fifty dollars a month and a bowl of rice a day.

I turned all that over and around in my mind, again and again, like a chipmunk turning an acorn, looking for the way to break it open, a way to make sense of it. I wondered what Jesus would say about it all. I fell asleep.

~ ~

chapter seventeen

That night I must have had one of my famously intricate dreams because I awoke the next morning with the small sense of confusion that often follows them. I showered and shaved, stretched a bit, sat in meditation for a while, and the confusion was replaced by a species of spiritual eagerness, a willingness to adhere to my good wife's advice and open myself to the possibility that Jesus might transform me in some positive and unexpected way.

I carried my bag down the three flights of stairs. Despite the positive mood, and the previous night's phone conversation, I could still feel one small tendril of doubt sticking to me. For some reason I saw this doubt in the imagery of football—a sport I watched occasionally but had never really played. It went this way: My spirit, the part of me that longed for liberation or enlightenment or salvation or a profound sense of peace, was a wide receiver. The Arkansas trip was my pass route. Anna Maria had thrown me a neat spiral, and I'd caught it in one hand, and I was running toward the end zone, still many yards away. I'd tucked the ball inside my elbow, made a feint and gotten mostly past the hefty middle linebacker of doubt, and was almost in the clear. But the linebacker lunged and got a grip on my jersey, just above the hip. He'd fallen to the turf, but still had a hold of my jersey. His grip was strong, but my legs were churning, I was spinning away, dragging him along with me, almost, but not quite, in the clear.

If that seems like an odd way to think about my road trip with Jesus, imagine how odd it seemed when, after not finding him in the lobby at the agreed-upon hour, I stepped out into the West Virginia day . . . and saw Jesus *tossing a football* back and forth with three tall young guys. I stood there and stared. He invaded my dreams, my imagination, knew my past . . . and looked like a pretty good athlete, besides.

The guys seemed to be members of a college basketball team. Their bus was waiting near the entrance, a few unusually tall young men climbing on. But these three—also tall and lanky—didn't seem to be in any hurry. They ran short patterns on the parking-lot tar, calling out happily when Jesus sent them a pass and they made the catch, or throwing their hands up in despair when they missed and the ball bounced off toward the road. Jesus was wearing running shoes, jeans, and a green and gold UWV sweatshirt I'd never seen. He'd draped his Army jacket over his red suitcase and left the suitcase beside my car. I could see, when he ran a long pattern to the far end of the lot, that he moved with a beautiful athletic smoothness, true grace, reaching up with one hand to snag a high pass and then tucking the ball in the crook of his elbow and pretending to run with it for a few yards, like a wide receiver eluding a tackle, making sharp cuts, tiptoeing along an imaginary out-of-bounds line. After a bit of that, he planted his feet, signaled for one of the guys to sprint left and deep, then threw a perfect spiral—forty or forty-five yards, I'd guess—that drilled through the air like a meteorite and straight into the young man's hands. The guy spiked the ball, right there on the edge of the asphalt, picked it up, and, laughing, he and his friends called out a happy goodbye to their older QB and headed for the bus. "You must have played!" one of them called out before he disappeared. "With an arm like that, I bet you played in college, man!"

Jesus greeted me with a huge smile on his face.

"Did you play in college?" I asked him.

He just laughed in a way that made me like him, said, "Yes, a football god!" loaded his suitcase into the trunk, and climbed in.

Kentucky was the one state in the lower forty-eight that I'd never been to, so I was pleased to cross the border near the hamlet of Canonsburg and check it off my list. Only Alaska remained unvisited, and I suspected it always would. My main association with the Bluegrass State was the famous Derby, the women in colorful hats, the men in suits, the Hispanic jockeys and their magnificent mounts, the mint juleps and inebriated people singing Old Kentucky Home. My main association with Alaska was frigid nights and Grizzly bears. End of discussion.

As I believe I've mentioned, in preparing for the Arkansas adventure, I'd done some research at home. From the first thought of making the trip by car, I'd known that I wanted to stop at the Trappist monastery in Kentucky. Gethsemane it's called, after the garden where Jesus was taken prisoner on the night before his death. And it's the place where the famous monk and writer Thomas Merton lived for some thirty-seven years. Anna Maria, who knew of my fascination with Merton, had made us reservations at a hotel in Bardstown, a few miles from Gethsemane. Not a chain this time, she said, but some-place with more character.

A short way beyond the Big Sandy River that marks the West Virginia/Kentucky line, Jesus began, without any preliminaries, to talk about his past. "My carpenter friend Jesse and I left our families and our jobs and headed off on what has come to be called the Silk Road," he said. "We had a small amount of money saved up and we were young and strong. There are various routes, as I'm sure you know, but it's incorrect to use the term 'road' for any of them. In places, there's just a lightly worn path through desert, a route from one oasis or one trading post or one simple inn to the next. The route we chose—by accident, really—took us through Damascus and south of the Caspian Sea and then through what are now called Iraq and Iran and Afghanistan. We had many adventures."

He fell silent there, lost in memories perhaps. Kentucky must be a beautiful state in the warm months, but it had been a cool spring, even that far south, and most of the trees were not yet in blossom. To either side of the Interstate stood gray, wooded hills. Smaller than the ones we'd driven through in West Virginia, they gave the landscape a certain gentle texture, a picturesque irregularity that made me think of returning with Anna Maria, in a warmer season, when we'd have time to wander the side roads and villages.

"Tell me one or two of them," I said.

He nodded, perhaps a bit surprised at my new tone, and looked out the side window. It seemed to me he was seeing, not the rollicking hills, but the landscape of memory. "We walked, mostly," he said in a far-off voice. "Mostly we walked, though every once in a while we were able to catch a ride on a cart drawn by donkeys or horses. There were camels, too, and a sparse if more or less regular stream of traders and nomads going in both directions. It's important to remember how unpeopled the landscape was, great swaths of desert and greenery, untouched mountainsides, massive trees, pure rivers—I'm not sure a modern man like yourself can fully imagine it."

I wasn't sure either, so I held my tongue and waited for him to continue.

"On occasion, we were able to pay for a room at an inn—there were some of those in the larger settlements—but on the night I'm thinking of, Jesse and I camped by the side of the road. We had cloth packs (my mother had made mine as a parting gift) with a rolled blanket belted on top, and we spread some palm fronds on the sand, pulled the blankets over us, and used the knapsacks for pillows."

"Were there thieves and bandits?"

"Yes, a few, but there were richer targets than two young boys. We weren't afraid in any case, not really. We were young and strong, as I said, both of us men of faith. We simply put our lives in the Great One's hands. On this night we'd laid out some palms and—it's cool in the desert once the sun goes down, you know—we'd made a fire and stayed up talking for a while. The fire had died to coals, and we were lying not far from each other, looking up at a tremendous array of stars, a sky so full of them it was as much white as black, when we heard footsteps.

"Boys," a man's voice said. "Would you have some water for me, boys?"

"We each had a little water left in our earthen jars and we shared it with the man. He sat down in the sand between us and seemed disinclined to leave. It was strange for that to happen. We'd met people on the road to that point, shared food and water, and been given some, too, but at night people usually left each other alone. Even the fact that he'd seen the embers and come over to us was somewhat strange. Jesse, I could tell, was uneasy."

"And you?"

"I'm protected. Always. Nothing can hurt me."

A dozen questions leapt to mind, foremost among them: if

you were protected, why had you let yourself be crucified? I remembered the book Janet had given me, and I remembered reading someone—Krishnamurti, it might have been—who insisted that a man of Christ's holiness would never have allowed himself to die in such a way. Against all logic, I wanted to believe that. Even as a boy, a good Catholic, I'd hated the idea of God letting his son be tortured to death. As we drove, I found myself cherishing a frail hope that Jesus was going to tell me it was all a mistake, the crucifixion a myth, a symbol; that, in actual fact, he'd lived to a ripe old age, teaching, curing, working miracles.

"Eternally protected," he repeated, and then: "In the firelight and starlight I could see the man's face fairly well. He was a darkly complected character, darker skinned than the people around whom we'd been raised, and darker and stockier than the people of the places we'd just traveled through. He spoke our language—Aramaic—but with a thick accent. He sat cross-legged and straight-spined and started to talk as if he'd been many days without companionship. "Boys," he said, "you may not yet be of an age to think about such things, but there are great mysteries in life, great secrets. Many people are fascinated by silks and jade and gold, and those are in fact beautiful. People are fascinated by wine, and people are fascinated by human beauty, by a shapely body or face. Those things you can touch, you can hold in your hand. And most people, as they grow older, concentrate all their energies on acquiring some or all of those pleasures. Once they've acquired them, they spend all their lives holding onto them, sometimes desperately, grasping at a false security even as they move inevitably toward the greatest insecurity of all."

"The man had a strange and poetic way of speaking," Jesus said, "and even with the thick accent we could tell he was well educated, and we guessed he was well traveled, too."

"They live in a city of those things," he went on, "and their thoughts travel back and forth along the streets of that city, over and over again, and they never realize that there are places beyond the borders of that city. Don't be fooled, boys. There are mysteries and secrets. There are ways of being on this earth that you cannot imagine."

"He paused there and drank, and we waited a long while for him to go on."

"I have seen people who can balance upside-down on their head, placing their whole face beneath the sand overnight, and not die. People who can endure tremendous cold, heat, or pain without crying out. People who can go days without eating and not fall ill or lack for energy. People who sit with open eyes at the moment of death and accept it with the purest and most unshakeable sense of peace. Do you believe me?"

"We said that we believed him, but in truth we harbored doubts."

"Don't let others set your limits," the man went on. "Don't let it happen."

"We promised that we wouldn't, but neither Jesse nor I thought he was anything but a half-crazed eccentric, the kind we'd seen wandering without clothes along the route, talking to themselves. The man asked if we minded if he slept there, near the warmth of the fire. We said that we didn't, but we worried he would steal what little we had. In the morning when we awoke, he was gone. Nothing had been stolen. He'd taken small stones and formed them into a square, and then taken two twigs and set them outside the boundaries of the square, as if to leave us with a visual image of what he'd said: The life of false security, and the possibility of standing outside that life and those assumptions. Jesse and I went on our way. And, in time, I came to understand that the man had been a prophet, a great teacher. Tibetan, perhaps."

"One of those important encounters in a life," I said pleasantly.

"Yes, exactly. I'll never forget him. A few weeks later, Jesse and I had to stop in Samarkand because we were about to run out of money. We found work, at first, as carpenters' helpers and found rooms we could rent, and then we began to learn how to set tile—they have such beautiful tile there. We were religious boys, as I said. I prayed, of course—upon rising, before and after meals, before going to sleep. And sometimes Jesse and I would go to services at Temple. In time, Jesse met a young woman and fell in love with her. I began to miss my mother—my father had passed on by then—and eventually I left my friend there with his woman and walked all the way back. The better part of half a year it took, and when I returned and had stayed home for some months, it began to seem to me, much as I loved my mother, that Nazareth was no longer my place, that the life I was living—working with wood, being with friends—wasn't the life I was destined to live. I remembered what the man had said. I remembered what my mother had told me about my birth."

"The three wise men, the star."

He nodded, far away again, it seemed. "There is so much in that simple story."

"Tell me."

"Where were the wise men from?"

"The East, that's all the Bible says. The East."

"Exactly. Consider that. Why would that be?"

"I have no idea."

He smiled, nodded, said, "The East," one more time and went on, "After another few months I took initiation in the monastery of the Essenes. Do you know the Essenes?"

"Only that they're connected to the Dead Sea scrolls."

"I moved into their monastery and lived with them as a monk for almost five years. It was a very simple life, one with few pleasures. Work, prayer, a little food, a little sleep. Not so different, perhaps, from the life Merton lived at Gethsemane. There, like him, I felt myself growing closer to the Divine and felt myself beginning to understand more clearly what that man in the desert had said to us, and the meaning behind what had happened at my birth. I knew that there was a world outside the monastery walls, but for those years it seemed a false world, one that led nowhere but to a disappointed old age. And then, in time, not so unlike Merton perhaps, it began to seem to me that I had gotten everything out of the monastic life that I could get. There was a dryness to my prayer, a repetitiveness. I saw that some of the older monks had attained to a great peacefulness, that no passion had hold of them any longer. But it felt to me, Edward, that something was missing, even in them. I couldn't guess what it was, but I trusted my intuition and knew I had to leave the monastery, and I did, though it was a difficult decision. I set out on the road again, taking the same route Jesse and I had taken, but determined to go further. I reached Samarkand again and stayed with Jesse and the woman—now his wife—and they had already two small children and he had become a skilled carpenter and tile artisan and his wife was very beautiful and very kind. It seemed like a wholesome life for me, what Buddha called 'the life of a householder', but, again, something was still calling me, and in time I left them, too, and went on, farther east, alone."

I want to note here that listening to Jesus wasn't anything like listening to Albert had been in the bar the night before. The "I" of Jesus's stories was smaller, the world around it larger; that's the only way I can explain it.

"What I don't understand," I said, "what I really can't wrap my mind around, is the idea that you were seeking anything, anywhere, ever. That you would listen to an eccentric old man giving advice, that you'd wonder about your destiny, after your mother had told you what happened at your birth, that you'd spend time in a monastery getting closer to God. My feeling about you has always been that, from the second you were born, even before that, you were God, or a piece of God, God's son, or something. Why would God's son have to seek? Why didn't you understand everything from the beginning? Why did you have to listen to some old guy or spend time in a monastery? Didn't you know all that already?"

There was a protracted silence. I took my eyes off the road just long enough to glance over at him. Many people have the capacity to sit still, but with Jesus there was another dimension to the stillness, a perfection to it, an absoluteness, as if he'd stopped breathing, the blood had stopped flowing through his arteries and veins, as if he'd moved into a realm beyond the reach of time. It was like sitting beside a dead man, but not really: a stillness, yes, but a vibrant stillness, if such a thing makes any sense. He did not seem dead. And yet, for that quiet minute, he did not seem quite alive either.

"Was that a stupid question?"

He made four small shakes of his head, eyes forward. "Do you follow basketball?"

"Only the last five minutes of a few playoff games every year, if the Celtics are involved."

"But you know who Michael Jordan is, correct?"

"Sure."

"Well Michael Jordan was born with the *potential* to be perhaps the greatest basketball player who ever lived, but at, say, age eight or ten or sixteen or even twenty-two, he was not yet that person. Do you see?"

"Okay, but Michael Jordan, in most circles at least, isn't considered God."

"The word makes me uncomfortable," Jesus said. "It implies a stagnancy, an exclusivity. What if God breathes inside everything, every human, every branch of every tree, every atom of every stone, every star and planet in every universe?"

"Polytheism."

He shook his head almost angrily. "If there's one root to the troubles humans endure, it's the false identification with the body. It's why death seems so terrifying to most people. You are not your body, Edward. Try to remember that at all times. You are a spirit, a piece of the Divine, and that piece happens to be inhabiting your particular body at a particular moment on the endless span of eternity. Think of what life would be like if you could expand your mind into that wider vision."

"Hard to imagine," I said.

"Yes, it is. But it's also the point of your being here, your work. It's the essence of the human challenge." He paused and abruptly shifted gears, "Are you hungry? The breakfast was very small."

I told him I was thinking of stopping in Lexington for lunch, that I liked variety in food, and we'd be more likely to find a wider option in the big city than in the smaller towns. "I have a hankering for Indian food today for some reason," I told him. "Do you like that cuisine?"

"My favorite of all cultures."

It seemed a strange answer. He turned on the radio and the day's top news story flooded into the car like a poison tide. A man wearing nothing but a jacket had gone into a Waffle House in Nashville at three a.m. and killed four people. A customer there had wrestled the gun away from him and he had fled and was being sought. His name was known to police by virtue of the fact that he'd been arrested weeks earlier after threatening to shoot himself because Taylor Swift was stalking him and had hacked his Netflix account.

There is only so much insanity you can take. And besides, the news made me drive faster, as if I might outrun it. I was worried about being stopped. A small-town cop. The Massachusetts license plate. The blood on Jesus's clothes.

I reached across and turned off the radio, but the story stayed on me like an oily film. I wanted to ask Jesus this question: if the Waffle House shooter were a piece of God inhabiting a body, why would he hurt another soul, another piece of God? I pondered it, trying to find the right way to ask, because Jesus's comment about Michael Jordan had been delivered with such certainty, as if it were the most obvious thing in the universe, and I was afraid of sounding stupid.

Everybody has their strong and weak points. I'm not exactly sure what my strong points are—vivid imagination, maybe, or compassion for the poor—but one of my weak points is certainly the habit of not reading road signs correctly, or not reading them at all, especially when my mind is worrying an idea or a plot line or going over something I've done that made me feel foolish. In general, I am the opposite of what is sometimes called 'a detail person'. My excuse for this is that I am an artist, a writer at least, and artists aren't supposed to be detail people. Our minds are elsewhere much of the time, musing, pondering, vainly attempting to organize the strange dream of human life into a sensible narrative.

We would make terrible accountants or surgeons.

On the moment in question, I was thinking about the story Jesus had told me, wondering about the 'mysteries and secrets' the dark skinned man had mentioned, wondering, still, why Jesus hadn't known them from the start. I was locked up in my original understanding of him, which was that he'd come to earth already perfect, God-man. In spite of his Michael Jordan analogy, it made no sense to me that, even as a teenager, he'd be a seeker, that he wouldn't have been born already knowing everything there was to know.

I was hungry, as well, and hunger is always a drain on the thinking mechanism. And because I tend to believe things will work out well, I'd assumed there would be a sign like this: LEXINGTON NEXT 8 EXITS, and I'd choose one of the eight that sounded like it would lead us toward a college, where the food offerings were bound to be exotic, or at least interesting. Without bothering to glance at a map or consult my GPS, I'd assumed, because I wanted it to be so, that I-64 leads directly into the big city.

It does not.

I did see signs for other routes, and they did seem to indicate that they would lead us to Lexington, but why should I take a roundabout route when I knew, I was almost sure, that I-64 went into the heart of the city?

And then, as often happens, little by little, mile by mile, I became aware of my mistake. Signs for Lexington disappeared, replaced by other signs for other places.

I said, "Shit."

Jesus said, "What's wrong?" as if he didn't already know.

I said, "Nothing."

Another little ways and I saw a sign for Bowling Green, and my perennial optimism kicked into gear again. Everything would be fine. Bowling Green was a college, I knew that from seeing football scores on Saturday afternoons. College meant college town. College town meant Indian food, or Thai, or Nepali, or very good Italian. I took the exit and, at the bottom of the ramp, followed the signs for Bowling Green. Two miles.

"Really starting to get hungry now," Jesus said, but I couldn't tell if he was saying it about himself or about me. If it was meant as a fact, or a criticism.

I went two miles, then another mile. I saw a second sign that said BOWLING GREEN, but the landscape was more farmland than college town, and after another little while I realized that something was wrong. Or, more correctly, that something *else* was wrong. I had missed Lexington, and now I seemed also to have missed Bowling Green. Cursing under my breath, I pulled into the parking lot of a convenience store and looked up Bowling Green University on my phone.

Bowling Green State University is in Ohio.

"Shit, shit," I said. Quietly.

I made a U-turn and sped down a two-lane highway, back in the direction of the Interstate. Halfway there, I changed my mind, pulled over, asked Siri for nearby eating options, and discovered that Indian food was not locally available. "But one of the ones listed," I told my traveling companion, "is a barbecue joint that gets superb reviews. Rick's Pig, it's called. Barbecue okay with you?"

Jesus nodded, but there seemed to be the wrinkle of a smile at the edges of his lips.

I checked the directions, checked them again, decided to put them into my GPS just to be sure, and then sped off down a two-lane, numbered road in the direction of Rick's Pig. After I'd gone half a mile, I saw blue lights flashing in my rear view. The fast heartbeat. The regret.

"When you grow more spiritually advanced," I said to Jesus, "do you become psychic?"

"Sometimes, yes," he said, and it was time to pull over.

~ ❦ ~

chapter eighteen

I fished my registration out of the glove compartment, pried my license from the little plastic wallet window, and watched the officer approach in the side mirror. She was on the short side, red-hair spiraling out from the sides of her police cap, and she unlatched the flap of her holster as she came. A routine gesture on her part, I'm sure, part of her training. But it did not comfort me.

Like most drivers, I've been stopped by the police a handful of times—headlight out, inspection sticker overdue, going 41 in a 30 zone in a careless moment, etcetera. No one thrills to the sight of sparking blue lights in the mirror, but at that point there's nothing you can do besides pull over . . . unless you're desperate or crazy or terrified enough to speed away. My strategy has always been to remember that I'm not a hardened criminal, to trust in the fairness of the officer in question, to present my license and registration without whining, and then to throw myself upon the mercy of the law. I know very well that I'm lucky to feel so optimistic about the encounter; I get that. I can imagine how different a black man would feel in that situation, and I know why. In my personal experience, there have been exactly two times when my faith in this approach has been shaken; two policemen—one a State Trooper, the other a small-town cop—who didn't seem to appreciate my politeness. We had words. I filed complaints. But nothing worse than that resulted. No tasers, no shots fired, no tragic deaths at roadside or in a relative's back yard. Whatever you look like, the encounter is always fraught with some degree of bad potential; the blue lights always bring forth a spurt of nervousness. Much worse for some of us than for others, yes; but never a pleasant sight.

As I watched the officer make her slow, careful walk toward the Camry, the familiar strategy kicked in on top of the nerves. I'd be polite. A speeding ticket, a critical remark—that was most likely the worst outcome.

And then I remembered the deer blood, and the unknown factor of what might be in my new friend's luggage.

While Jesus sat with his hands folded in his lap, the officer and I had the usual exchange. I handed over the documents. She took them back to her cruiser and ran a check—which I knew would show nothing of substance. A few minutes later she returned with a speeding ticket, $75, and that would have been the end of it if, just as she was handing back my license, Jesus hadn't piped up: "We are without sin, woman."

I cringed, tried to smile, managed to say, "My friend thinks he's a comedian."

The officer did not so much as force a miniature grin. She gave us the once-over with her eyes, my face, Jesus's scar, the console between us. "Either of you been drinking?"

"Just hungry," I said.

"No alcohol at lunch?"

"No lunch is the problem. I was heading for Rick's Pig and we're—"

"No recent use of marijuana or other substances?"

"Nothing. Zero."

"Less than Zero," Jesus added.

"What brings you to Kentucky?"

"We're on our way to Arkansas. I have a book talk there. I picked up my friend here in Massachusetts, he was hitchhiking, I—"

"Your friend have ID?"

Jesus leaned across the front seat, long hair dangling, and pronounced these memorable words, "I have a false ID. I am everyman, and everywoman. I inhabit every soul. Surely, even in Kentucky, such a spirit needs no actual ID."

That did it. A bad two seconds and then, "Step out of the car, please. Both of you. Hands on the roof."

The officer—BRITTINBANE was the name on her badge—called in reinforcements, and while we were being patted down, the town's other cruiser came speeding toward us with lights flashing. It skidded onto the gravel shoulder behind us as if we were the most exciting thing to happen there since the UK Wildcats won the NCAA basketball championship in 1997. Officer Brittinbane asked if we'd be willing to take a breathalyzer test. Jesus looked at me for guidance. I said that we would be, yes, of course, no problem. Jesus readily agreed.

Tests performed.

Alcohol level: exactly .000.

So we had that going for us. Still, it was a slow day in that small Kentucky hamlet, and they were dealing with a wise-mouth longhair with a fake ID, and a driver from Massachusetts who seemed all too compliant.

"Mind if we search the car?"

In winter I work out at the local health club, and because I get bored doing my thirty minutes on the stationary bike, I usually flip through the channels on the small screen in front of me, and because I get tired of the political news and because the only sports on at that late-morning hour are ten-year-old college football games, I sometimes watch COPS. I knew what happens when an officer asks that question and you refuse. So I didn't refuse.

As we lingered off to the side, half-leaning, half-sitting on the guardrail there, Edward Valpolicella furious at Jesus Christ for opening his mouth, the fury exacerbated by hunger but tempered by my urge to be more respectful than I'd been in the past, the two officers went through the car as carefully as if they'd gotten a tip that we were carrying seventeen hundred bags of meth from my lab in Western Mass to a biker headquarters in Jonesboro. My golf clubs were taken out of the bag, one by one. The golf balls, tees, ball markers, divot tools, extra gloves, old scorecards, rain gear, and a mostly empty bag of potato chips were laid out on the top of the trunk like exhibits ready for photographing. The second officer went through my suitcase, checked my dress shoes (I'd wiped the blood off), and then opened the suit bag hanging from its loop and examined the pockets with his eager fingers. Jesus, leaning on the rail beside me, was maddeningly calm. The male half of the police duo—they were both wearing blue medical gloves—pulled Jesus's red suitcase out of the back seat, placed it on the ground, and started meticulously going through it. It took him fifteen seconds to discover the bloodstained dress shirt. He drew it up and out of the suitcase with a dramatic flair and held it there until the female half—placing objects back into my golf bag—looked over. She let out a low whistle.

"Care to explain?" she asked us.

"We hit a deer. Look. You can see the dent in the front of the car. Jesus was dressed up. He—"

At that moment, the male half lifted another object from the suitcase, Jesus's hunting knife.

"'Jesus', you called him?" The woman said.

And before another minute had passed, my traveling companion and I were handcuffed and sitting in the back of her cruiser. We were read our rights. I was informed that my Camry would be towed to the local pound, and that I would have to pay the $200 towing fee, plus $97 per day if storage was required due to incarceration. While the officers consulted behind the vehicle, and I moved my wrists to ease the discomfort of the pinching metal, Jesus said, in a disturbingly serene tone, "So much for Rick's Pig."

I couldn't look at him.

~ ~

chapter nineteen

For those who aren't familiar with it, the jail in the township I will call Salvation, Kentucky, is about what you'd expect of a small-town hoosegow. Two cells, wooden beds, stainless steel toilet and sink, all of it sitting five steps down from street level in a building that also houses the police headquarters and the offices of town clerk and county commissioner. As soon as the door was opened, Jesus and I, still in handcuffs and being led with great courtesy and care, could hear a man shouting. He was clearly insane, or drunk, or both, and he was extraordinarily angry. "Let me out, let me out, LET ME OUT! I didn't ask for this! I've had a hard life! I didn't even know what it was!"

When Jesus and I were led past his cell, the man went silent long enough to fix us with a malevolent stare, then started up again in the same vein. "LET! ME! OUT!!!!"

Officer Brittinbane ignored him, opened the door of our cell, and we stepped in. She released us from the cuffs but confiscated my cell phone.

"I'd like to make a call," I said, though as soon as the words were out of my mouth, I realized there was no one I wanted to call. Anna Lisa? Her violence-prone brother, Reggie? My sister? Our lawyer, whose work to that point had consisted of helping us write up a will and sell my mother's house?

"You'll have that opportunity in a few minutes," the good officer said. She locked the cell door and walked up the stairs.

The man in the adjacent cell, separated from us only by a row of bars and a few yards of floor space, was rail-thin, with ears that stuck out like small wings, a very high forehead, and tattoos on each of his bare forearm. JESUS on one and IS LORD on the other. Naturally. He stepped over to the bars, clasped them with his hands and, like a character in a TV sit-com, demanded to know what we were in for. I could smell the alcohol from twelve feet away.

"Blood and a knife," Jesus told him matter-of-factly. He and I were sitting side by side on the only bed, as far from the man as we could get.

"You're killers then. I'M IN HERE WITH KILLERS!" He slapped his hands against the bars, so hard I was sure he'd break a bone. "I DIDN'T DO IT! THEY DID! I'LL MAKE A DEAL! I'LL FLIP!"

After a few seconds of this—I was sweating under both arms—Jesus stood up and walked straight at the man, who first shrank back into the middle of his cell and then rushed forward again. "I AIN'T AFRAID OF YOU! KILLER OR NO, I AIN'T AFRAID! YOU AIN'T GONNA INTIMIDATE CONSTANTINE REPSON! Jesus held out his hand in a friendly way and pushed it through the bars. "Jesus Christ," he said. "What's your name!"

The man shrank back again. "I'M HERE WITH THE DEVIL! WITH SATAN! A BLASPHEMER! LET ME OUT, GODAMMIT!"

Jesus stood there a moment, hand still sticking through the bars, and then the male officer came through the door and down the steps, holding two tin trays.

"Don't you eat it, Jesus," the man in the next cell advised, in an eerily friendly tone. I noticed that he had another tattoo—an open-mouthed snake on the left side of his neck. And I noticed, too, that he had intelligent blue eyes. If you looked only at his eyes, you'd think he was bright, sober, even kindly. "They'll poison you, man. AND YOU'LL BE IN THE FLAMES FOR ETERNITY BECAUSE YOU KILLED JESUS CHRIST!" he shouted at the officer who pointedly ignored him at first, opened our cell, handed in the two trays, then said, to our neighbor, "Calm down Todd," and left.

Inch-high squares of corn bread, scratched plastic glasses filled with what appeared to be lemonade, hamburgers that might have come from the local McDonalds, though they were unwrapped, and two apples.

"NOTHING FOR ME?" Todd shouted at the door.

Jesus and I sat side by side on the bed with the trays on our knees and began, in desultory fashion, to sample the food. Todd seemed to have temporarily exhausted himself. He sank onto his cot and sat there with his head in his hands, moaning.

"They'll test the blood and see that it's deer's blood," I said quietly, "and they'll let us go."

"I think you're right."

"Here's what I don't understand. You say you *think* I'm right, but other times you seem to know the future—the Delaware license plate, the idea of grandchildren, the package for Ellory. You're not consistent."

"Half man, half God," he said, gnawing on the cornbread, which had the consistency and taste of pressed sawdust glued together with rancid margarine.

"Cute."

"We'll be fine, Edward. And it will give me time to tell you more of the story without distracting you from your driving duties."

I realized at that moment that I was furious at him for his foolish comments to the female officer, but also that it had been my fault, not his, that we'd been stopped. 44 in a 30 zone in a small Southern town. As Anna Maria would say, "Not wise, hon."

With the exception of the lemonade, the lunch was basically inedible. I tried a bite of the hamburger, a second bite of the cornbread, looked at the apple—it was small and bruised—and set the tray on the concrete floor. "I'd welcome the distraction right now," I said.

Bite by bite, Jesus finished all his food. I waited patiently. He stood, set the tray on top of the mattress, and began pacing back and forth in the cell, head slightly lowered, hands in the pockets of his pants. "Where was I?"

"The man at the campfire. The time in the monastery. Then you stayed with Jesse and his family and went on, east. How old were you at that point?"

"Twenty."

Todd looked up, then buried his face in his hands again.

"It was difficult traveling then, east of where Jesse lived. Desert at first, and then foothills, and then the highest mountains on earth. But the world was different than it is now, Edward. This is something you are going to have to convey when you write the story."

"I haven't agreed to write the story."

He ignored the remark. "People had very little, but they were so much less suspicious. They would let you stay with them, sometimes in outbuildings with the animals, sometimes in their home, and they would often feed you in exchange for work, or simply because they saw that you were hungry. There were criminals, yes, of course, but crime and bad behavior weren't in the news every hour, so the human mind still had an unspoiled, hopeful, innocent aspect to it. It helped, of course, that I had skills. One whole winter, near Dushanbe in what is now Tajikistan, I stayed with a family, helped them with their animals, built a platform in their barn. In many places there was a kindness, a willingness to share, that has become almost extinct in your world."

"Why?"

He ignored the question. "Between there and India, where I eventually ended up, there are very high mountains, the Southern Himalayas you call them now, and once I left that family, when it was warm enough for the snow in the passes to melt, I went along very slowly, sleeping in the open many nights, sharing meals with nomads and herders. Sheep's milk and cheese, a type of flat bread, sometimes ferns or other greens, sometimes a bit of fruit. I spent many hours praying under the stars in the early morning. Dawn is the ideal hour for prayer—the close of darkness and the promise of hope. For weeks at a time I would travel with certain people, and then we'd go our separate ways." He stopped pacing and stood in front of me. "You can use that as a metaphor, if you wish."

"For what?"

"For the way we pass whole lifetimes with loved ones and then move on, perhaps to see them again in another millennium."

Todd started pounding his fists on the tops of his thighs. "I'M IN HERE WITH KILLERS! WITH BLASPHEMERS!"

Jesus' quiet recitation of his travels, the stained concrete floor and iron bars, Todd's bright eyes and maddening screams, the $275 in fines and the possibility of some kind of mistake that would connect us to an actual crime, the thought of calling Anna Lisa and telling her the story, my growling stomach. . . . I felt as though some kind of bizarre circus were at play in a mental amphitheater, and I sat there, staring at Todd, listening to Jesus, squinting, hoping it was all a terrible dream.

"Often," Jesus went on, "often I would stop and share tea or a jug of water with traders going in the opposite direction. I was able to give them information they needed—about weather, trail conditions, hospitable people, water sources, places they could feed their animals, and so on. In return, they would sometimes give me a small, imperfect piece of jade, or a silk scarf with blemishes. I would later trade those objects for a month's lodging, for food or clothing, or I would give them, in turn, to people I came across who seemed hungry or poor or bereft. The time in the monastery had hardened me to discomfort—a great advantage in this world—and so, if I had to go a day without eating, or if I had to sleep in the cold, or on a hard bed, it didn't bother me."

"The beds here are brutal," Todd said from the other cell.

Jesus glanced at him and went on. "There are two important things that happened to me," he said, "and these must be told in some detail. The first was that, after I had crossed the mountains, in Gupis, which is a small place northwest of Srinagar, I fell in with a couple of young men who had traveled from Egypt and whose native tongue was close to my own. These were highly spiritually evolved souls, and they were following a certain instinct they hoped would help them to pierce the final barriers."

"What final barriers?"

"Well, they are not precisely final. But from the standpoint of the human mind, they appear to be the last obstacles between what you think of as your normal state, and what might be called 'liberation'. There are countless examples in various spiritual literatures and oral traditions of demons guarding the gates. What does this mean?"

"It means the fucking cops!" Todd said quietly. He seemed to have regained some of his energy and was sitting back on his bed with his spine against the concrete wall, his eyes fixed on Jesus with an intensity that terrified me. Jesus did not seem to care.

"It means that, as you progress on the spiritual ladder, at each level there are going to be obstacles. At the lower levels these obstacles might be a tendency toward violence, and then toward anger." He glanced pointedly at our neighbor, then turned to me again. "As you climb, lifetime by lifetime, lesson by lesson, and transcend those base urges, you may have to deal with addiction, lust, greed, or multiple obstacles at the same time. But once you have ascended to a certain point, once, for instance, you no longer use violence, your sexual behavior is under control, you have begun to calm your mind, then the obstacles are subtler. They have been depicted as dragons guarding the gates or, in Christianity, Satan, the temptation of the devil, and so on. By whatever name, these obstacles can be devastatingly clever. For example, you might be living an extremely pure life, doing good deeds, selfless in the extreme, but then into your river of thought flows a thin polluted stream telling you how good and holy you are, how much better than others. You begin to form judgments, and those are nourishment for the ego. This is why you sometimes see very highly evolved spiritual teachers who suddenly turn and become dictators to their disciples and followers, who abuse them, sexually and otherwise. It's a grave temptation. Does that answer your question?"

"It does, but it also makes it seem impossible to ever really, I don't know, go to heaven or become enlightened, or be *liberated*, to use your term."

Todd had gotten up from his cot, walked across the cell

and resumed his previous position, hands grasping the bars, high forehead pressed against them. He was working his lips and eventually out from between them spouted these three words. "The Good Book."

Jesus continued to ignore him. "So I fell in with these young men," he went on, "three of them, and we traveled together, down out of the mountains. Srinigar sits in the midst of an exceptionally beautiful high valley, a ribbon of greenery bordered by snow-topped mountain ranges. Our instincts led us there, and it was there that we came upon a great teacher, a woman somewhat older than we were, a master of yoga. We settled in that town and studied with her for the next six years."

"Hot babe?" Todd asked.

Jesus interrupted his tale and walked across the cell. Todd shrank back at first and then pushed himself forward again, determined to convince himself that he wasn't a coward. Jesus walked up close, reached out and tapped him once in the middle of his forehead, with his second or third finger—I couldn't quite see from where I was sitting. Todd jerked his head backward a few inches, and then a change came over his face. "A pretty woman, is what I was asking."

"Yes, beautiful," Jesus said. "Now sit down and listen."

Todd backed across his cell and plopped down on the edge of his cot like an obedient pet. When Jesus turned back to me, there was something new in his face. A veil of politeness had been stripped away, and for a moment I was more afraid of him than of Todd. It wasn't anger, but a concentrated form of attention, or power, as if he were blasting me with bright light.

"Studied what?" I was able to ask.

"The magic arts the man at the campfire had told us about. Self-control. One-pointedness. Transcendence."

At that point, the metal door at the top of the steps

squeaked and banged open, and the redheaded officer came down the stairs in her black boots and uniform. No readable expression on her face. I thought she was going to allow me to make the phone call, but she walked to our cell and put a key in the lock and turned, then held open the door. "Deer blood," she said. "We tested. You're free to go, but the speeding fine and the towing charge need to be paid upstairs. Your phone's at the desk, your car's at the curb. We take MasterCard and Visa."

Jesus thanked her. I held to an insulted silence. Todd followed us with his eyes and, when Jesus reached in to give him a goodbye handshake, he accepted it warmly, pushing out his lips, nodding, standing tall. At a desk on the street-level floor, I presented a credit card and received a stamped, official-looking receipt. Officer Brittinbane escorted us to the front door, stepped through and held it open. "You know," she said, "in this part of the world we don't much appreciate people telling us they're Jesus Christ. We don't just throw that name around. We're more respectful than that. And we don't like people saying they have a fake ID when they are a real and searchable person."

We were standing on the top step with her, cars passing on the tree-shaded street nearby, the ordinariness of the day seeming to reach out to us, to call us back into a more or less pleasant reality. I was happy—overjoyed would be a better word—to be out in the air again, to be free. $275 seemed a small price to pay for that privilege, and I hadn't the smallest urge, not the slightest urge, to engage the good officer in some kind of religious discussion. I was leaning toward the car. I might even have taken a step. Perhaps I had hold of Jesus's sleeve and was tugging on it. But he'd stopped still, facing Officer Brittinbane at close range, and I could see that light, that power, that force in his eyes. She seemed not to. "Which would be easier," he asked her quietly, "to call oneself Jesus Christ, or to free a man from his demons?"

"Hunnh," was the noise she made, and I worried for a moment that she was going to arrest us all over again. But there was something else in her face now, something beside scorn. A small flicker of doubt around the eyes, a softening of the mouth. Perhaps even a note of fear.

Jesus reached into his pocket and pulled out a thick wad of bills. He peeled off two hundreds. "When he sobers up sufficiently, kindly use this for his bail. I can assure you that you'll never have trouble with him again."

And then we were safely in the car, pulling—very slowly—away from the curb, yours truly breathing normally again, but the circus still playing in my inner world. I felt weirdly shaken, changed, humbled. Perhaps jail time—however brief—does that to everyone, I don't know, but it was a new feeling for me. I glanced sideways. Jesus had gone still again and was looking straight ahead, half there, half in some other world.

~ ~

chapter twenty

From Salvation to Bardstown was a drive of only about forty-five minutes, and for at least the first half of it I floated or swirled along in that state of mind, an overcooked noodle of a man, part nothing, part everything. Jesus slept, or meditated, eyes closed, hands folded in his lap, a perfection of stillness. It required an act of will not to pull to the side of the road and call Anna Maria, just to retouch some kind of solidity, just to remind myself that I was myself, that I existed in a familiar form. But I drove on as if under a spell.

By the time we arrived in Bardstown, it was already late afternoon and my ordinary self was partly reassembled. Jesus had opened his eyes and he suggested that, instead of checking in at the place of lodging Anna Maria had arranged, we should head right out to the Abbey at Gethsemane and try to get there before darkness fell. I agreed.

We crossed a bridge and headed out into the countryside again on a winding, two-lane highway, past a few ranch homes at first, and then through a lush spring greenery. The monks hadn't made their place easy to find. When I pulled onto the shoulder and checked again online, I discovered that there was no street address. I opened Rand McNally to the Kentucky page, and used that as a guide, but the road that seemed to lead in the right direction was numbered for a while, and then not. The GPS worked for a while and then didn't. It was as if the brothers had made a deal with the tech companies to keep their place of residence invisible. Almost as if they wanted no link to the world of commerce and rush. Almost as if they felt it might somehow hinder their liberation.

So there we were, in God's hands so to speak, plying the winding back roads of the Kentucky countryside without benefit of assistance from the satellites or the mapmakers. Naturally, I expected Jesus to use his psychic powers to help us find the place, but, though his eyes were open, he seemed, as he sometimes did, distracted and distant, pondering our jail time, perhaps, or caught up in his memories of the Kashmiri yoga teacher.

"You missed it," he said suddenly, as if having roused himself from a nap.

"I'm famous for that. All I see is trees."

"At that last intersection, the road that veered off to the left. I saw a sign."

I made a U-turn on the gravel shoulder and backtracked as far as the intersection. The sign there—GETHSEMANE—was tilted and rusted, about the size of a shoe box, perched on a flimsy metal pole that leaned to one side, up to its shoulders in a growth of roadside weeds. Easy to miss. Years ago, the Pope had instructed the brethren to make their location known for delivery trucks, and they'd complied, but begrudgingly.

I turned there. The road, unlined now and not well paved, wound through a shallow valley, with woods and small patches of farmland to either side. The few homes we passed were set back from the road and modest—a cabin, a trailer, a one-story cape. And then, rising up from behind the trees on the left like a Bavarian castle or a Hollywood Oz, we saw white turrets. And then a huge bulk of a building. And then, beyond the trees, a lawn, more buildings, and an actual sign:

Our Lady of Gethsemane
Trappists

The circular drive was shaded by a large oak, not yet in leaf, with a trunk as thick around as a truck tire, and branches like muscular arms reaching across the gravel and as far as the wrought-iron fence. There were signs along the fence: MONASTIC ENCLOSURE DO NOT ENTER. A few cars were parked out front beneath the tree and we saw another sign: BOOKSTORE. "Hurry," Jesus said, "they're about to close."

Inside, we found displays of various religious books, as well as shelves of products made by the monks—fudge laced with bourbon, twenty flavors of jam, medallions representing every saint and Catholic deity, rosaries, statuettes, greeting cards. A woman stood behind the desk thumbing through the day's receipts. Behind her, propped up conspicuously and standing out like a pitchfork in a college classroom, was a shiny hardcover: *Success is the Only Option,* by John Calipari.

Jesus browsed. I found the Thomas Merton section, five shelves of paperbacks authored by the famous monk. It would be hard to overstate the influence Merton had had on my spiritual life. I'm sure millions of people feel similarly. I'd become aware of his books not long after I finished college and had joined a Merton reading group at a progressive Catholic church for a few weeks before leaving the faith entirely. If you trace his many publications, from the best-selling memoir, *Seven Storey Mountain*, written while he was new to the monastery, through *The Asian Journal,* which was truncated by his sudden death, you follow a person who starts out as a more or less agnostic party-boy, moves through a period of intellectual questioning and nascent artistic expression, leaves behind his wild ways, converts to Roman Catholicism, embraces his new calling with the fervor of a young lover, joins the Trappists, becomes a hermit, then moves, through decades of the most austere monastic practices and without abandoning his own faith, gradually to an embrace of other ways of looking at creation. He was many things: A monk who had a love affair with a local nurse; a hermit who became world famous; a poet and essayist; an environmentalist long before the term was popular; an anti-war activist. He was a radical in five different directions, a fact that accounts for the lukewarm reception he's always received in conservative Catholic circles. When addressing the United Nations, the present pope, another radical, mentioned Merton in a select group of three.

To me, he was a bridge—*the* bridge—from the strict Catholicism of my youth, to a broader view of life. He confessed to practicing Zen meditation. He carried on a dialogue and wrote a book with the famous Buddhist, D.T. Suzuki. He had kind things to say about Sufism, a religion I'd never heard of but have since come to admire. He lived a life of great austerity but famously criticized his fellow monks for "thinking they'll go to hell if they enjoy a dish of ice cream once in a while." For me and millions of others, he chiseled out a window in the thick wall between East and West. And at the end of his life, having finally been granted permission to leave the monastery for a trip to Asia, he had some kind of an enlightenment experience, a liberation maybe, at once so mysterious and so modern that his very brief description of it in *Asian Journal* would stay with me forever.

Although I owned a copy of the book that included that description, I pulled another one from the rack. I decided to buy some bourbon-laced fudge, too, and carried both items to the counter. The woman there was eyeing the long-haired Jesus as if she thought he might slip a silver rosary into his pocket and walk out. She started ringing up my purchases and I asked about the Calipari book.

"He had a friend who was dying of cancer and he used to fly his helicopter out here and land it on the hillside across the road and pray with the monks," she said, flicking her eyes—twice—in Jesus' direction.

Jesus ended up buying a bronze crucifix on a chain and peeling bills from the same thick wad of cash he'd used for Todd's bail. He left the box on the glass countertop and draped the loop of beads over his head, then tucked it inside his shirt, grinned at the woman, and told her he thought she was beautiful.

She became flustered, caught, it seemed, in a bad territory between enjoying the praise, hoping it was sincere, worrying it was a come-on, and not wanting to be seen as some kind of art object. I was hoping he wouldn't say something else and send us to jail again. He seemed oblivious, asexual, or somehow beyond sexuality. "Who's this Calipari?" he asked her, in a friendly way.

"You don't know?"

"A famous basketball coach," I put in.

"Ah. Give me a copy then, please."

She rang him up a second time, slid the hardcover into a paper bag and handed it across.

I was ready to leave. Jesus, apparently, was not.

"I have a question," he said to the woman.

She looked at the phone as if hoping it might ring.

"Do you mind?"

She shook her head, earrings swinging, eyes and mouth saying: *yes, I mind very much.*

"What do you think is the most important commandment?"

She pressed her lips together, narrowed her eyes. "They're all important."

Jesus nodded thoughtfully. "Okay, thank you. Just curious."

And outside we went.

"You're a little out of practice dealing with people," I said. "You say strange things. With Mason you seemed okay, normal even. And with Anton. But then you say stuff like what you just said to that woman. You made her uncomfortable."

We were wandering past the large oak tree, taking in the feeling of the place, the peacefulness. Jesus considered my remark for a moment and then said, "It's been a problem of mine forever. Look at the Bible. I'm constantly saying things that either offend or confuse people. You can't imagine the kind of trouble it got me into."

"Actually, I can."

"They asked me that same question, you know. In the old days."

"I know, and I know what you answered. 'Treat your neighbor as you would wish to be treated'."

"That was only half the answer. The other half was love God with all your mind and all your soul."

"Which has always confused me. Why, for one thing, would God care about being loved? And, for another, how are you supposed to love someone or something you can't see?"

"Love is attention, Edward. The more you refine your attention, the more capable you are of loving."

"How do you pay attention to God then? Go to church?"

"You cleanse your mind, you look around. You get outside yourself. You stay present. You appreciate the fact of your existence. It's very simple."

"In the modern world, not so simple, I think. Not simple at all."

"Then eschew the modern world."

"How? Tell me. I have a house, kids and a wife I love. I have to make a living. I can't join a monastery or go off into some cave somewhere and—"

"Eschew it *interiorly.*"

"But how?"

I felt he was about to give an answer, but just then bells sounded in the building to our right. I saw a couple get out of their car and start walking in that direction. They passed close to us on the lawn, and Jesus asked them if there was a service we might attend. "Sure, Vespers," the woman said, in a lovely Kentucky accent. *Vaisprs.* "We're going, we'll show you."

They led us into a white stucco building and up a set of stairs to a steeply slanted bank of wooden pews that looked down, through thick plate glass, upon one part of the monastic enclosure. As the bells continued to ring, monks in white vestments with black shawls over their shoulders came filing in. They sat below us in their own rows of pews, facing each other, not forward, and I studied them with great attention, wondering if it had been exactly the urge to eschew the modern world that had brought them to their vows. The average age looked to be about seventy, though there were a handful of others in their thirties and forties. To a man, they looked stooped and exhausted, and I thought about their daily routine—up at four a.m., hours of choir and prayer, interrupted by more hours of physical labor, small meals taken in silence, more prayer, a little time for reading. Year after year they went on that way, their lives bereft of any measure of comfort or luxury. No sex, no exotic meals, no sporting events or favorite TV shows, no movies, no lunch dates, no hope of travel to a beach resort for a week in the sun. I wondered, again, if that was what Jesus had in mind, if that might be the narrow path to liberation or salvation, the only way, the best way. But at the same time I knew I couldn't have lived that life even for two weeks. I had my pleasures all lined up in front of me—a good meal at the restaurant, a conversation with Anna Maria or one of the girls, a night's rest in a comfortable bed, breakfast of coffee and whatever else I wanted, potatoes, eggs, meat, pancakes slathered in butter and drenched in Vermont maple syrup. The joy of driving, of talking, of golf, a planned vacation. It was all strung out in front of me like bullet points on a tour itinerary, and if it were interrupted by illness—mine or someone else's—or by bad weather on a golf day or the lack of a particular food on a menu, by a financial setback or family troubles, I knew that, though I'd try to suppress it, I'd feel a kind of righteous indignation. How dare the world mess with my plans! How dare the Lord let my people suffer and die!

Looking down at the monks, I kept thinking of Todd and his, "Get me out of here!"

There were hymns and prayers led by a monk at a pulpit. His brethren sang along, exhausted, beaten down, shriveled. Not one of them raised his eyes to the small group of laypeople in the upstairs pews. Not one of them smiled. I wanted to ask Jesus if this was the way to show one's love for God, if God wanted this degree of abstemiousness, some kind of proof of one's devotion, as if He were jealous of earth's many pleasures. But he was deep in prayer, hands clasped in front of him, eyes closed. He seemed not even to be breathing.

Somehow, the person I believed myself to be had now fully reassembled itself. I was Eddie Valpolicella again, semi-well-known writer, husband, dad, good citizen of the U.S. of A. But behind or beyond that person, I could dimly sense another possibility. It was almost as if Jesus had led me to a place where I could stand on the shore of a sea and look across, beyond death. I had the distinct sense that something waited there, some other form of being, some other state of mind, some other formation of the atoms I called "me". It was there, yes, beyond a foggy horizon. I could sense it, but not see it, and the exhausted monks seemed like citizens of that world, ghosts maybe, with merely a wisp of themselves visible, the rest already gone.

I sat there, quiet and still, bathed in this strange new awareness. Vespers went on for most of an hour and then the final prayers were said, the monks filed out, and Jesus and I and the Kentucky couple went down the stairs and back out into the mild evening air. Beyond the circular drive was a bench that looked across the road to a hillside field. I told Jesus I wanted to sit there for a few minutes and think about things and he said, "Good, Edward. Excellent. I want to give these rosary beads to a friend. I'll meet you at the car."

I went and sat on the bench, took *Asian Journal* out of the paper bag, and paged through it, looking for a particular passage that described an experience Merton had while kneeling in front of the huge stone reclining Buddha at Polannaruwa, in what was then called Ceylon. It was near the end of the book, not difficult to find:

"Looking at these figures I was suddenly, almost forcibly, jerked clean out of the habitual, half-tied vision of things, and an inner clearness, clarity, as if exploding from the rocks themselves, became evident and obvious. The queer evidence of the reclining figure, the smile, the sad smile of Ananda standing with arms folded (much more "imperative" than DaVinci's Mona Lisa because completely simple and straightforward). The thing about all this is that there is no puzzle, no problem, and really no 'mystery'. All problems are resolved and everything is clear, simply because what matters is clear. The rock, all matter, all life, is charged with dharmakaya . . . everything is emptiness and everything is compassion. I don't know when in my life I have ever had such a sense of beauty and spiritual validity running together in one aesthetic illumination. Surely, with Mahabalipuram and Polonnaruwa my Asian pilgrimage has come clear and purified itself. I mean, I know and have seen what I was obscurely looking for. I don't know what else remains but I have now seen and have pierced through the surface and have got beyond the shadow and the disguise."

When I'd read it twice, slowly, I looked up and realized that a cool April dusk had settled over the monastery grounds. On the other side of the road I could see the field where Coach Calipari had landed his helicopter, and I wondered who his friend had been, and where the famous coach's prayers had gone, and if they'd helped the person in his or her suffering. I wondered, too, how it was that a Catholic monk, a man who had lived for twenty-seven years in these buildings (in fact, he died exactly 27 years after the day he entered), worked these fields, ate so little and prayed so much, a hermit bestseller—how it was that the experience he'd sought through all those arduous years had come to him, not in Jerusalem, not in Vatican City, not before a statue of Mary or a wooden cross, but as he knelt in front of a huge stone Buddha on the island then known as Ceylon. I would have given a great deal to have been able to ask him about that, the experience, yes, but also why it had come there, of all places, and how he had felt writing about it. There was a particular intensity to my desire for that; it wasn't just an idle thought, but something stronger, something that grew out of my own striving and seeking, my own upbringing, my own doubts. It was connected, in a way I could not quite understand, to the sense of that other world, that other dimension of life, and I felt the urge piercing me as I sat there, cutting into the center of me like a blade.

And now I reach the place where, if I haven't already come to seem like a well meaning flake, I certainly will do so. I'm a writer, after all. And one of the skills writers are supposed to possess is a sense of their audience, a sense of how far you can push your readers before they abandon you in disgust. I can't help it, however. I've sworn to myself that I would tell the truth here, and that's what I shall do.

Just then, holding the closed *Asian Journal* in my lap, in the quiet and the fading light, with that powerful sense of being pierced by my own desire for something greater than the self I believed myself to be, I had the distinct sense of someone sitting beside me on the bench. So distinct that I didn't have the courage to turn and look. All the fight or flee reflexes kicked in: the fast heartbeat, the sweating hands, the awareness of the skin on the back of my neck. Jesus playing another trick, I thought, I hoped, because, while, in the abstract, I believe in ghosts, and believe some of the people who claim to have seen them (one very sane New Jersey friend, for example), I'd never had the pleasure, myself.

I tried to keep my eyes straight ahead, but couldn't. I turned to look. For one second what I saw there was a bald man with a very familiar smile on his face, and a robe with black shoulder scarf that was identical to what I'd seen from the choir loft. Without hesitation, from the depths of me, in a fear-choked voice that frightened me even more, I blurted out: "Help me understand."

And then he was gone.

The ghost, if that's what it was, had looked exactly like Thomas Merton.

~ ~

chapter twenty-one

As full darkness fell over the monastery grounds, I sat on the bench for another fifteen minutes and tried to let my breathing and heart rate return to normal. Though the skin along my spine prickled and clenched, I made myself twist around in the seat to see if the apparition might be lurking there behind me, or if a monk was wandering the grounds, tasked with chasing off loiterers. I turned forward again, balancing the book on my legs, squeezed the tops of my thighs in both hands, bent over and ran my fingers across the earth between my running shoes, bit the inside of my cheek—anything to reclaim a sense of normalcy. As the minutes passed and nothing else happened, I began to be able to tell myself that I'd fallen asleep for a few seconds and had a flash of dream. But I was lying and knew it. When the first monastery bell started ringing the hour, my whole upper body twitched once, as if the nerves there had been filed raw.

I stood up, and in darkness broken only by a single spotlight high up on the building where we'd attended Vespers, found my way back across the lawn to the car. Jesus wasn't there. I waited, leaning against the driver's door at first, and then sitting behind the wheel. No Jesus. I checked my phone to see if, though he didn't seem to own a phone, he might have sent a message, but the only message was an email from a company that arranged marriages with Russian brides. How it had gotten through my spam filter, I had no idea. The bookstore windows had long ago gone dark. I was ravenous and treated myself to a large chunk of bourbon fudge. After I'd waited there for the better part of an hour, I went back to the pews above the monks' choir, thinking he might be there, lost in meditation. No one. One full hour I waited, and then I told myself I had little choice. I'd been reasonable, generous even. He must be playing another one of his tricks. I started the car and, completely sober and tremendously hungry, headed back to Bardstown.

A feeling of emptiness, almost loneliness, overtook me on that winding dark drive. I found a parking space in front of The Old Talbott Tavern, rolled my bag into the building and up to the front desk, checked in, climbed a set of creaking stairs to a room with a four-poster bed and a tiny TV, and stood for a few minutes at the window, looking down on the street. It felt as though the walls of normalcy, which had been bubbling out away from me from the minute I'd let the strange hitchhiker into my car, had now ruptured completely. I was seeing ghosts. I was believing that they were real. Describing his experience in Sri Lanka, Merton had written that he'd been "jerked clean out of the habitual and half-tied vision of things". I wasn't feeling that, exactly. I hadn't been jerked clean, but I had been knocked sideways off the perch from which I'd always viewed the world. My assumptions had been shaken like palm trees in a hurricane, tossed this way and that, almost uprooted, coconuts thudding into the sand on every side. Strangely enough, there was no thought that my sanity was in question. I felt perfectly sane, hyper-sane, in fact. To use a different metaphor, it was clear that Jesus, with his series of shenanigans, had caused the chess board to wobble, and now, suddenly, the pieces seemed set in an impossible configuration. I'd had the smallest taste of some other reality, or some expanded version of this one. A glimpse beyond death, perhaps. I wanted more and, at the same time, I was afraid to be wanting more. I wasn't ready either for death or for the kingdom beyond death. I was hoping I could procrastinate.

Another quarter of an hour passed—still no Jesus. I showered away the concrete and disinfectant stink of our time in the jail cell, changed into fresh clothes, and by then I was so hungry I could have eaten the rest of the fudge for dinner.

As Anna Maria had promised when she texted me the reservation, the hotel boasted a restaurant on the ground floor. I descended the creaking stairs, was seated there at a table with a view of the bar, and perused the many offerings, half expecting to see Jesus stride across the room with a sly smile on his face, pull up a chair opposite, and tell me he'd been out playing basketball with some guys he happened to come across near the monastery.

I discovered that I missed him.

On the back page of the menu was a list of bourbons from probably seventy-five different distilleries. I asked the waitress for the one that had a distillery closest to town—1792 it turned out to be—ordered the barbecue ribs with mashed potatoes, and then, when she walked away, sat there feeling like an alien just off my spaceship. At a nearby circular table sat four men in the early part of middle age, golfers, it turned out, down from snow country on a junket. They were very loud. With each new round of drinks, they grew louder, spilling their newfound freedom from the cold across the crowded room with tales of marvelous approach shots and missed putts. The word that came to mind was *raucous*. I was happy for them, possibly even envious. I often feel distanced from loud groups of men, but what I felt, looking at and listening to them, was something else. There was no judgment in it; I didn't feel superior in any way, but I did feel alienated, distanced, different. I suppose I was thinking of the monks, focused as they seemed to be on the promise or the hope of something more than a glass of bourbon and eighteen holes of fun. I felt like I had touched, however fleetingly, a land beyond the body, beyond death, and I knew that Jesus had pushed me over to the edge of ordinary Americana and told me to reach out my hand. But if that were the case, what strange methods he had! The dead deer, the visit to Mason and his family, the brief time in jail. What kind of divine teacher did such things?!

Though I waited and watched and hoped, he didn't show. My food arrived. The bourbon tasted like the syrup from the tree of the knowledge of good and better; it seemed to transcend time. I understood what all the fuss was about—the Bourbon Trail signs we'd been seeing, the glorious descriptions of different flavors. This wasn't booze. It wasn't crafted for the purpose of inebriation. It was nothing less than a divine instrument, designed to bathe chairs and tables and loud northern golfers in a new and kinder light. I sipped and kept sipping. No need for caution; my room was upstairs and I wasn't planning to drive. And I felt very strongly that I needed something to soothe me after a day—jail, hunger, ghosts—that had shaken me to my bones.

By the time I'd enjoyed my fourth glass, finished the delicious ribs and potatoes, topped things off with a slice of German chocolate cake, paid the bill, and added a ridiculously large trip, the stairs felt like a mountainside trail in ancient Galupistan. I made it back to the Daniel Boone room, collapsed on the bed, fished the phone out of my pants pocket, and hit the link marked HOME.

~ ~

chapter twenty-two

"Hey, Bueful One," I said, when I heard Anna Maria's voice.

"You're drunk!"

"Not exactly. I—"

"What is wrong with you, Eddie! What is going on! You're with Jesus Christ and you get drunk! Are you lying to me?! Are you . . . is something going on?!"

"Stop yelling at me."

"I AM NOT YELLING!"

"STOP YELLING!"

She hung up. I began to count. Because we've been married a long time and love each other very much, I counted only to 11 before the phone buzzed.

"Sorry," she said.

"I am a little drunk."

"But why, Eddie Val?"

"How are you? How's your mom?"

"Good. Everything's fine. I had a half-day job shooting at the museum and Mom went out onto the porch and sat in the sun for a couple minutes. What's going on?"

"Long sorry," I said. "Story."

"I have time."

So, as well as I could through the bourbon haze, I filled her in on the events of the previous twenty-four hours. The ping-pong-ball man, the time in jail, the monastery, the story of Calipari—something I knew she'd enjoy since she's a big fan of college basketball. I left out the part about Jesus's one-finger touch to Todd's forehead, and I left out the part about the ghost, and I even left out the part about Jesus's story about traveling to India. I don't know why. I wanted us to get our feet on the ground—phone-wise—before I delved into the more difficult subjects, and my brain was tilting and whirling. I sat up against the headboard and tried to focus.

"Jail? A real jail?" she said.

"Mayberry-ish."

"Thank God they let you go."

"Right. And not at the same time as Todd. He would have asked to come along."

"Who's Todd?"

"I really should have stopped at two."

"Two what?"

"Bourbon. I like it now. I'm going to bring a bottle home. Todd was in the other cell. A nut. Jesus tapped him on the head and he calmed right down, maybe changed for life. I think it was actually like a miracle."

"What else, there's something else. I can hear it even though you're disgustingly drunk."

"Not disgusting. I'm almost . . . I'm starting to sober up, I think."

"It's not like you. Something must have happened."

"I'm in the Daniel Boone room," I said. "Good hotel choice, thanks, and the food was good."

"What happened, Eddie?"

"Uh."

"Hon?"

Without realizing it, I was squeezing my free hand into a fist. I was tightening my arm muscles, pressing my lips together hard. At last I said, "I saw a ghost. Thomas Merton. He came and sat down next to me on a bench."

"It's just the bourbon."

"This was pre-bourbon. B.C.B."

"I'm worried."

"Don't. There's an election soon. November. Things could change."

"You might need to see someone, honey. Or it's the pressure of the talk. You should have taken a plane, we told you."

"I'm fine. Glad about the photo job."

"You're not fine. You say you're traveling with Jesus, you're drinking, you're seeing ghosts. I don't call that fine. I'm going to tell the girls. We want you to get help."

"This is why I can't talk to you," I said.

"Don't you dare hang up. I swear, if you hang up—"

"I'm not." I made the mistake of standing up, because I sometimes do better on the phone when I'm pacing. My head whirled and I sat back on the bed. "Strong stuff. Listen, Anna Maria, my beautiful wife, I'm a little drunk, not crazy. Everything I told you is the truth, and I haven't even told you some of it because I was worried about how you'd react."

"Nice. We tell each other everything."

"Jesus went to India."

"Meaning what?"

"That's what I haven't told you. He's been telling me a story, in chapters. When he was a young man, he went on the Silk Road to India, by way of Uzbekistan or one of the Stans. Or someplace. Who can keep it straight without a map? Things had one name then, a different one, then another one. Mountains, old guys by the fire, a beautiful yoga teacher. He's filling in the Gap."

There was a stretch of silence. Five or ten seconds, or maybe a minute, I couldn't be sure.

"You still there?"

"Yeah. Hon, I think . . . I think that, if you're not crazy and not lying—"

"I don't lie!"

"Don't yell. I think that, if you're not crazy, and if he's not a scam artist or a criminal, then something big is happening. I'm sad I can't be there. I think it's like, I think . . . it's one of those things you read about."

"It is."

"What are you going to do?"

"One thing more," I said, and I sank back against the pillowed headboard. "Jesus is gone. Disappeared. At the monastery he said he was going to do an errand, he'd meet me back in the car, and then . . . gone. I waited, I booked everywhere."

"Looked."

"Right."

"Maybe he turned into Thomas Merton. Maybe his spirit takes different shapes. Maybe he and Buddha were the same spirit or something, or all the holy teachers have been the same spirit and we just give them different names. Could that be?"

"Hon, right now the way I feel is . . . anything could be. Anything. My belief system is shaken right to the core of me."

"Maybe that's the point. Maybe it was supposed to be."

"Then it is. I'd send you a plane ticket if I thought you could get away, but I know you can't. And don't tell the grills, please."

"Girls."

"Yes, don't."

"Maybe he'll come back."

"He's been supposed to be coming back for two thousand years."

"You know what I mean."

"Yes. I'll keep you reformed."

"Allright. Love you. Drink a lot of water and take ibuprofen or you'll wake up miserable. I know you."

"And I know *you*. Biblically."

"Sleep, hon. And don't worry, okay? Things will work out."

~ ~

chapter twenty-three

From exhaustion, not stubbornness, I went to sleep without drinking water, without taking ibuprofen, and without removing my clothes. Next morning, there was a price to be paid. Nothing feels quite like a hangover. There's the headache, the queasy stomach, the weariness, and it's all combined with a sense of having sinned and been poisoned. The liver complains, an organ not to be messed with. A chorus of regret plays loudly in both ears.

Hydration, medication, a long shower, fresh clothes, and I felt well enough, if barely, to carry my bag out of the Daniel Boone room and down the steep set of stairs of The Old Talbott Tavern. There was bourbon fudge for sale in the lobby and, considering it a sweet version of hair of the dog, and forgetting that I had some in the car, I bought a big piece and, along with a cup of the Tavern's free coffee, made that my breakfast. Outside, the Kentucky morning held a chill. I decided to take a *passeggiata,* clear the toxins from my bloodstream, and see if maybe Jesus would magically appear before I was ready to hit the road.

Bardstown—which Merton mentions in his writings as a place the monks would sometimes go to, riding in a farm cart, to buy supplies or deliver hay—had apparently been voted the prettiest small town in America. Where, exactly, this vote had been taken I don't know, and I'm suspicious about those polls in any case, but there were several signs in the downtown area claiming that title. It wasn't unjustified. Set in neat lines along both sides of the main street's commercial section stood small shops selling everything from stylish clothing to souvenirs, and the municipal building near my hotel had a classic look to it, all brick turrets and large paned windows perched above a grand front stair. Half a mile further along, the downtown strip's two and three-story buildings gave way to a varied selection of Victorian homes, all of them meticulously kept and set apart from each other on parcels of mowed lawns that were rich with shrubbery and small flowering trees. In all, the town looked like a kind of Eden, an advertisement for an imagined America of olden times, simpler, kinder, easier to grasp. A better place, perhaps . . . as long as you hadn't been black or gay or an ambitious woman. Or Irish, or Italian, or a Jew.

Across the street from the inn was this historical marker, the first of three interesting signs in Bardstown:

SUCCESSFUL SURGERY

The first successful amputation of a leg at the hip joint in U.S. Done here by Dr. Walter Brashear in 1806 without any precedent to guide him. The patient was a seventeen-year-old boy whose leg had been badly mangled.

I took a picture with my phone and said a prayer for the young man's spirit.

And then, after I'd completed my tour of the village and had turned back toward the hotel, ready to grab a large iced coffee for the road and feeling maybe ten percent less poisoned, I came across a store—closed at that hour—with a typed sign in the window. I took a photo of it, too:

THIS IS NOT A
POLITICALLY
CORRECT STORE!
We say, "Merry Christmas", "God Bless You," we salute the flag, we support our troops, our police, our firefighters.
If this offends you don't come in
Or feel free to leave this store, this town,
& country!

And then, a little farther down the same block, as if the full range of American opinion was on display:

> This is the beginning of a new day. You have been given this day to use as you will. You can waste it or use it for good. What you do today is important because you are exchanging a day of your life for it. When tomorrow comes this day will be gone forever. In its place is something that you have left behind. Let it be something *Good.*

Another couple of doors down I did stop for coffee, was given a tall takeout cup by a very friendly woman about my own age, and then I retrieved the damaged Camry and set off, west. Just a touch of bourbon still in the bloodstream. Some of the spiritual shakiness gone. Memories of Bardstown in the cerebellum. No Jesus.

I started out on back roads, as I am wont to do, curving and meandering along a winding, two-lane route. At one point, not long before I joined the superhighway, I passed a tiny, sad-looking log cabin that claimed to be the place where Abe Lincoln had been born. A tourist attraction now. Large parking lot, cars already rolling in. I moved on and soon reached the Interstate.

Where I-64 met I-65 I turned south toward Nashville and finally, near the infamous Bowling Green, started to see the first real indications of spring. Here and there some trees had blossomed into displays of pink and white; it would be weeks before we saw such things in the hills of Western Massachusetts.

As I went along, sipping coffee and trying—unlike so many of my fellow travelers!—to keep a steady speed, I thought about home, and Anna Maria, and filled the emptiness left by Jesus's disappearance with thoughts of how our own belief systems had evolved. Both of us had been raised devout Catholic, she in Wooster Square, the Italian section of New Haven, Connecticut, and yours truly at the northern end of the Boston subway line. Both of us had gradually drifted away from the faith without much anger or guilt (though certain relatives judged us harshly), holding on to the tenets that had helped us—the discipline, the regular consideration of another life, the habit of prayer, the emphasis on self-sacrifice and compassion—and letting go of those that had not—the guilt, the sense that ours was the One True Faith, the man-in-the-sky idea of God. In her case, that evolution had been directed East by a remarkable Religion course she took senior year at Brown. In my case, as mentioned, it was the Thomas Merton reading group and then Ram Dass.

Prone to argument as we sometimes were—especially over the phone—in two important places our ideas aligned almost perfectly: raising children and the spiritual life. I had a regular meditation practice; she did not. But, though we never claimed to be sure, we both suspected that reincarnation was the only reasonable explanation for the manifest unfairness of the world; we both believed there had to be some consequence for one's actions; and we both understood that the important thing, the main practice, was to do unto others as you would have them do unto you. We'd only rarely taken our girls to church services, and they'd ended up as two of the kindest and most compassionate people we knew. We talked about the Big Questions, and said a prayer before bed, but gave them space to figure out their own answers.

Both of us kept our spirituality to ourselves and didn't much care for proselytizers.

As I was thinking of our girls, the phone rang. I pushed a button on the wheel and heard Juliette's voice. "You okay, Dad?"

"Fine, you?"

"Mom's worried."

"Without cause. What's going on at that fancy school for rich kids?"

"Dance last night. It was fun. Softball practice this afternoon."

"Courses okay?"

"Yeah . . . Mom wrote me and Sis and said you went to jail. What'd you do?"

I never lie to my children, but at that moment I wasn't ready to divulge the full truth (tell me, what is the best way to reveal to your child that you have been on a multi-day road trip with Jesus Christ?) so I tiptoed across a factual tightrope. "A deer ran in front of the car. I hit it, got some blood on my clothes. Then I was hungry and speeding a little bit and got pulled over and they saw the blood and jumped to a bad conclusion. Once they tested it, they let me free. I'm planning to sue."

"Really?"

"No. It was nothing. *Mayberry RFD.*"

"Huh?"

"Small town stuff."

"Cool, though. Not many kids here have dads who are in jail."

"As it should be."

"And Dad?"

"What, honey?"

"Mom thinks you're having like a mid-life crisis or something."

"Too late for that."

There was a pause, voices in the background. "Okay then, gotta head off to class. Don't go crazy or anything."

"Sane as Santa," I said, which made no sense, but that's what I said. "Love you, kid. Enjoy the day."

"Love you, Pops. Bye."

One thing I resolved to ask Jesus, if I ever saw him again, was how it could possibly be, as some scriptures of various faiths suggested, that you were put together on earth with other spirits, you loved them to the extent Anna Maria and I loved our children, and each other, and then you died, and the connection was broken forever. What kind of God would do that? No, my dream God—may I be forgiven—was sensible, logical, a God who presided over a system that incorporated the idea of earthly love, not just of some untouchable spirit in the sky, but love of your kids and food and golf and being alive on a spring day.

I remembered Jesus saying that it wasn't important what you believed; what was important was what you did, how you acted. *That* was my kind of God. Everybody had a belief system, even if it was only a firm belief that there was nothing to believe in, it was all random, you died and ceased to exist in any form. A system of belief might govern how you behaved, but it certainly didn't change the existential situation. Believing it wasn't going to rain tomorrow wouldn't change the forecast by one drop.

I suddenly realized, again, how much I missed him. That I wanted him there in the passenger seat. That I had a thousand questions I should have asked when he was around.

There was nothing to do but go on and hope for the best. What I was thinking about, on the ride south through Kentucky and toward the Tennessee line, was a question that had poked its head into my interior room from time to time over the years: Was trying to lead a decent life enough, or was there something else we were supposed to be doing, some other dimension, some hidden purpose we were supposed to discover and act upon? I'd read that there were various paths one could take in the direction of enlightenment or salvation or wholeness or actualization, various personality types that fit one approach more than the others. Contemplation, devotion, scholarship, service—those were the ones I could remember. Of course, they weren't mutually exclusive; most people who were serious about their spiritual life had a little of all of them. But if I had to place each of us, I'd say Anna Maria fell into the service category, and I was more of a contemplative.

Complicating all this was the idea—another one I'd come across in my reading—that if you tried too hard to be a 'spiritual person' or to attain enlightenment, you could so easily turn it into a competition and start comparing yourself to others. I had a Merton quote to that effect up on my office wall.

So where did that leave us?

~ ~

chapter twenty-four

I'm sorry, I'm sorry, I'm sorry. I see now that I've gotten away from the story! But this is exactly the kind of person I am. I can't help it. From the time I was old enough to put on a Little League uniform, I've been obsessively pondering the existential predicament, wondering how we got here, what we're supposed to do here, what happens next. I know that lots of other people share this obsession. Probably I wouldn't change it even if I could, but sometimes I overdo and wind myself up into a wet knot of curiosity.

At which point I have a glass of wine, or an ice cream sundae, or I read one chapter of a classic novel. . . . Or, if the weather cooperates, I play a round of golf.

Roughly halfway between Bardstown and Nashville, just over the Tennessee line, I pulled off the Interstate and into the parking lot of a Dollar Tree. A quick search on my phone indicated that there was a golf course ten minutes away, The Legacy Club in Springfield. The day was mild and sunny. My clubs were in the trunk. Jesus was nowhere to be seen and I told myself I needed some salve for the unexpected ache of missing him. I very carefully plugged the club's address into my GPS system, checked three times to be sure I had it right, and, I'm proud to say, I did not get lost on route.

The people at the Legacy Club were extraordinarily welcoming: they squinted at but did not comment upon my Boston accent. I paid, used their men's locker room to change into shorts and a collared shirt, rented one of their push-carts, and wheeled my bag to the first tee. A little stretching, a few practice swings to loosen up, a moment to look around and appreciate the manicured landscape and beautiful blue sky, and I set my tee in the ground.

This is the finest moment in a golfer's life. At the start of a round, you're still free to imagine that great things will happen. And once in a while they do. Part of the addictive nature of the game comes from the fact that on any given day you might make a golf shot worthy of a great player—Sam Snead or Gene Sarazen; Annika Sorenstam or Tiger Woods. Tell me any other sport where that's true. You're not going to hit a 90-mile-an-hour slider 400 feet in your Saturday pickup game. Playing with a friend on the local courts, you're not going to blast a 102 mph serve that just catches the line and gives you an ace. You're not going to have a lucky day and run the 100 in 9.1 seconds. But in golf, even if it's only one time out of five hundred, you can send the little white ball across a pond the size of a football field and land it within a body-length of the flagstick. A shot worthy of any great professional.

The game is fodder for ridicule, I know that. And from the outside that ridicule seems justified—a bunch of old men who shouldn't be showing their legs, driving around in funny little carts, smoking cigars and chewing up clods of earth with long metal sticks. It has an ugly side, too. Country club golf can be connected with the worst kind of elitism and privilege, martinis on the verandah after a hard week of inventing ways to screw people out of their money, while your spoiled kids argue with each other in the shallow end of the pool.

But, for millions of people, golf is a working person's sport, a kind of outdoor bowling. The greens fees as the Legacy were $34, half the price of a bleacher seat at Fenway. The course had an Audubon certification, which meant that its designers and greenkeepers took the environment into account—using less fertilizer, protecting certain plant species and wetland areas, perhaps using filtered gray water for their grass-growing. And the female golfer who came walking up to me just as I was about to tee off looked to be the farthest thing from a Master of the Universe. "Hi," she said, "mind if I join you?"

A true golfer never says no to this question; it is part of the dignity of the game. You embrace the opportunity to embarrass yourself in front of complete strangers.

The woman and I shook hands. She introduced himself as Mary Catherine and stood quietly by as I laced a desultory tee shot that curled lazily right, bounced twice, smacked into a tree trunk, and popped back into the fairway. We then walked up to the forward tees—where most amateur women and some older men play from—and she hit a hard grounder that traveled 150 yards right up the middle. On those two somewhat sour notes, off we went our adventure.

Mary Catherine—she asked me to call her MC—was a trim, athletic woman of Asian heritage, somewhere in her mid-thirties, that blessed decade I could almost recall. She had dark hair cropped very short and wore long trousers and a long-sleeve golf jacket, as if the day—so warm and welcoming to a New Englander—still seemed, to a native, part of the Tennessee winter. We reached her ball first. I stood aside and watched her swing. She took the club back with a smooth motion, then exaggerated the pause at the top and brought her club down against the ball as if it were a bitter enemy. It worked. She blasted a low line drive that ended up just in front of the green.

"Nice," I said. "Nice swing, too."

"Thanks. My wife and I play three times a week and we both think we should be better than we are. We both played sports in college."

"Me, too," I said. "It's a brutal game."

She laughed, we walked up to my ball and she returned the favor of standing still and quiet while I flew one into the green-side bunker.

Her "my wife" remark caught my attention, of course, but wasn't exactly astonishing. Anna Maria and I live not far from Northampton, Massachusetts, which has a significant lesbian population, as well as a fair number of gay men. Our kids grew up with classmates who had two moms, or two dads, and no one we knew ever made a fuss about it. Watching MC chip on-to the green, and then curse quietly and laugh at herself because the ball went skittering well past the pin and almost to the far apron, it occurred to me that we are all creatures of habit, programmed to cling tight to certain opinions. If we come of age around families with two mothers, even a minority of such families, it blends into our world. If we grow up eating a tilapia, plantain, and hot pepper stew, like a Ghanaian friend of mine, then that seems an ordinary dinner, not exotic in the least. If we're raised with violence and shouting, then that will be part of our view of how things are. There are many normals.

MC and I putted out, we walked over to the second tee, and all the while I was wondering if there might be another dimension to the idea of becoming accustomed to things. Maybe we get plopped down on earth, where all we know is earthly life—the sights and sounds and smells and tastes and behaviors—and we become accustomed to that, and more or less just go along, unable to push our minds out past the familiar boundaries. Maybe the great teachers are sent to us precisely in order to do that: make us aware of other possibilities. Not that we could suddenly decide to flap our arms and fly, but that there might be something beyond the necessary struggle for food and shelter, and then, once we've secured that, the long list of pleasures and worries that fill most of the modern mind. Something beyond the idea of death as a sad thing, the demolition of every joy. Maybe, in lesser fashion, artists are always trying to do that, too—move us to see the world differently by using paint on a canvas, or words in a book, or movement on a stage, or music.

Thinking about such things, I hit an embarrassingly bad tee shot, a crooked dribbler that bounced and wobbled to my right and took up residence at the base of a flowering bush. I tried to laugh.

MC held to a respectful silence.

Though I can't say I appreciated it at that particular moment, the best part of golf, and a part that remains invisible to the eye of the non-golfer, is that it humbles you. If you let it. You have to stand up in front of your friends, or complete strangers, and try to get the explosive ball three or four or five hundred yards into a four-and-a-quarter-inch hole in as few strokes as possible. Mistakes—horribly embarrassing mistakes like the one I'd just made on the second tee at The Legacy Club—are built into the game the way wet feet are built into surfing. Your playing partners stand still and silent. You address the ball, mind whirling with advice from golf magazines, lessons with a pro, tips from pals, theories about the boundaries of the earthly mind, memories of disaster and glory, and you swing, and sometimes the round white demon dribbles off sideways into the shrubbery and sometimes it flies in a magnificent trajectory straight and far and lands dead center in the fairway two and a half football fields away. There are players, men mostly, who respond to this potential humiliation by puffing themselves up even more. They strut around the course, they talk too loudly in the snack bar, they huff and bluster and make every manner of excuse. They cheat. Most of the men I've golfed with, though, allow themselves to be humbled by the game. They learn to laugh at themselves, learn to compliment others on a good shot; they master the complex dance of etiquette that's part and parcel of a decent golfer's round.

I made a good recovery shot, paused to take a very quick photo of the flowering bush, and both of us ended up with a respectable score of bogey, one shot over par. The course was uncrowded. We stepped along in tandem for a few holes, good shots and bad, silence and conversation. MC had a nice way about her. She took the game seriously enough to try, but not so seriously that she swore and grumbled and slammed clubs back into her bag after a mistake. When she asked what had brought me to Tennessee, I told her about the Arkansas talk, and it turned out, first, that she was a reader, and second, that she'd read *Breakfast with Buddha* and had *Lunch with Buddha* on her night table. I was flattered, of course—that kind of thing happened every once in a while—and asked her what she did for work.

"Yoga teacher. Thalia and I have a studio downtown. Was that hilarious yoga scene in *Breakfast* from your own experience?"

"I confess that it was, yes."

"I read it aloud to my advanced class. They loved it."

"You wouldn't know it from today's golf game, but I'm fairly coordinated. Yoga is about the only physical activity where I sometimes really feel like a klutz."

"It's magical, though, isn't it?" she said.

That word—*magical*—caused me to remember Jesus's encounter with the old man on the Silk Road, and his comment about the amazing feats of people in the East. And then about his yoga teacher in northern India. And then I connected it to the previous line of thought—about familiarity. And all that, along with a gorgeous tee ball on the par 4 seventh hole, caused this to come out of my mouth: "Where does the spiritual path lead a person, do you think? I mean, if you don't mind me asking. I mean, sorry, but—"

MC was smiling. She'd also hit a gorgeous tee shot, maybe that was the reason. We walked toward the green, silent at first, yours truly wondering if I'd just put a golf shoe squarely into my mouth, but then she said, "It's so funny you should ask that. Thalia and I were just having that discussion the other night and that exact question came up."

"Good, I'm relieved. I'm not a proselytizer or anything. Something made me ask. What kind of answer did you and Thalia come up with?"

MC stopped right there and turned to look at me. For a moment it almost seemed we'd forgotten about golf entirely. She tilted her head sideways, as if making sure it was a sincere question. "We decided," she said, "that you have to live the life you've been given. We're gay women living in a pretty conservative part of the richest country on earth, and our job is to live out that life as best we can. She had breast cancer a few years ago. No one likes that, of course. It scared us both. But after the first shock, we just said, "Okay, we're going to deal with this," and we did.

"I read once in a Zen book that the monks advise you to say 'yes' to everything."

"Exactly. Not, 'oh, yes, wow, breast cancer, how great!' But this is the deal. This is the situation right now. This is my life. I'm going to take hold of it and live it as fully as I can, as well as

I can. That's what we came up with."

"My feeling precisely," I said. "Though it's not easy."

"Which is the whole point."

We turned our attention back to golf and played along peacefully, happily, taking the good with the bad. Near the end of our eighteen-hole tour, on the par 3 17th, 167 yards from the tees she was playing, MC chipped in from the fringe for birdie. I gave her a fist-bump and we played the final hole in bright sunshine, shook hands on the last tee and went our separate ways. But as I was loading my bag into the Camry's trunk, she came over for a last word. "You're a good person," she said. "I can see that. You should know that."

It was an absolutely tremendously odd thing to say, and for a second or two I couldn't think of a response. And then I said, "You, too. Nice meeting you. And great birdie on seventeen."

MC went off to her SUV and tooted the horn a last time as she drove away.

I reset the GPS for the hotel Anna Maria had found in Jackson, and then sat there for a bit, staring out at a trio of women playing the 7th hole. "This is why you decided to drive," I said aloud. I'd met the ping-pong ball maker, Anton at the Greenbrier, Mason and Emma and Ellory, and now Mary Catherine. In between, there had been shorter encounters with clerks at gas stations and waitresses at coffeeshops. In a world filled increasingly with robocalls, maddening phone trees, a continual diminishing of human contact, I loved those kinds of connections, snippets of human unity, reminders of the fact that we are all spinning around on the stone in the middle of space. In the same spacecraft.

~ ~

chapter twenty-five

And I love driving, too. It's like being at an elaborate visual buffet, one interesting sight after the next laid out for the viewing pleasure of an insatiably curious man. I like the challenge of it, the need to stay attentive, to be aware of others and strike a mix of confidence and self-awareness. A kind of meditation, really. I wished that Anna Maria and I were making the trip together, not in April but in a hot and humid mid-summer, when the landscape would be painted in various greens, the hillsides and fields bursting with life. April offered a subtler enjoyment, though, and like most northerners, having suffered through months of cold gray lifelessness, I took an extra pleasure in the first stirrings of spring.

Climbing a rise on I-65, I was astonished to see the Nashville skyline materialize before me. Never having been to Music City USA, I'd envisioned it as a sleepy little southern town with folk and country venues scattered here and there. But what faced me on that afternoon, backlit by the setting sun, was a miniature Manhattan. Because my high school daughter had heard that students at Vanderbilt University were the happiest in America, I stopped there for a quick snack and wandered around the campus, taking snapshots for her and asking the occasional student what they thought of the place. The reviews were favorable, the kids admirably open to an old stranger walking up and saying, "Excuse me, I have a daughter who's thinking of applying. How do you like it here?"

That kind of ordinary interaction has been polluted, of course, by a small number of what both daughters would call 'creepers.' I'd heard that, in the place where I'd once worked as a paperboy, the exalted profession no longer existed: no parent wanted to put their child at risk . . . and understandably so, given the horror stories. Innocent physical contact—a hand on a shoulder—has been rendered nearly extinct by similar creepers. Ticket holders at ballgames and concerts have to pass through metal detectors. Schools need armed guards at the doors, and sometimes even that doesn't protect the students. Bottles of everything from milk to vitamin C tablets come with protective inner seals to prevent poisoning. In order to have access to a sick elderly parent's medical information, you practically have to mail in your fingertips first so your identity can be verified. Passwords and security cameras, malware and pepper spray—there were good reasons for all of it, yes, definitely, but it seemed to me sometimes that the culture was being shaped by the worst among us, and that we were undergoing a slow, deadly dehumanization.

Wandering the aisles of the thought-supermarket in that fashion, I somehow became lost again on the pretty Vanderbilt campus and had to ask directions of a trio of hefty guys—football players, I guessed—loitering on the green. "What street did you park on?" One of them asked.

"I didn't notice."

"Any stores or anything near there?"

"A convenience store, I think. A little row of shops."

"Try West End Ave," and they pointed me north.

With their kind assistance I managed to find my car, and

with the assistance of the GPS, managed to free myself from Nashville's world-class traffic and make it to the city of Jackson before the dinner hour had passed. When I checked into the hotel Anna Maria had reserved online I was surprised to find two smaller beds in the room instead of the usual king, but that didn't matter much: the hotel sat on a busy street lined with every imaginable kind of outlet store and chain restaurant, and it was a five-minute-drive to the kind of food I had a hankering for: Indian.

'Sizzler' was the name of the place, according to Siri. I found it without trouble, tucked back off the road in a strip mall. Didn't get lost, didn't get stopped for speeding. By then, it was near enough to closing time that a young couple and I were the only diners in the place. I found a booth, perused the menu, ordered my favorite meal—mango lassi and dal tarka with Naan bread and basmati rice. The waiter brought a small basket of the wafery, chick-pea-flour papadum—and, while I waited for the meal to arrive, I watched a Bollywood film on a TV attached to the top of the far wall. Below the TV was a short corridor leading to the restrooms and, as the beautifully costumed men and women danced and sang on the screen, I saw a familiar face appear there beneath them. Jesus was wearing jeans and running shoes and wiping his hands dry on a gold UT VOLUNTEERS sweatshirt.

He sauntered across the room and slid into the bench seat across from me.

"Order yet?" he asked, as casually as if he'd been with me all the way from Gethsemane and had just stepped out of the bathroom.

"Just now."

"Good, we'll share. How've you been? I missed you."

"Fine, good," I said, playing along, cool as could be. "Still a little wrung out from a bourbon adventure in Bardstown. You?"

"Excellent."

Why did you disappear? I wanted to ask. Of course. But I felt, well, *vulnerable* isn't a word I like, especially when it's used to describe me, and I felt vulnerable then. I'd gotten accustomed to being around him. I'd come to like him as a person, and I'd come to believe it was possible that, with his tricks and questions, his unpredictable behavior—tossing a football one minute, meeting with strange Russians the next—he was leading me toward some interior destination. I'd begun to realize how badly I wanted to go there. He irritated me, worried me, angered me . . . and pushed me, in the strangest ways, to a deeper consideration of what it meant to be alive.

Exactly what a spiritual teacher is supposed to do.

I watched him—the intense eyes—gray blue at the moment—the long flowing hair, the racial ambiguity and perhaps even a bit of what we used to call androgyny. I was remembering Gethsemane, trying to be ready for whatever happened next, and it made me feel . . . vulnerable.

"Only twenty-four hours until the big talk. You ready?"

"Stopped being nervous years ago."

"Amazing what practice can do, isn't it?"

I had the sense there was a double meaning in the comment, that he was pointing my thoughts in a certain direction, working another angle. *Practice.* Maybe he meant spiritual practice. Maybe I hadn't been practicing enough, meditating enough, thinking properly, acting appropriately with my wife and children and friends. Maybe I was out of practice, spiritually.

But he didn't elaborate. He took off the cap and ran his fingers through his thick brown hair, pinched it behind his neck, left it there unclasped. And then he said this: "You know, I really enjoyed that birdie on seventeen," and punctuated that line with a smile that was half-bashful, half-sly.

Our waiter brought two mango lassis to the table. I studied Jesus's face more intently and at last saw the resemblance to Mary Catherine, faint but clear, if you were smart enough to look, which I hadn't been.

It seemed to me then that I'd been led into a bizarre world, one that was becoming more and more strange by the hour. The seat beneath me seemed suddenly unstable, gently shifting, like the deck of a sailboat in a not-quite-calm bay. "Are you . . . can you, you know . . . can you turn into anybody you want?"

"There's a bit of me in everyone," he said casually, factually, lightly, not exactly flippantly but as if he were saying *this mango lassi is tasty.* He leaned forward over the sweet orange drink and sipped from the straw. He sat back, grinned, raised and lowered his eyebrows like a comedian who'd just made a goofy joke. For a second he was Groucho Marx, no cigar. The features of his face—lips, eyes, eyebrows, jaw muscles—had gone suddenly elastic.

"Thomas Merton?" I pressed.

He shrugged, seemed about to laugh, but caught himself. His face solidified, became almost severe.

It was very difficult for me to pose the next question, but I was remembering something Anna Maria had said in our most recent call, and I felt pushed somehow, shoved into a new and risky territory. I could almost feel the Sunday School nuns, sixth grade, hovering nearby, glaring at me, ready to play the Eternal Punishment card. I forced out the word. "Buddha?"

The flippancy, if that's what it was, evaporated instantly; the severity intensified. For one moment I thought he was angry and would explode at me, or lean across the table and growl:

Listen, Edward, there is one Lord, and you are looking at him! Don't you dare suggest that my spirit and Buddha's were identical!

Catholic guilt, I suppose. Or the old idea, shared by every religion on earth and drilled into the heads of its children, that their way is the only way. In Jesus's eyes—now as green as a Christmas tree—I saw the same fiery intensity that I'd seen in the jail cell. "I don't know why you haven't understood this yet," he said, quietly but forcefully, in a tone that admitted no argument. "From the second I sat in your car in downtown Williamsburg, I've been trying to show you that the cardinal sin of being human is that humans do not understand who they actually are. Don't you see?"

I shook my head. The table made another slight shift, as if a tugboat wake were lifting and dropping my flimsy craft.

The waiter came and set our food down in front of us, the lentil dish and rice, each in beautiful brass bowls. Neither Jesus nor I thanked him.

"The pure spirit resides in every living creature, every atom in fact. In human beings it is covered, hidden, a vein of precious ore in a mountainside. Your work, lifetime after lifetime, dimension after dimension, challenge by challenge, is to uncover it. Do you not understand?"

I shook my head.

"You are fixated on your body, Edward. Your personality, your appearance, your name, your so-called *identity,* when, in fact, you are a spirit composed of a temporary association of molecules swirling in an unimaginably massive sea of other swirling molecules. Do you see?"

"No," I managed.

He pressed his lips together. "On the seventh tee you hit your ball beneath a large rhododendron bush, just in bloom, its lavender blossoms a kind of feast for a variety of bees. Did you notice it?"

"I did. I even took a quick picture with my phone and later I sent it to Anna Maria and the girls. I—"

"Well, the people in your circle of acquaintance in this lifetime—your wife, your daughters, your closest friends and relatives, you yourself—are like the flowers on that bush. All individual-seeming, yes?"

"Yes."

"And yet all part of something larger. They burst into blossom and then die. They nourish the bees and hummingbirds. They are *associated* with each other for a certain period of time. They share a fate, you might say, and yet there is an apparent separateness. When the blossoms die and fall, they nourish the bush. They decay, and then the molecules become part of the roots, the stems, the leaves, see? They *apparently* disappear, the way I just did at the monastery, the way Buddha and all the other great teachers did. And then they return and are united in the same growth, the same plant. Eventually, in a day, or after a hundred summers and a hundred winters, some of those molecules will be carried away on the wind, or in the fur of a rabbit, or the feather of a bird, and they will then become part of another association. Another universe, you might say. *Seemingly separate,* and yet, in fact, part of the whole, a kind of enormous and always-changing family. Do you see?"

"Starting to."

"What happened at the Last Supper, do you remember?"

I nodded. "You predicted you'd be taken away from your friends. You held up the bread and said, "This is my body, eat this in memory of me." Then you held up the wine and said, "This is my blood, drink this in memory of me." It's why there's communion in Christian churches. The priest blesses the wafers and wine and—"

Jesus was nodding vigorously, happily it seemed, and, at the same time, spooning rice onto the plate in front of him. He looked up and his eyes made me stop right there, with that 'and.'

"This is my body," he said. "Think about it. In other words: *this piece of bread is as much my body as this assembly of flesh and bones and blood that you are so worried about not seeing again!!*"

"That's kind of a different take, if I understand you right."

"You do, finally. I was trying to tell them not to be so obsessed with my physical body, especially because I was about to disappear, so I just reached for the objects closest to hand—bread, wine—and held them up and said that."

"But we took it literally."

"Exactly. As you have done with so many of my words. When you write this story, I expect you to make it clear that you are using the sacred tool of *metaphor*."

"So you *were* Buddha then. I mean, your spirit inhabited the person we think of as Buddha, is that correct?"

He had been spooning some of the soupy dal tarka onto his rice, but he stopped and glared at me. "Are you truly stupid?" he asked.

"I'm beginning to think so, yes. I—"

"What did I just tell you?"

"The rhododendron bush, the bread and wine, the . . . molecules."

"You have eyes but do not see, ears but do not hear."

I nodded again, stupidly.

"Eat," he said, in a slightly kinder tone. "Indian food isn't as tasty when it's cold."

So I spooned the rice and lentils onto my plate, and broke off pieces of the buttery, delicious Naan, and sipped at the succulent mango lassi, and avoided looking at him. My mind was absolutely whirling, a nine-ring circus, a carousel with ringing bells and flashing colors and jumping plastic horses. Everything I looked at—the bread, the sweet drink, the water glass, the grains of rice, my own hands—seemed to be winking at me. I was having difficulty swallowing. Strangely, perhaps, what came to mind was a feeling I'd had many times when the four people in my family were together. There were four distinct faces, four personalities, four bodies. A kind of separateness. And yet, there was also a sense of connection that transcended the separateness. A feeling. "Love" we called it, but that was merely a label for something we couldn't possibly explain.

After a fairly long silence, Jesus said, as matter-of-factly as if there had been no interruption in the story, "The yoga teacher's name was Choden—it means 'the Devout One' in Tibetan. At first, I and the other young men I mentioned—we all studied with her. We lived together in the city and worked just enough to pay our way, and we spent half of every day practicing our asanas and various meditations, learning how to withdraw from the five senses and so on. In time, one after the next, my friends moved on and I was there alone and became Choden's primary student. Nine years in all. She was a very special soul, one of the earth's great teachers."

"But not famous."

"All great teachers aren't famous, Edward. It's the height of foolishness to believe that. In fact, most of them aren't known as teachers and do not care to be. There are thousands of them living on the earth right now, in disguise you would say. Grandmothers. Farmers. Basketball stars. Librarians. Nurses. People picking up garbage or driving a bus. All doing their secret work."

"Why did you leave her?"

"I had a certain destiny, a commitment to the Jewish people, and she knew that, but it was a very sad leavetaking."

"A relationship?"

"A very deep friendship."

I tried to ask if it had been a sexual friendship, but I couldn't bring myself to do that. "I wanted to ask you about that, about leavetakings. I spoke with one of my daughters by phone this afternoon, not long before I saw you. I miss her and her sister so much. What happens to love like that, you know, after?"

"It persists."

"Good. It wouldn't make sense otherwise."

"Exactly."

"So did you see Choden again, after you left?"

"Oh, yes. She was with me when I died."

"No mention of her in any of the gospels."

"Exactly," he said. "That's my point, the whole reason I wanted to talk to you in the first place. It's part of the Gap."

The waiter stopped by to refill our water glasses and shone a gorgeous smile on Jesus.

"Sorry, I'm a baptized Catholic. I'm still wrestling with the Buddha idea," I said. "The Thomas Merton ghost."

"It's not complicated.

"For me, it is. For us. One time, years ago, we were in Miami on vacation, me, Anna Maria and my mother and the girls—who were small then. My mother wanted to go to Mass, so we found a Catholic church and took her. Actually, the church was undergoing renovations, so the Mass was held in the gymnasium of the Catholic school next door. During the announcements, I remember the priest saying that there would be a yoga class starting up on Wednesday nights, and then reassuring the congregation, as if making excuses for the announcement, that practicing yoga didn't mean you were worshiping some false god, some Buddha or anything like that. Those were his exact words."

"Not yet an enlightened being," was all Jesus said.

"Which begs the question: what is Jesus doing practicing yoga with a beautiful woman in Kashmir?"

A one-note laugh, a sip of his mango lassi. He broke a small piece off the papadum and chewed thoughtfully before answering. "I'm trying to think of the best way to explain it to you. Why did Thomas Merton have that vision in Sri Lanka and not Kentucky?"

"Okay, I was thinking the same thing. But, I mean, why yoga? Why not mountain climbing or Bollywood dancing or ping pong?"

"Because yoga," he said quietly, "is magic. The people who developed it, thousands of years ago, were the most highly developed souls on the planet. Similar to the great scientific geniuses of the Western world. They saw beyond the veil of assumption, beyond the presupposed limits. Eat while I talk, please. You'll need it. Tomorrow we're fasting."

"We are?"

"Yes, until dinner. I want to show you something."

"What? The amazing things my body is capable of?"

"More the mind actually, but yes. It will be fun."

"I still don't see why Jesus would take yoga lessons from anyone, anywhere."

"It was part of my destiny. Without the yoga, the crucifixion couldn't have happened the way it did."

"Kindly explain."

"Eat. We'll get into it later if I feel you are ready to hear it. For now, let me just say this: The West is marvelous in its use of the mind. The spaceships, the medicines, the incredible and bridges and airliners. But for thousands of years the

East has used the mind differently, and there's very little recognition of that in your culture, except perhaps among the West's aboriginal peoples and a very small number of mystics. You're all about the exterior world—inventions, machinery, weightlifting, hockey, spaceships—while the interior world is not only ignored, it's ridiculed or trivialized. Meditation is navel-gazing; it's laziness. Yoga is stretching; it might improve your sex life. Meanwhile, among all the wonderful things the West has accomplished, you also have massive levels of addiction, depression, and violence, not to mention what has been done to the sacred earth. And you go on praising yourself as the superior civilization! Certain people of the East and certain of the aboriginals have, for thousands of years, been able to cure themselves of diseases by the power of their minds and do what you'd consider magical things with their bodies. And they've also been able to live on the Earth and not harm it. I know Tibetan monks who can be tortured by the Chinese invaders and not scream or feel pain. These aren't tricks, they're very real. Exceedingly rare, of course, but real, and they would point you in that direction if you would only stop with the 'worshipping of false gods' and 'navel-gazing' stuff, and the constant rush for more, bigger, faster, and open your hearts and minds to a different way of being."

"There's nothing wrong with weightlifting and new medicines."

"Of course not! The blend is the thing. Exterior and interior. Action and contemplation."

"Yin and Yang," I said, suddenly remembering the business card he'd given me as I was leaving Northampton.

"Now I see a glimmer of hope."

Jesus waved a hand as if to signal the end of the conversation and I accepted that without resistance. Not long before left the restaurant, he said, "The Gap is all about this, Edward. Think about it: What was left out? The East, the interior, the magic, the metaphor! And what was kept in? The West, the exterior, the concrete! This is what you have to include in your story!"

"Westerners accept the miracles in the gospels."

"Yes, somehow it's been perfectly acceptable for centuries, the idea of my turning water into wine, curing diseases, and yet—"

"Because people, even great yoga teachers, don't do those things. God does."

"There are people who have always done them. Every religious tradition tells those stories, every single one."

"No one I know has done them."

"This is the great conceit of the Western world," he said. "You're imprisoned by logic. You make up your own narrative. If the facts don't fit, out they go."

"Which leaves us with the Gap, am I right?"

"Precisely! What happened in those seventeen years simply didn't fit with the limited understanding of Western historians and the powerful men of the Western Church, so it was set aside. Reincarnation was part and parcel of Christian theology until the Council of Constantinople, *six hundred years after my death!* Think about that, Edward. Ponder it!"

I tried my very best to do that.

~ ~

chapter twenty-six

Interesting, yes, even fascinating, but that wasn't an easy conversation for me. Maybe I was, as Jesus said, 'imprisoned by logic,' but I thought it was better than being imprisoned by illogic, by wishful thinking, by the notion that I could somehow transcend my human limitations simply by wanting to. I drove him away from the mall parking lot in a stubborn silence, not so different from some of the silences Anna Maria and I had driven through after one of our restaurant tiffs. It's not that I was angry at him. It's more that, whenever he started talking to me about his Gap, I experienced a bristling resistance, exactly the way I feel when someone challenges my politics in a way I don't like. No, no, no, a childish voice was saying. You're wrong, I'm right. I know how things are.

But how did I know? Why was I so sure that what he called "the Western way of thinking" was the only right way? Because I was used to it, I'd grown up with it; because all my life I'd been surrounded by a kind of propaganda. Because the Bible said so and the Bible was the only divinely inspired spiritual writing and therefore could not hold a wrong word.

Of course, certain members of certain non-Christian faiths felt the same way: their religious texts spoke the truth; everything else was heresy or foolishness. Punishable by death, in some cases. And, of course, atheists were just as guilty: No, no, no, they said. You're wrong. I'm right. I know how things are! There's no God! No afterlife! There can't be!

The reality is that none of us really knows how things are. We cling to our theories because they help us get through the day; they explain the inexplicable; they give us the comfort of the company of like-minded souls.

How did the Bible put it? "For now we see through a glass, darkly."

Amen.

We returned to the hotel to discover that the place was booked.

"No room at the inn," Jesus quipped, of course, and the clerk shot him the nastiest look.

I suppose the outlet stores had drawn a lot of visitors, or maybe there was a musical event in town that night; I didn't ask, just told the clerk that Jesus would stay with me and he could add any extra charges to my bill. This drew another not-so-kind look.

I wasn't keen on sharing the room. I liked my privacy, my peace, my alone time, and felt particularly in need of it after our dinner conversation. I was sure that, just as Jesus knew where I'd be stopping for the night and where I'd be having dinner, he knew that there would be no extra room for him. I was beginning to see a pattern. Not only was he challenging some of my most securely held ideas about history, he was working things so that I was being continually pushed out of other comfort zones. I'd been anticipating a nice solitary road trip, lots of thinking time. No.

I'd been anticipating a life without time in jail cell. No again.

I'd been anticipating, especially after the upsetting conversation at Sizzle, some private time to speak with my wife by telephone. No, a third time. And as we walked from the elevator toward the room, I remembered his fasting idea. No to breakfast the next day apparently. No to lunch.

I bought a bag of chips from the vending machine.

We settled in. I assumed my usual position—back on the floor, legs hooked up over the mattress—and he sat quietly, in meditation I suppose, in the armchair near the window. I was thinking of ways I might call home—step into the bathroom, or out into the hotel parking lot. But the phone rang and I drew it out of my pocket and answered.

"Weren't you going to call?"

"Sure I was, Hon. I'm just, I just got back to the hotel and I'm stretching a little."

"Is it okay?"

"Fine, great. Two beds instead of one, but it's great."

"What did you have for supper?"

"Indian, you?"

"I made eggplant parm. Not so much fun eating alone. I miss the girls."

"Same here."

"What's wrong, Eddie Val, you sound funny."

"Nothing's wrong. I'm just upside down."

"Is somebody there with you!"

"No, hon," I said, and then, "Yes, I'm sorry, yes."

"Well God dammit!" she said, and the line went dead.

I took a deep breath and began to count. It was my fault, I knew that. The "No, hon," had been a lie, clearly an instinctive lie, the exact wrong message to send to my wife, even though I'd cancelled it almost immediately. Still, the reflex had been to lie, and she's sensed that, and was right to be angry. I hit the home button and it went to the message machine, so I said, "I'm sorry again. Jesus is with me. Call please."

Thirty seconds later, the phone buzzed. "Sorry," I said.

"He came back?"

"He did, and there was no room at the inn so—"

"Let me talk to him."

I held the phone up in the air. Jesus walked over and took it from me and spoke to Anna Maria as he paced from the bathroom door to the window and back again.

"Listen," was the first thing he said, "it's all right. The lingerie model that was traveling with him for the last few days has gone back to D.C. I've forgiven him. I suggest you do the same because he says nice things about you."

There was a long pause. I closed my eyes. I was feeling the pile of the carpet against the back of my head, and the pressure of the mattress against my calves, and I was thinking that Anna Maria would certainly be expecting something different from the Jesus of her imagination. Someone joking about lingerie models wouldn't fit the mold. It might even make her suspicious, make her think I was traveling with just another guy, an old college friend, a golf buddy, and one with a bad sense of humor on top of it.

The long pause, my mind whirling, and then, "Yes, yes. It was a joke, perhaps a bad one but . . . no, a joke, really. Yes, I am *the* Jesus. Yes, I know it's hard to believe. But you dropped your fork at dinner, that was unlike you. Wiped it clean with your green and gold napkin then changed your mind and fetched a fresh one from the strainer. And you still have a quarter glass of that Barolo left, and your Edward will be slightly bothered that you opened it without him, so drink it up now."

Another pause. I was struggling to picture her, phone in hand, standing in the kitchen, stunned into an atypical silence. Jesus went on pacing. I *was* slightly bothered by the Barolo, which had been a gift from a well off friend for my birthday, and something we should have enjoyed together.

"Yes," Jesus said. And then, "No." And then, "Of course. Your faith is much stronger than your husband's. He's riddled with doubt about me, no matter what I do."

More pacing. His beautiful laugh. "Yes, but I think you should tell him that yourself. Here, I'll hand him the phone. Love you, too."

Jesus handed the phone down to me. "You opened the Barolo?" I said. "Nice."

"You're an ass. He knew I dropped the fork! He knew how much wine I had in my glass! He knew the color of the napkin! You're traveling with God! And you're such an idiot that you keep making him prove himself. Are you truly and really crazy?!!! You should be on your knees asking forgiveness."

"That was quick," I said.

"How much proof do you need?"

The question caught me. Jesus had his back to me and was standing looking out the window. I could hear Anna Maria breathing loudly on the line, the way she did when she was massively frustrated with being married to someone like me. "I'd pretty much gotten there," I said.

"You still don't sound convinced! *Pretty much!!!* What is wrong with you, Eddie?!"

"Nothing," I said. "Too logical, maybe. This is all outside the boundaries of my experience."

"Oh, for God's sake!" she shouted. "Open your mind. Open your heart!"

And she hung up. Then called back five seconds later, said, "I love you, sorry about the Barolo," and hung up again. I set the phone against my chest.

Jesus said, "Everything okay at home?"

~ ~

chapter twenty-seven

When I awoke the next morning, Jesus wasn't in the room. I showered and shaved and as I was packing up, he returned. "Nice breakfast downstairs," he said.

"I thought we were fasting today."

"We are. Let's meditate before we hit the road. You've been neglecting your practice."

"I have. I usually do a half hour every morning."

"Right, you'll be on the road, what? Five days? So today we'll do two-and-a-half hours."

I'd had a lousy sleep. During the night, I must have awakened six or seven times, and each time the first thought that entered my mind was Anna Maria saying, "How much proof do you need?" In the shower that morning I'd come to the conclusion that something was fundamentally wrong with me. Not that I considered myself an evil person; I did not. Despite my various imperfections and failures, I knew I was a decent husband and father, and that I tried to put good into the world, tried not to be too selfish, tried, in the great Catholic tradition, to examine my conscience and my behavior and see how I might alter it for the better. It occurred to me then, not for the first time, that there's more to life than that, that there are countless layers of any person's psychology. Most days, when we swam in the lake near our house, the water would be chilly but comfortable. A minute or two and your body adapted and you could stay in for a while. But if you happened to dive down eight or ten feet, you encountered another layer of chill entirely.

The mind, I decided, was like that, except there was layer upon layer upon layer, all of it laid down in geological fashion—to choose a better metaphor—by the years of your upbringing. And—who knew?—perhaps by countless earlier incarnations. It had seemed to me for a long time that the vicissitudes of daily life—what the great modern monk and writer Thomas Keating called 'our spiritual homework'—served to scrape away the top layers and lift the others into the light. Anything—someone blaring the horn at you in traffic, an illness, an argument with your spouse, a dashed hope, a critical review or unexpected illness—could force you to face a part of your mental geology that you'd been able to keep buried until that point. Maybe that was the purpose of suffering, harsh as it seemed. Maybe we were such stubborn creatures that, if our lives went along unruffled, we'd refuse to consider the possibility that we might need to make adjustments. Maybe we were afraid to drill down into that vein of precious ore that Jesus had mentioned.

What occurred to me in the shower, pressed as I was by my wife's question, was the notion that, at some profound and very subtle level, I felt unlovable. Or at least unworthy. Even Anna Maria's warmth (and I feel I've given an unfair picture of her here; she's actually incredibly kind and loving . . . though sometimes not as much on the telephone) and the love of my daughters couldn't completely salve some hidden wound. I suddenly remembered another line from Merton: "Modern man doesn't believe that even a God could love him." The truth was that, while Jesus had certainly pushed me outside my comfort zone, irritated me, puzzled me most of the time, he had been offering an unexpected friendship. What was it about me that prevented me from simply accepting that? What if some great spiritual figure, some prince or princess of love, climbed into your car one April morning? And then showed you, repeatedly, that he or she had some extraordinary powers and wasn't out to steal from you, or trick you, or convince you to do anything beyond accept the fact that you were worthy of a brief visit from the beyond? What would you do?

What I did was agree to the 2.5-hour meditation without complaint of any kind. Well, there was an interior complaint, a loud chorus of it, but when Jesus moved a pillow from bed to floor, and sat cross-legged on it, and then suggested I'd be more comfortable in the armchair, I didn't fight him.

But, however . . . but, however, agreeable as I was, on some level, to allowing myself to be pushed out of another comfort zone, as soon as I sat in the armchair and closed my eyes, up rose the complaints from another level of the mental geology. Two and a half hours! It was crazy, ridiculous! I had places to go, things I wanted to see. I had to be in Arkansas by that evening and we were still several hours away!

And no eating?!

These complaints linked themselves smoothly to thoughts about the conversation with Anna Maria, and then to wondering if the hotel maid would interrupt us. Had we hung out a Do Not Disturb sign? Did I have a five-dollar bill to leave her as a tip? What had I done with those potato chips? Was having a few chips cheating, or just the idea of cheating? Were they almost the same? I was hungry. Was the breakfast downstairs good, or had Jesus been teasing me? Why had he gotten into my car in the first place? Who was he, really? What had he done with the rosary and the Calipari book? Was I hallucinating?

Losing my mind? Was I subconsciously nervous about discussing a novel with Buddha in the title in front of a congregation of Protestants? Would they laugh at my accent? Was my older daughter okay over there in Southeast Asia? How much time had passed? Was I a fool? Was Anna Maria naive? What was Jesus's mind like?

And on and on and on and on and on.

I'd catch myself and try to return to the moment.

The mind would skitter off again.

I'd return.

More skittering, some of it logical, some of it about food, some of it absurd.

I'd return.

Eventually, a certain amount of settling occurred. Instead of an Interstate of thoughts at rush hour, my mind began to resemble an Interstate at six a.m. Then four a.m. Then a two-lane highway. Then the Interstate again. Then the two-lane highway on a quiet evening. For about ten seconds it was the gravel road to Mason's house, and I was standing there, not moving. Then I was thinking about Mason and Emma and Ellory and a minute or two passed in complete distraction.

Return.

This was the drill, and from decades of practicing, I knew it very well. I did not see any visions. My mind did not go blank, except, perhaps, for a few seconds here and there. I kept doing it because I knew by then, after all those years, that there were layers of psychological sediment that needed to be dug up, and exposing them to the light of meditation would be the start of cleaning out whatever poisons might be lurking there. I had faith in that, if nothing else.

There were stretches of relative peace, and stretches of restlessness, but somewhere after the hour and a half mark a pleasant calm settled over me and I cruised along the two-lane highway on a motorcycle, with only the occasional car hurrying past.

Eventually, I heard Jesus stretch, then stand up. I opened my eyes. For one second I thought I saw, not a halo exactly, but a faint glow surrounding him. One second.

"Let's hit the road," he said. "It's eleven a.m. and I believe there's one more place you want to see before we get to Little Rock."

There was.

~ 🕊 ~

chapter twenty-eight

I had been a sophomore in high school when Martin Luther King was killed. There were riots all over the country, America burning on the news every night, an immense frustration and fury pouring into the streets. At that point in my life I had exactly one African American friend, and if I hadn't gotten a scholarship to a Catholic prep school, the number would have been zero. Racial segregation was so pronounced in those years in America, maybe especially around Boston, that black people simply did not venture into our small city, and we simply did not venture into Boston's black neighborhoods. But on April 4, 1968 you didn't have to have a lot of interaction with African American culture to realize that something hideous had happened, something to push you—whatever the color of your skin—into another dimension of possibility. Yes, black people had been being tortured and murdered in America from the 1600s—we all knew that—but this was modern America, a famous man, a minister, someone who hadn't just talked about fairness and kindness, but put his life on the line to promote those things. And these were the enlightened late Sixties. And now he'd been murdered in the light of day and his killer had not yet been caught.

As I mentioned earlier, just before going to bed on the eve

of my departure for Arkansas, I'd gotten out my dog-eared Rand McNally and scouted out possible routes. I wasn't sure what I might find along the road, but I knew I wanted to stop in two places: Merton's monastery, and the Lorraine Motel.

I'd heard that the motel had been turned into a museum, and guessed it would be a simple memorial like others I'd seen—a roped-off bedroom, you could stand in the doorway, spend a few seconds looking at the open Bible or a pair of shoes on the floor, let your imagination take in the moment, and move on. Still, I was drawn to see it.

On a glorious spring day, guided by the magical GPS, Jesus and I left I-65 and drove through part of downtown Memphis, took a couple of side streets, and ended up in a large parking lot presided over by men who politely guided you to an open space. From there it was a short walk to the entrance, more blacks than whites, but men, women, and children of all races and ages moving along the sidewalk. On a nearby corner several people stood behind a large banner that said:

BOYCOTT THE CIVIL RIGHTS MUSEUM NOW
If you agree with spending $27 million
to celebrate death and violence
ENTER
STOP!
If you feel the money should be used to help the poor and needy

I took a photo of it and texted it to my daughters.

We walked on by. I paid for both Jesus's ticket and my own and then we entered a world of such incredible sorrow that it has left a mark on me to this day.

The entire motel had been turned into a series of exhibits, and it wasn't just a museum of King's legacy, but of the history of black people in America—everything from recordings made to sound like the horror of the slave ships to modern day movements for justice. There were no Gaps. Room by room, historical fact by historical fact, we read America's history book, open to some of its worst pages. Rape, lynching, beatings, a mockup of the Woolworth lunch counter, a piece of the burned bus that had held the Freedom Marchers. Photos, video, audio. We went through it slowly and somberly, spending over an hour there, and when we emerged into daylight and stood for a while near the vintage cars parked out front—cars in which King and his entourage had traveled, all I could say to Jesus was "Why?"

He stood there beside me, leaning on the barrier, looking up at the balcony where King had died, and said nothing.

"Why is there evil? What is the purpose of it, the reason behind it?"

Nothing.

I couldn't seem to stop. "You know, of course, that this is what makes it so hard to believe in any kind of loving God. What kind of God would allow this?"

He turned his eyes to me for a moment then looked at the motel again. It occurred to me that, if he was who he said he was, and if things had happened the way they were reported to have happened, then I was demanding an answer of a being who was without sin and had been tortured and murdered. Even then, I couldn't stop. "I want God to be fair," I said.

He blinked.

"If it's all set up, as you say, then these people must have done something to deserve their misery. What, then? They were all racists in a past lifetime and needed to go through hell in order to understand that they'd been evil? Kids who get cancer? Friends—good people—who die of ALS? Millions slaughtered in a war, or starved to death in a famine? The Jews who died in the death camps? The kids killed at Stoneman Douglas High and all those other places?"

"My Lord, my Lord, why have you forsaken me?" he said at last.

"Even your faith was shaken then, okay. But can you give me some kind of answer for it, something to hold onto? Something beyond what they used to say to us in Sunday School: we have free will?"

"You do have free will."

"I would like something more, if you don't mind."

"Why do you meditate?" he asked me after another few seconds.

"Why? I don't know."

"I would like more than 'I don't know'. Why do you meditate?"

"I guess because I have a sense—maybe it's fear, maybe wishful thinking—that there's something else beyond what my rational mind and my senses tell me."

"Why do you think that?"

"I watched my daughters being born. I watch the sun go down. I have a birdfeeder outside the window of the room where I write, and I watch the birds. The ocean, my own breath, the leaves coming out in spring. I get a sense of something . . . larger."

He nodded.

"Not enough," I said. "That doesn't explain," I waved my arm at the building in front of us. "This."

"You were patient today in the long meditation."

"Right."

"Extend that sense of patience."

"Still not enough. Give me something to hold onto here."

He sighed and looked at me. "It's not simple," he said.

"I'm not asking for simple."

Another sigh. "Humans—self-centered creatures that you are—cannot learn, cannot make spiritual progress without suffering. Suffering, pain, misfortune, disappointment, frustration, illness—those things are endured for various reasons. Yes, in some cases, it is a consequence for having done evil in a past life. Yes, in some cases, a person is born black, or female, or poor, or rich, or ill, because he or she wasn't compassionate enough to members of those groups in a previous life. But it can also be true that a particularly courageous and generous spirit chooses a difficult life—as my friend Martin did, for instance—in order to spare another beloved spirit or spirits a degree of pain, in order to inspire or soothe other sufferers. Are you familiar with the idea of the *bodhisattva?*"

"Yes, some Buddhists—"

"Martin was a *bodhisattva.*"

"But still."

"Lastly, some people choose to put more suffering into a single lifetime in order to get finished with it, and others choose to stretch that suffering out over a number of lifetimes. A matter of preference." He paused and stared at the motel balcony. "And these explanations are very simplistic. The whole pattern of suffering and pleasure is much more complex. I've given you the equivalent of the leaves on one sapling. The world is covered with forests, and each leaf corresponds to a piece of the truth here." He burned his eyes into me. "Satisfied?"

"But why are we made this way? Why do we need to suffer in order to learn?"

"Why did Adam eat the apple?"

"I don't know."

"Lack of humility. A kind of greed. A kind of hubris. It is part and parcel of the human configuration."

"We're a sad species. But why?"

He glanced at me again and then back at the balcony. "No one remains on the human plane forever."

"Thank God," I said, trying for a joke.

Jesus smiled, sadly it seemed. "Work out your salvation with diligence, that's my advice. Beautiful as human life can be, it's a kind of prison cell." He turned away from the motel. "And now let's go back to the car and drive on. Unless you want to be late for your talk."

~ ❦ ~

chapter twenty-nine

Anna Maria had texted, asking if I was all set for getting to Little Rock that night, and letting me know she'd made a reservation at a special place. She gave the name and address of the special place, wished me good luck on the talk, and ended her text with, "BELIEVE!".

I was starting to get a little nervous—not about the talk itself, but about getting there on time. Before one of these presentations, as mentioned, I like to have a few hours to myself. What I do, during those hours, is shower and meditate and stretch a bit, play music from YouTube, favorite songs that put me in a certain mood. John Hiatt's "Buffalo River Home," Lady Gaga's "A Million Reasons," Dire Straits's "Sultans of Swing." Garth Brooks, Led Zeppelin, Arkansas' own Lucinda Williams, The Temptations, Junior Walker and the All Stars, old Springsteen. But it was past noon by then, and, while we were only three hours from Little Rock, Jesus had said we had a stop to make, and I was hoping the fast would end by late afternoon and I'd be able to take a little nourishment. The last thing I wanted was to pass out on the stage and have to tell the kind people who'd arranged the talk, "Well, I was weak because Jesus made me fast."

Jesus told me to take State Route 70 rather than I-40 because the Interstate in that section was filled to overflowing with tractor trailers. Trying to leave Memphis behind, I made two wrong turns, but then found Route 70 and kept the Camry at three miles an hour over the speed limit. Even the nastiest small-town cop wasn't going to stop someone for three miles an hour over the speed limit.

Almost from the first mile, I liked that road. Flat, straight, running through rice and soybean fields with old feed stores and storage bins on the shoulders and a sense of the earth you never feel on the raised and too-busy superhighways. We'd gone along for a bit when Jesus said, "You're a writer. Talk to me about metaphor."

I was sure he knew the definition, but I played along. "I think of a metaphor as the opposite of literal. A word, or an image, that stands for something it really isn't but gives you a different way of thinking about it."

"For example."

"For example, right now the sun's laying down a blanket of gold over these fields. There's no blanket, and no gold. It's a metaphor."

"Ah," he said, in a way that bothered me. Because I hadn't eaten, maybe. He lowered his window and let in some fresh air. It smelled like just-cut grass. "I didn't tell you where I went after I left Choden."

"Right, you didn't even really tell me why you left her."

"I left her because she felt she'd taught me everything she could. From northern India I headed further north and east, to Tibet, because I'd heard wonderful things about the people there, and the teachings, and I wanted to see for myself. What do you know about the place?"

"Dalai Lama. Big Mountains. Chinese genocide."

He grunted. "It was a difficult journey. I went along the

southern edge of the Himalayas—spectacularly beautiful land—as far as Kathmandu, and then over the mountains to a place called SangSang. You can still find it on a good map. The name hasn't changed. Two years, it took me."

"So by now you're how old?"

"Mid-twenties."

"Prime of life."

"Physically, perhaps, but not spiritually. I still didn't feel quite . . . what's the word?"

"Ripe," I suggested.

"Exactly. Choden's teachings had lifted me to a new level, but they'd also awakened me to the understanding that there were so many levels, even on the human plane. Deeper and deeper states of meditation. In SangSang, I found to my surprise that monks in a certain monastery had been expecting me. Apparently, their ancient writings predicted that a Jew from the West would arrive one day, wearing a gray scarf with a bit of blood on it. Choden had given me the scarf as a going away present, and just that day I'd cut myself on my left cheek", he pointed to the scar there—"when a piece of ice slid from a roof and hit me. They welcomed me, gave me a few days to recuperate from the long journey, and then a monk named Kukkun Rinpoche began to initiate me into their most secret teachings. His order wasn't nearly as austere as the Essenes had been. No fasting, no lifetime commitment. You stayed until you felt you'd learned what you had to learn, and then you were free to go out into the world, marry and have children if you felt called to such a life. Find a job, and so on."

"No fasting," I said. "Sign me up. And I've heard a lot about 'secret teachings' but can't imagine what they could be."

"The aforementioned magic."

"Okay."

"I studied with Kukkun Rinpoche for another several years. Sometimes he and I and one or two others would climb into the high mountains and stay there for a week or two."

"I'm afraid to ask: What did you do for food and shelter?"

"We took a little food and water with us. We didn't need much. We slept where we could. Caves, high fields. Once Kukkun Rinpoche slept on a glacier with only a blanket wrapped around him, and we all did the same. . . . Don't try this at home," he said, and laughed.

"What happens?"

"What do you mean?"

"I mean, when you're at that level of attainment, or whatever the word is, and you go off like that and hardly eat anything and sleep on ice. Or when you went out into the desert for forty days. I've always wondered what happens, what it's like."

"You are immersed."

"In what? What does it feel like?"

"Imagine the greatest physical pleasure on earth."

"Imagining."

"And imagine the greatest emotional pleasure, the birth of your children, for instance."

"Got it, the two pleasures are linked, by the way, in my mind."

"By design. Now imagine them at the same time and multiplied by a factor of a hundred but with no sense of you, yourself, feeling that pleasure. The 'you' is simply immersed in it."

"Incredible."

"And what you want to do after that, all you want to do is *give*. To try and lead others to that place, and to give. For yourself you want exactly nothing."

~ ~

chapter thirty

Here's how I knew I hadn't reached that level:

I wanted to eat.

And I wanted to get to Little Rock on time.

Not far beyond Forrest City on SR 70, Jesus told me to turn onto a numbered side road. Somewhat concerned, I did that, and following his instructions, headed off into the fields. I am not allowed to give the number of the road here, to mention the towns we went through, and I'm certainly not permitted to give out the address of the person we visited. Suffice it to say, we drove through the Delta's rice and bean fields, with levees to either side, and storage bins, and hoses and pumps and small trucks, and here and there old wood-sided houses with a big shade tree out front and a porch and the sense of the passage of time. I'm not someone who glorifies the past. Many of the things that happened in those places a hundred or two hundred years ago would have horrified and disgusted me. At the same time, a wood-frame house with peeling paint and a rusted old Studebaker in the yard does something for me that no gleaming 90-story New York City apartment building could ever do. The ultra modern world, with its voice-recognition software and Russian hackers, its rush and glitz and advertising madness, often seems to me the antithesis to the spiritual world. At least the people in the houses we passed once had a chance to sit still and look out at life and possibly even come to believe there was some force at work that was greater than the human mind. Yes, there were horrors then, and particular horrors on that fertile landscape, and some of those horrors had led to the Lorraine Motel and what happened there. I'm not sentimental about those days. I only wonder, for all its many benefits, what modernity has cost us.

Speaking of the passage of time, with each minute I was growing a little more worried about arriving in Little Rock on schedule. The people who'd invited me had been kind to do so, and the money was important to my family, so the very last thing I wanted was to arrive late, or—God forbid—miss the event entirely. I said this to Jesus, three different times. "Don't worry, don't worry," he replied, but I did worry. In fact, one of the hidden flaws in my programming that I'd noticed over the past few years was how *much* I worried, how often I envisioned a negative outcome, how intensely I feared being late—by so much as three minutes—for a dentist appointment or dinner with friends. It was a weird mix of negative projection and pride in being punctual and so, of course, Jesus was pushing my face down into that muck and making me look at it.

Despite the sense of rush building in my arteries and veins, I stayed close to the speed limit. No more jail time for me. No more blinking blues in the mirror. Jesus, calm as ever, started to talk.

"There are two problems with these states of mind," he said. "The first—as you've no doubt noticed, even at your level of meditation—is that there's a pleasure associated with the quiet mind. It's almost physical, isn't it? And so, like any pleasure, it can become addictive. You can start to engage in meditation, not as a spiritual exercise, but in the same way you'd eat chocolate, or smoke marijuana, or indulge in sex. Pleasure is fine. It's designed, like road signs, to guide you toward something beyond itself. If you sink too far into it, however, if you indulge to an excessive degree, then you're just enjoying reading the signs, you're not going anywhere, do you see?"

"I think so."

"And the second potential problem, for a devoted meditator or any devout person, is that you start to believe you are special, so much different than others, so far superior. Just another trick of the ego."

We approached an old man on an old bicycle, pedaling along the old road as if he had an eternity to arrive at his destination. For no particular reason, I tooted the horn at him as we passed, and he raised his left arm in a friendly wave.

"Is the ego the same as the devil then?"

"Bravo, Edward!"

"Thanks. So we could substitute 'ego' for 'Satan' in the Bible—during your time in the desert, for example, and pretty much be on the right track?"

"Exactly the right track. Wonderful!"

"Thanks."

"This was the other lesson Kukkun Rinpoche taught me—not to be proud of our meditative states, not to indulge in them. They aren't an end in themselves, but simply a means to enable us able to give more to the world, to escape the prison of self-consciousness."

"So why didn't he leave the monastery and go around feeding people or something, healing the sick?"

"Because he was already giving to the world the greatest gift that could be given. He was teaching the most important lessons. That was his place in the world, not giving food or healing."

"No women, though, right?"

"There were famous women teachers there, too, like Choden, but, yes, the men and women were separated. Both were treated with respect, however. The female teachers in that town were revered. But let me continue, because we're running short on time. I stayed with Kukkun Rinpoche at SangSang until I was twenty-eight, and then one day he called me to him and sat me in front of him and we meditated for a time and then he told me this: "Now you are ready. Go back to the place where you came to earth. Do what you are destined to do. And then return here." And he touched me on the forehead in the same way I touched Todd in the cell, do you remember?"

"Yes."

"That's my story then. That's the filling of the Gap."

"And you walked back to Palestine and were crucified."

"Yes."

"But what about the "And then return here," comment?"

Instead of answering, Jesus said, "We've arrived. Turn left here, on this street, and you'll see it."

At first, I didn't see anything. The street was flat and unlined, fields to either side. Four or five hundred yards farther along I noticed a pair of oak trees, and tucked in behind them a shack. Unpainted boards. Sagging porch. All of it set up on concrete blocks and looking like a thirty-mile-an-hour wind would blow it into matchsticks . . . and this was tornado country.

A confession: Despite everything, all the lessons, all the progress I felt I'd made in the past day or two, Satan, or Ego, was still with me. I looked at the shack and found myself thinking: Perfect place for a gullible northerner, weakened by lack of food, to be killed and buried.

There was no driveway, only a patch of bare dirt out front.

No other cars visible.

"Nobody's home," I said, and my voice broke.

Jesus didn't speak. When I stopped the car, he got out and walked toward the porch, but I sat there behind the wheel, the last threads of doubt, like some Lilliputian system of restraint, holding me. "Believe," Anna Maria had texted, but she wasn't sitting there, in the vast Arkansas Delta, down a road that saw maybe three cars in a month, being asked to walk into a dilapidated shack with a person she'd known for four days.

As Jesus approached, the front door of the house opened. I thought I could see a person there, a very small person it seemed, though, with the tree trunks, porch posts, Jesus, and the half-open door, I didn't have a clear view. He turned and waved for me to join him. I could feel the fibers of doubt holding me. All I had to do was back the car out onto the road and leave. I'd make it to Little Rock with plenty of time to have a shower and prepare, and Jesus, I knew, would take care of himself. Whatever he and the small person—was it a child? Mason's daughter, Ellory maybe?—had planned for me, good or bad, would never come to pass. I decided to say another Hail Mary. I'd gotten as far as, "Hail Mary, full of grace," when the small person came across the porch, down the two uneven wooden steps, and started across the dirt yard toward me. It was a woman, tiny, black-haired, with the facial structure of the South American native people. She seemed unthreatening. I opened the door and she smiled and said, "Being afraid won't get you very far."

Not the most comforting line. And something about her made me uneasy. Small as she was, she had the air of someone who never in her life had taken the smallest amount of abuse from any living person. There were three dime-sized gold earrings in the lobe of her left ear, and a tattoo on the inside of her right forearm. A panther, it looked like.

"Hi," I said, to stall for time.

"Hi, I'm Luisa, an old old friend of Jesus. Please come into my house."

Sometimes we make decisions, poorly considered decisions, simply to avoid embarrassment. That was one of those times. I had two options: get out and follow Luisa into the house, or slam the door, put the car in reverse, and speed away. In the few seconds I had to decide, I imagined calling home that night and explaining to Anna Maria that I'd left Jesus at a shack in the Arkansan wilderness because I was afraid of a woman about the size our daughters had been in fifth grade.

So I got out.

Luisa immediately hooked her arm inside mine and, talking all the way in a soothing voice, led me to her front door. "Everything will be fine, you'll see. There's no need for worry. Jesus is my friend. The house looks poorly from the outside, but inside it's nice."

I felt like I was at a sales pitch for a Belizean time share. In another second, someone—Luisa's muscular boyfriend waiting inside, perhaps—was going to shove a pen into my hand, slide a contract in front of me and point to the dotted line. Or do something much worse.

But there was no muscular boyfriend inside. No husband. No girlfriend or kids. No one. As she'd promised, the interior was not a reflection of the exterior. In fact, it was weirdly modern, with shining hardwood floors, granite kitchen countertop, and carefully painted walls with framed photographs of various Andean landscapes. Besides my anxiety, hunger, and worry about getting to Little Rock on time, the only problem was olfactory. Luisa was cooking something on the kitchen's gas stove, and it smelled like a rat was being boiled—not that I've ever boiled a rat. A nasty combination of smokiness and rubber. Maybe it wasn't from the pot on the stove; maybe her husband was an eccentric artist, working in a back room singeing old car tires and gluing them to bloodstained plywood, but it was awful. She didn't seem to notice the smell and neither did Jesus. My empty stomach noticed. I felt a bad clenching there and was preparing my "I'm not hungry, but thank you," defense, as absurd as that might have been for a man who'd missed breakfast and lunch.

"Please, sit," Luisa was saying, but at first, I didn't see any place to sit. Although she'd escorted me into what I supposed was a living room, there was no TV, no couch, and no chairs, only a circular glass table maybe five feet across, with three round cushions beside it. After a moment, I realized I was supposed to sit on one of the cushions. Jesus was smiling. He lowered himself onto a cushion and sat cross-legged, effortlessly. I am not young, not a yogi, not God or God's representative on earth. Plus, I suffer from an inherited, systemic arthritis that causes my tendons to become inflamed and requires twice-daily doses of medicine and twice-monthly self-administered injections. For those reasons, lowering myself onto the cushion was accomplished without panache. I knelt and more or less slanted my hips and butt sideways onto the cushion which tilted beneath me and tossed me off to one side. I hoisted myself up with both hands, shifted into the new position, and crossed my ankles beneath the table. One knee rested uncomfortably against a metal leg. Instead of moving myself, which would have been precarious, I took hold of the table and shifted it left eight inches. I was settled. I looked at Jesus. He was smiling. "Not that hungry," I said, and he laughed.

"It's just tea," Luisa announced from the kitchen, and I could hear her taking cups from a cupboard and settling them onto saucers there.

It should be remembered that recent headlines had carried accounts of expatriate Russians, living in London, who'd been assassinated by Putin's thugs. With poison. Tea was the vehicle. Working against this particular concern was the idea that anyone preparing a poisonous tea would never make it smell like poisonous tea.

Jesus had closed his eyes and folded his hands on the glass tabletop. Luisa was humming, or chanting. While the tea was steeping, she brought in a plastic bucket—the kind of bucket you might see in a custodian's storage closet—and placed it on the floor beside me. I wanted to ask why she had done that but could not make myself speak. Another half minute and she was carrying in three full teacups—a delicate porcelain set not unlike one my mother's mother had owned. An Englishwoman, a tea lover, she'd been fond of welcoming her guests with freshly brewed tea and Oreo cookies. But her tea had smelled nothing like this. Nothing. The steam wafting up toward my mouth and nose was unbelievably disgusting. I couldn't help myself—I peeked into the cup to see if there were any rat parts in the bottom. "So what's this?" I managed to say.

Luisa took her place on the third cushion and smiled. She reached up and tucked a strand of black hair behind her ear and said, "Vision tea."

"Ah. I've never had it."

She and Jesus both laughed. "It causes us to have visions," she said. "It releases a truth that's winding around deep in our thoughts but cannot quite be expressed."

"A snake," I said foolishly.

She laughed gently. "Sometimes, especially the first few times you try it, it can cause you to vomit, which is why I brought you this." She reached over and touched the top of the plastic bucket. "Please don't be embarrassed if that happens. It might not."

"I've never enjoyed vomiting," I said.

Jesus put his hand on my left shoulder, and I flinched. "You'll be fine by tonight's performance. Clear headed. No worries there."

He and Luisa hooked their index fingers inside the teacup's looped handle. She lifted it to her mouth and took a small sip. "Not too hot."

"The trick for a novice," Jesus told me, "is to drink it all up quickly. It doesn't have a pleasant taste."

"Is it poison?" I asked, and they laughed again.

"Only for the worst among us," Luisa said. "Only for those with evil in their thoughts."

Everybody has a little evil there, I wanted to say, but they'd lifted their cups, and Jesus motioned for me to do the same. "I've been preparing you for this for days," he said, fixing his gaze on me. "For lifetimes." His eyes seemed to be sending forth a beam of light. "Just drink, relax, and go where the tea takes you."

Though I knew I should, I did not have the courage to get up and walk away. All those years of telling our daughters to leave high school parties and sketchy concerts if they had a bad sense about things, all those fatherly lectures were coming back to haunt me in the clearest tones. "I'll try, Dad," Allie had promised after one of those sermons, "but it's not that easy."

"Doesn't matter. If you have a bad feeling, leave."

And now I couldn't leave, and I felt clothed in the robes of a hypocrite. I lifted the cup and tried to breathe out through my nose. "May the spirits shine on us," Luisa said, in the tone of a prayer. They were waiting for me to drink. It was the cannoli scene in *Godfather Part III*. "All my pleasures are finished now,"

Eli Wallach was telling Talia Shire, as she offered him the poisonous cannoli. I opened my mouth and drank the tea down to the bottom and they did the same. I was the only one who vomited, however, immediately and forcefully and cleanly into the mouth of the big bucket.

"It's fine, it's all right," Luisa was saying in a soothing voice.

One moment I was worrying about asking for a napkin to clean my lips, and the next, the room was swirling and tilting and I was riding a roller coaster, upside-down, through the interior worlds. My thoughts no longer took the form of words, but of images, swaths of color like the canvas of a Rothko painting, except that the colors seemed to have particular meanings. There was a stretch of cowardice in a yellow streak across the middle of my vision. There was bold blue, a sense of myself as a powerful spirit, with a dark black band of bravery. Then a flash of red, orange, and pale green, a kaleidoscopic display that seemed, as if in the most vivid of dreams, to be making an insistent argument. But about what? The argument went on, the colors shifting, some sense of a buried truth being unearthed. I could feel what I felt for Anna Maria and the girls, that deep and unshakeable love, presented in a sky as clear and bright as the finest winter day. For a moment, that love seemed the most solid of things, the most dependable, the one image-feeling that underlay the others. And then, behind it, something else, even deeper, a shimmering silvery gold. I could suddenly feel my body in a way I'd never felt it before, the cells vibrating from toenails to eyebrows. A sense of my inner workings—the heart pumping; the organs, so finely tuned, playing in concert with each other. And then, on the heels of this, the exhilaration similar to what a moving piece of music gives you, but in this case a mix of rock and roll and opera, great soaring sweeps of emotion, and so positive that I could feel my lips stretched tight in a smile. *Orgasmic* is not the right word, but I struggle to come up with something more accurate. It was as if all possible pleasures were playing together at once. A great, deep joy took hold of me, the sense that I was absolutely beloved; that, no matter what happened, I would remain safe and at peace. I felt myself turn and look at Jesus. To my shock, my utter astonishment, he'd turned into Buddha, hands in his lap. Eyes closed. The famous small smile at the corners of his lips. The beard and long hair were gone and he was shimmering. I watched, absolutely rapt, as he then morphed into the Jesus in the mural above the nave at St. Anthony's of Padua in Revere. I turned to Luisa, and all smallness had disappeared. She was enormous there, a vapor in pale blues and golds, wavering, oscillating, a feeling flowing from her that made me think of the first moments when Anna Maria had held our girls. There had been such a pure, such an absolute love there. It was a love I couldn't imagine, could not summon, something so innate to her that it almost seemed a vaporous umbilicus connected them. I'll never forget it. That same love poured out of Luisa's eyes and bathed me. I had never felt a happiness like that, one that must have made some kind of physical impression on my brain because I can summon a distinct memory of it even now.

The swirling and shifting slowly, slowly settled and shrank, and I was vomiting repeatedly into the bucket and Jesus was holding the back of my neck and Luisa was holding my hand on the tabletop. And then I seemed to very gradually come back to a more or less normal consciousness. She carried away the bucket and carried back a moistened cloth and tenderly washed my mouth and chin. Jesus was squeezing my neck in a comforting massage. I was shaking my head, very very hungry but not weak, just addled, stunned, shredded. I started to speak, to ask, but Luisa put a finger to my lips and shushed me.

"Now just a brief meditation, and we'll be going along," Jesus said to her. "He has a speaking engagement tonight in Little Rock."

"On what subject?" Luisa asked, and they both laughed, as if it were an inside joke and the subject was well known to them.

I was instructed to close my eyes, and I did so, and for four or five minutes I enjoyed the most peaceful meditation of my forty-year meditative career, one or two thoughts straggling past like small clouds drifting through a clear pastel sky, with long stretches of a kind of echo of the peace I'd felt a few minutes earlier.

When it was finished, we stood up. Because of the aforementioned inherited arthritis, I have particular trouble with the tendons on the outsides of my knees, but they didn't hurt at all. I felt lithe, young, nimble. Luisa brought me a glass of cold water. They stood there and watched as I drank, and then they were embracing each other, and she was embracing me, and I was behind the wheel again and driving back toward SR 70. Just as we reached that road, I seemed to recover the ability to speak. "What on God's earth was that?" I asked.

And Jesus said, "Your mind as it actually is. A preview of the moment of death."

"Nothing to worry about then," I said.

"Not in the slightest."

And on we went through Delta farmland.

~ ~

chapter thirty-one

Shortly after we rejoined Route 70, Jesus said, "Good eating place up ahead on the left. You hungry?"

"I could eat three horses."

"Not on the menu."

"Or some barbecue."

The place Jesus had in mind was called Craig's and it stood only about twenty feet off the dusty edge of SR 70. Addled though my mind and body still were from the experience at Luisa's, I was beginning to understand that the lesson of that particular day—or one of the lessons—was that surfaces deceive. Luisa's house, so shabby-looking from the outside, had an interior that could almost be called luxurious. The person or spirit riding along with me, who called himself Jesus and sometimes looked like the common depictions of Jesus Christ, could, apparently, change himself into Buddha, or Thomas Merton, or a lesbian Asian American golfer, or God knew what else. And Craig's, which, from the dusty, four-car parking space out front, looked like the kind of eatery you'd avoid at all costs, especially if you were traveling with little kids, turned out to offer a plate of barbecue brisket, coleslaw, and beans that should have earned Michelin stars.

You can find it if you drive that road: a little, white, cinder block-and-stucco shack of a place with a red roof and red-trimmed windows, and a glass sign above that looked like it came from the era of Teddy Roosevelt. In short, Craig's would win no prizes for aesthetics—unless, like me, you find beauty in the old and tattered. Inside, it was more of the same: A half dozen Formica tables and mismatched chairs scattered around a linoleum-clad floor; a counter where you ordered; a menu above the door to the kitchen in black clip-on letters.

I had never been hungrier in my life. Jesus and I, the only customers at that late lunch hour, ordered, and took seats at one of the tables, and I kept looking anxiously at the swinging door that led to the kitchen, hoping it wasn't one of those places that sport a note on the menu saying: *Good food takes time. At Craig's, we cook everything the old fashioned way* . . . etcetera.

But it was.

To distract myself, because my mind was absolutely roiling with questions, and because, to add another strange twist to the day, the African American woman behind the counter had clearly seen something in Jesus that most of the people we encountered did not see (while he was ordering his ribs and beans, she'd reached out to touch his arm, tentatively, as if he were an apparition and not flesh and bone; it reminded me instantly of the way Ellory had first touched him), I asked him a question that had been rattling around in my brain since we drove away from Luisa's. "What do I do now?"

"You do what Mary Catherine suggested on the golf course."

"Embrace my life, exactly as it is."

He nodded, glanced at the kitchen door as if he, too, were hungry, then brought his fiery dark eyes back to me. "You play your role in this life with courage and complete sincerity. Your role as husband, father, friend, citizen, writer. Tonight, you give your talk at the church, and you do that with as much humility and presence as you can summon. In short, you be yourself."

I cannot explain how, exactly, but this advice felt as if it had its roots in the place I'd traveled to at Luisa's. It was as if the vision tea had shown me . . . well, *heaven* would not be too strong a word. The place where my destiny, our destinies, were designed. The brain trust of life, the center of all universes.

As if he could read my thoughts, Jesus said, "Try to imagine the number of fish and other creatures in all the oceans. Multiply that times a trillion and you would have something like the possible characteristics of any human birth. Nationality, race, gender, size, shape, facial structures, bodily makeup, financial standing, health details, plus the innumerable and completely unique aspects of any given psychology. And then, of course, you have the trillions of other possible incarnations that are not human—insects, reptiles, birds, animals, fish. And then you have the other universes, world without end."

"Mind boggling," I said. "But how does it work? How is it decided, the place you land in all that?"

"This is where 'free will' comes in, my Edward. Each soul has some say in his or her next incarnation. The purer the soul, the greater the say. Some spirits are new to the human realm. Over millennia, they've worked their way through the various sentient realms, from a flea—just to choose one example—through snakes, fish, birds, beasts, and finally have attained rebirth in human form. Some of those souls are pure, but many of them are crude, and so new to the freedoms and powers of humanity that all they can think of is taking advantage of the pleasures human life affords. They rape, they steal, they accumulate vast sums, they may even kill, or, obsessed by power, attain to positions of leadership and ignite wars, and so on. The suffering they cause results sometimes in their being reverted to more primitive forms of life all over again: they have to spend another few million lifetimes in the lower realms, suffering in untold ways, for what seems like an eternity, and then, sometimes, once they reach humanity again, they appreciate the great blessing that is human life, and life in general. They are less selfish, more kind. Are you following me?"

"Yes," I said, glancing at the kitchen door. Another five minutes, I told myself, and I was going to go back there and eat the food right off the grill, future lifetimes be damned.

"At the higher, *cleaner* levels—for lack of better terms—you have some say, some input. You, yourself, realize the lessons you must learn, and so you choose, or have some agency in choosing, the womb into which you shall be born."

"And for the others, God makes the choice."

"I dislike the word 'God' but, yes, the Divine Intelligence makes that choice. But it happens according to Divine Law, not the whims and moods of a man in a long white beard. It happens as automatically as water turning to ice at 31 degrees Fahrenheit. All of it arranged like a complex architectural plan."

"And then what?"

"And then free will comes into play again, because once you are born into that life, you can decide how to behave, how willingly you embrace the lessons—some of which are exceedingly difficult—or how carelessly and fearfully you flee from them. Those decisions, some small, some enormous, will then determine future births."

"According to some computer algorithm."

"It's not the worst comparison. In fact, the minds that developed the computer had a faint touch of memory—like an ink stain on fingers, or the scent of onions on a burlap sack that once held them—of the complexity of the realms beyond this one. That small coloration or scent, that vague subconscious memory, led them to their inventions, as if the human world were a small child mimicking its father's morning shave or mother's hair brushing, carrying a toy suitcase off to 'work', do you see?"

"Yes."

At that moment, thank God, the food was brought to our table. Jesus prayed over it silently. I attacked it without mercy or delay, cutting into the tender brisket with my plastic knife and fork and bringing it, dripping, to my mouth. One taste, and I felt as though an opera of gratitude were being sung in every one of my cells.

"Stunningly good," I said, and then I attacked the coleslaw and beans, and took a long draught of the iced root beer. "But life can seem so unfair."

"*Seem* is the operative word. Remember what I was saying about the concept of bodhisattva."

"The idea that someone who could have remained free of rebirth and all its suffering decides to come to earth for the benefit of others."

"Exactly. It's more complicated than that brief description, but what you said is essentially true. 'Angels' or 'saints', Christians call them."

"I think whoever is cooking in the kitchen is a bodhisattva."

"She is, in actual fact."

I finished off the meal with a piece of chocolate meringue pie, something I'd never heard of before. I sat back in the chair and sighed, my belly distended, worries about making it on time to Little Rock temporarily set aside. Jesus was still only about halfway through his plate of ribs, lifting them one by one to his mouth, nibbling delicately, appreciatively, wiping his lips after every mouthful. When he was at last finished, he piled his plastic utensils and napkin on the plate and gazed across the table at me. "You're wondering now where you are in the process. How many more lifetimes you must endure before your liberation from this planet of pain, what you can do to speed things up."

"Yes. I mean, this is a great life I'm having. Lot of illness and some other troubles, but all in all, considering where I could have been born . . . I'm grateful every day."

"Excellent. It doesn't help to think about future lives. A good motto is: "Ten thousand years, straight ahead."

"Right."

"For now, I'd suggest you put a twenty in the tip jar and compliment Eliza on the food. And then, we should really be going. There's a big traffic tie-up on the road to Little Rock."

Jesus went out to the car. I used the bathroom and then thanked the woman at the counter profusely and slipped a folded bill into the jar.

"You're from up north, aren't you," she said.

I admitted that I was and told her there was still a little snow in my yard, in the shady spots.

"See, that I could never live with."

"You get used to things," I told her, and then a mother and her grown daughter came through the door, talking about wedding dresses, and I realized, with a sudden twist of anguish, that I was going to be late for my talk.

~ ~

chapter thirty-two

We traveled on SR 70 only as far as the town of Hazen and then zigged north and rejoined I-40. There were, as Jesus had predicted, a lot of eighteen wheelers, but I was able to go faster than I would have on the side road.

As if the story had been interrupted only minutes before, Jesus said, "When it came time to leave Kukkun Rinpoche, I felt a deep sadness come over me. Life there had become so blissful that it was like—"

"Like tearing yourself away from heaven in order to come to earth," I suggested.

Jesus laughed and looked out the window, turning his face away, so I couldn't see the expression there. "I could so easily have become attached to my life in SangSang. Bliss upon bliss upon bliss. The company of some of the most elevated souls that have ever walked this good earth. You read about my being tempted in the desert, yes? Well, in SangSang there was a terrible temptation of exactly that kind, the temptation to indulge in my own pleasure instead of fulfilling my destiny. To this moment I remember the pain of leaving and starting off on the journey back to Palestine."

"You knew what awaited you there, too."

"I did. But I knew I could cope with that. I had been given

the tools, by Choden, by Kukkun. I'd been born with the tools inside me and they'd shown me how to sharpen them."

"So you weren't afraid?"

"Never."

"And you went back along the Silk Road alone?"

"I had a companion. A female spirit."

"Spirits have genders?!"

"For the duration of a lifetime, yes."

"A lover?"

Silence.

"Sorry," I said. "Not my business."

"It took us almost two years to make the trip back to Palestine. She was from what is now called Pakistan. Her name was Qudrah. Along the route we were afforded hospitality by scores of men and women. Qudrah was a healer, and everywhere we stopped she encountered someone suffering—children, elderly people, all of them suffering with every imaginable illness and affliction. The only thing she requested of them was that they never tell anyone she had cured them."

"Tall order."

"I requested the same, of course, as you know from the Bible. But there were those who could not be quiet."

"What happened to them?"

"Nothing happened to them. Stop thinking in terms of punishment."

"Right."

"She was there at the crucifixion."

"There's no mention of her."

"No mention of so much of what actually happened, before and afterwards. How many paintings of me as a young boy or teenager have you seen in the great museums? Almost none. I'm an infant, and then a grown man. Think about that, my

Edward."

Traffic choked up badly then and brought us almost to a dead stop. I looked at the clock, at the GPS. Twenty-seven miles to go and we had an hour and eighteen minutes before I was supposed to show up at St. Mark's, washed, dressed nicely, and prepared to speak.

"I'm trying to tell you something important and difficult and you're worried about being five minutes late. They can't start without you, you know."

"Sorry."

"I'm not sure you're ready."

"Sorry again, don't punish me."

He let out a one-note laugh, but when he started talking again I had the distinct sense that he'd changed course, or was purposely omitting certain details, and it pained me.

"You're a writer, do you know of a relatively recent novel called *A Flag for Sunrise?"*

I shook my head.

"You should read it. In it, there is a priest character, a Roman Catholic, something of a radical. When asked why he doesn't recite certain prayers, he answers, "I consider them wrongly written down." This is one of the wisest lines in all of American literature. You should ponder it. The Bible is a great work, of course," he went on. "As are the Upanishads, the Vedas, the Sutras, the Koran, the Torah. They are all, in fact, divinely inspired, but there are omissions and bits of propaganda tossed into all of them, errors in certain of the details."

"What happened to Qudrah?"

"Qudrah, like all great spiritual teachers, lived a long life and died peacefully before entering the very depths of old age."

"You died much younger, though," I said.

He ignored me.

"She's now healing and teaching on another plane. There are billions of dimensions to life, states of being that are unimaginable to the human brain. And creation is constantly evolving, changing, expanding. Even your scientists suspect as much."

"My mind can't go there. It's a mush when I start thinking about that. And why did you die so young if spiritual teachers live a long life?"

Jesus fell silent. Someone cut me off. I sighed instead of cursing. After at least a minute, he asked me, "Do you know what a koan is?"

"Sure. A baffling question some Buddhist teachers use to open their students to a new understanding."

"Good. Yes. So here is a koan for you: It comes from Matthew 7:13. After the resurrection, I appear to the disciples. I ask them for something to eat. Now, please tell me: If I were, in actual fact, a resurrected spirit on my way to heaven, why would I ask them for something to eat?"

"I have no idea."

"Ponder it. And now, please, keep a steady speed. Concentrate on driving, and then concentrate on giving the best talk you can give, on loving Anna Maria and your girls—divine and highly evolved creatures, all of them. Concentrate on being kind and generous. On doing your writing, keeping your home, being compassionate to your friends, accepting illness and disappointment and old age and death. Ten thousand years straight ahead. Just play your role here, now, as faithfully as you can. The structure of the universes will take care of itself. You're on the right track, my Edward. You are a good man. Do not worry."

~ ~

chapter thirty-three

Those were the last words Jesus said to me. I pulled into a MacDonald's on the outskirts of Little Rock, slipped into the men's room there, and changed into dress pants, a dress shirt, and good shoes. Washed my face, ran a wet hand through my hair, hurried back outside. When I reached the Camry, I noticed immediately that he wasn't there. His red suitcase was gone. Lying on the passenger-side seat was a note in elegant handwriting:

Good luck tonight, beloved Edward!

For a few seconds I sat there, enveloped in sadness, staring out the windshield at a man on a bench. The man was talking loudly to himself and gesticulating with both hands. A mangy-looking dog trotted up and sat down at his feet, and the man reached down to pet it. I wondered if the man might be Jesus, playing games, taking a new shape for a while to teach someone else a lesson. And then I remembered his last advice. Play your role here, now. My role, that night at least, was to give a talk. I put the car in gear and drove to St. Mark's.

I like giving talks. I enjoy the back and forth with people who care about books and about the Big Questions. I like the attention, too, I admit that, the feeling of being a minor celebrity for an hour. At the same time, I was raised in a place where one of the cardinal sins was thinking too much of yourself (the other cardinal sin was cheapness; I remember my father and uncles fighting over who would pay the restaurant bill, grabbing it from each other, or slipping the waiter money beforehand) and I have tried always to remember that. The truth, of course, is that, beyond a small circle of admirers, I am not famous, nor do I want to be. Apart from these occasional talks, I sit in an upstairs room in part of our house and scrawl words on a yellow legal pad, or tap them into a computer. It's hardly world-changing. And yet, as Jesus reminded me, it is what I do, and the point is to do it as well as possible. Sincerely, he'd said. Humbly. Without being puffed up by the attention, and without shrinking from it. That's the deal.

The good people at St. Mark's had set up everything perfectly—wine and cheese and snacks on a patio for the first hour, mingling and chatting, and then I was led into the church itself and I stood at the pulpit and did my thing. I scanned the crowd, hoping I might see Jesus there, but I did not.

I told the story of how *Breakfast with Buddha* had come to be, tried to make it funny, but not just funny. Afterwards, as planned, there were questions. They ranged from ones I'd heard many times before: "How do you get your ideas?" and "Which of your books is your favorite?" to less familiar ones "You write a lot about food. If you had to have a last meal, like a condemned prisoner, what would it be?"

Familiar or not, I tried to answer each question as well as I could, sometimes joking with the questioner, sometimes going on too long with an answer (I'm a novelist, after all, and we're not known for terseness). It's my favorite part of those presentations, the human connection, the way words on a page can reach people you don't even know. But sometimes there are awkward moments. Near the end of the night, a woman stood up from the third row, the mic was passed to her, and she said, "What gives you the right to have Jesus or Buddha or your other characters tell us what we're doing here? I'm sorry if this seems rude, but who do you think you are?"

She sat down abruptly and there was a bit of muttering in the crowd, and then a pregnant silence.

"It's a good question," I said. "I ask that of myself all the time, and I have moments of feeling worried that some day I'm going to have to answer for those kinds of things. I try not to preach. I hope you don't think I'm doing that here, or doing it in my books. But I feel like we all have a Jesus of Our Imagination, or a Buddha of Our Imagination, or a Krishna or Mohammed or Moses of Our Imagination. We've never met those teachers, we've only read their words and read about their lives. We might have a vivid image of them—from paintings or sculptures or just from the holy books—and I think we all have slightly different interpretations of what they might want of us, what they'd advise. I feel like I have as much right as anyone to imagine Jesus or Buddha, to interpret their teachings for myself. And I'm a writer. I make stories. So in those stories I'm just exerting my right to imagine those great teachers, but it's not like I think I know."

A few people applauded at the back of the room, which embarrassed me slightly and might have made the woman feel badly. So I went on a little bit. "That's a perfectly fair question. I'm glad you asked it."

She was frowning at me.

The mic was passed to a man sitting a few rows behind her and off to the side of the room. He had a shaved head and was wearing a maroon robe, and I worried for a second that he was going to tell me that the way I'd described the Buddhist teachings in the book were all wrong, bad karma, the height of conceit. But he had a big smile on his face, and what he said, in a fairly strong accent, was, "I like these books *wery* much! When we gonna see more?"

"I'm working on that," I said.

"Well work more faster, man!"

The remark brought out a wave of laughter in the church, the sound echoing up into the rafters like a hymn. It seemed like a good place to stop. Just as the person who'd introduced me was coming up to the podium to signal the end of the talk and the start of the book signing, I looked up and saw Anna Maria. She was standing in the doorway between the nave and the vestibule and had apparently been sitting back there the whole time. She offered a lovely wave and flashed me two thumbs-up.

And then the presentation was finished and I was sitting at a table in a nearby room with a line of people waiting to have a book signed. Someone brought me a glass of water and a plate of cookies, and many of the people in line said kind things. A little flood of gratitude washed over me, as it sometimes does at those moments. I could sense Anna Maria standing off to the side, texting the girls. *Dad seems more or less sane,* I imagined her writing. *Call off the intervention.*

~ ~

chapter thirty-four

Afterwards, she and I went out for a nice meal of cioppino and red wine in downtown Little Rock and we shared a tiramisu and decaf coffee for dessert. She looked as beautiful as I'd ever seen her look. Gray hair, green eyes, wondrous smile. "It was so nice of you to send me the plane ticket, Eddie Val," she said. "I was totally surprised, and, this is weird, my mom seemed to really perk up the last couple of days and this morning she told me she was fine, I should go see you, she'd be okay on her own. You're a real romantic sometimes, you know that? A real sweetheart."

I hadn't sent her the ticket, of course. Didn't think she'd be able to make the trip. But, and perhaps this was some kind of sin, all I said at the time was, "Well, I missed you." Which was not a lie.

She wanted to hear all about my conversations with Jesus, and I gave her the report in as much detail as I could, maybe shading things just a bit so I didn't seem like a complete fool. Even though, truth be told, I was feeling that way just then, already sensing that I hadn't made the most of an extremely rare opportunity, had left scores of questions unasked, would be replaying and regretting my fearfulness for the rest of my days on earth.

Later that night, lying in the hotel bed, touching along the length of our naked bodies and drifting toward the world of sleep, Anna Maria said, "Ever since you told me all that at dinner, I can't seem to stop thinking about it. It's crazy, isn't it?"

"What part?"

"The gap. I mean, there's so much we don't know about what really happened. We have the Bible stories, we make them into Christmas carols and sermons and Sunday School lessons, and then we basically just stop wondering about everything."

"Yeah, it's what we do. We all like to think we know."

"Are you going to try to write it all down?"

"He asked me to."

"You should then, Eddie Val. You'll probably get in trouble for some parts of it, with certain people like that woman tonight, but I think you should."

"He gave me a kind of koan to figure out first."

"Tell me."

"Why did Jesus ask his disciples for food after he'd risen from the dead? He was a risen spirit, on his way to heaven. How could he be hungry?"

There was a moment of silence and then Anna Maria said. "That's such a strange thing, isn't it?"

"Among many strange things."

"We'll think about it right before bed every night and maybe we'll dream the answer."

"Sure, great idea. And thanks for coming."

"Glad I could."

"Love you."

"Love you, too, hon," she said.

Some time after that—who knows when exactly?—Anna Maria nudged me rather forcefully, lifting me to the edge of wakefulness. "Eddie Val," she said, "you're jumping all over the place. You're having one of your dreams."

"Sorry," I mumbled.

"Try not to snore if you can, okay?"

"I'll do my best."

A squeeze of the hand, echoes of forty years of love and two other spirits in the room, the dark hotel ceiling, the sound of her breathing.

And then, once more, the gift and the mystery of sleep.

The End

Little Rock, Arkansas, April 6, 2018
Conway, Massachusetts May 1, 2021

Acknowledgments

My heartfelt thanks to Peter Sarno and the people at PFP for their hard work, to Robert Braile for his careful reading of a draft of this novel, and to the kind souls at St. Mark's in Little Rock, for their hospitality.

About the Author

Roland Merullo is an awarding-winning author of 26 books including 19 works of fiction: *Breakfast with Buddha,* a nominee for the International IMPAC Dublin Literary Award, now in its 21st printing; *The Talk-Funny Girl,* a 2012 ALEX Award Winner and named a "Must Read" by the Massachusetts Library Association and the Massachusetts Center for the Book; *Vatican Waltz* named one of the Best Books of 2013 by *Publishers Weekly*; *Lunch with Buddha* selected as one of the Best Books of 2013 by *Kirkus Reviews*; *American Savior,* a Massachusetts Center for the Book, "Honor Award" winner; *In Revere, In Those Days* a Booklist Editors' Choice Recipient; *Revere Beach Boulevard* named one of the "Top 100 Essential Books of New England" by the *Boston Globe*; *A Little Love Story* chosen as one of "Ten Wonderful Romance Novels" by *Good Housekeeping* and *Revere Beach Elegy* winner of the Massachusetts Book Award for nonfiction.

Merullo's essays have appeared in numerous publications including the *New York Times, Yankee Magazine, Newsweek,* the *Boston Globe, the Philadelphia Inquirer, Boston Magazine, Reader's Digest, Good Housekeeping,* and the *Chronicle of Higher Education.* Merullo's books have been translated into German, Spanish, Portuguese, Korean, Croatian, Chinese, Turkish, Slovenian, Bulgarian, Czech, and Italian.

He has been a frequent contributor of commentary for National Public Radio affiliates.

Some Other Books by PFP / AJAR Contemporaries

a four-sided bed - Elizabeth Searle

A Little Love Story - Roland Merullo

Ambassador of the Dead - Askold Melnyczuk

Big City Cat: My Life in Folk Rock - Steve Forbert

Deadly Sweet - Sterling Watson

excerpt from Smedley's Secret Guide to World Literature - Askold Melnyczuk

Fighting Gravity - Peggy Rambach

Girl to Girl: The Real Deal on Being A Girl Today - Anne Driscoll

Lunch with Buddha - Roland Merullo

Make A Wish But Not For Money - Suzanne Strempek Shea

Moments of Grace & Beauty: Forty Stories of Kindness, Courage, and Generosity in a Troubled World - Roland Merullo

Music In and On the Air - Lloyd Schwartz

Temporary Sojourner - Tony Eprile

The Indestructibles - Matthew Phillion

The Winding Stream: The Carters, the Cashes and the Course of Country Music - Beth Harrington

This is Paradise: An Irish Mother's Grief, an African Village's Plight and the Medical Clinic That Brought Fresh Hope to Both - Suzanne Strempek Shea

Tornado Alley - Craig Nova

Waking Slow - Ioanna Opidee

Who Do You Think You Are? Reflections of a Writer's Life - Joseph Torra

Made in the USA
Coppell, TX
24 August 2023